PRISONER OF GOD

PRISONER OF GOD

Michel Benoît

Translated by Roger Clarke

ALMA BOOKS

ALMA BOOKS LTD
London House
243–253 Lower Mortlake Road
Richmond
Surrey TW9 2LL
United Kingdom
www.almabooks.com

Prisoner of God first published in French as *Prisonnier de Dieu*
by Fixot in 1994
First published by Alma Books Limited in 2008
Copyright © Michel Benoît, 1994-2008

Printed in Great Britain by CPI Cox & Wyman, Reading

ISBN: 978-1-84688-052-0

To the memory of my uncle Maurice, who is dead.
To Monique, who is living.
To Isabel Ellsen, my sister,
without whom I should never have had
the courage for this book.

All resemblance to characters or situations in real
life is inescapable. The identity of persons still living has
therefore been disguised. For the dead – may God preserve
their souls – real names are used.

PRISONER OF GOD

I've set the alarm for five in the sixth-floor bedroom I'm using. Yesterday I lunched with Uncle. He asked me:

"It's to be tomorrow then?"

His tone was anxious, with a pretence of detachment.

"Yes."

"Does your mother know?"

"No. Please don't tell her."

The alarm has gone off. It's still dark. I'm acting like a robot, with all the time in the world... I sit down at the table and write my mother a note. The manner is theatrical, like everything that's been said this last year: "When you read these lines I shall be gone..."

I've descended the dark staircase and placed the keys by the kitchen sink. The bedroom upstairs is empty now, just a sheet of paper on the table...

I've not been able to eat. It's as though the climax of so much tension and strife has left me crushed. Every action is charged with significance: I'm leaving the keys where she'll notice them. She'll understand, go upstairs. I don't want to think of her shock at seeing the empty room. Without closing the door, she'll go to the table; sit down sideways, uncomfortably, to read. She'll not finish, as tears will cloud her eyes. Then she'll slam the door shut, collapse onto the bed, and sob.

She'll go downstairs and start boiling a kettle for tea, looking away – moving slowly, wiping the lonely tears.

I've taken the metro: the station's grey and cold. The carriage is empty to start with, then one passenger, I think. I'm leaning against the window, letting the suburbs and dismal countryside pass before my gaze. I'm carrying within me a whole world of longings and of struggles.

* * *

9

Suddenly there before me stands the abbey, utterly still, awesome. A moment of hesitation: I step forward and ring the monastery bell. Nothing but silence.

It's Brother Roger who's let me in. Once inside, I put down my suitcase and say simply: "Right, then." He's wearing a broad smile that lights up his pale face beneath a close-shaven scalp. I wait for the Father Guest Master; his mysterious whisper is my introduction to the world of the abbey. He leads me to a reception room – bare, cold, where the voice makes weird echoes. We don't know what to say: he jokes, I give mechanical replies.

The Novice Master arrives: a large man in a black habit, he seems to take everything as a matter of course. He picks up my case, not heavy. He conducts me to an internal chapel and kneels; I copy him, my mind a blank. Then up a well-lit staircase, the treads covered in dark-green plastic.

On the first floor, at the end of a vast, broad corridor, is a glazed partition labelled in yellowish letters "Novices". We've not exchanged a word since the reception room. Six doors open onto this area (from which there's no other exit), and into each door at eye level is set a window of rough glass. He stops at the first door on the right and opens it. From now on this is my cell.

I'm twenty-two years old, with two degrees and work experience. I speak four languages. I'm what they call a "bright lad", with a high market value.

I step gingerly into the cell ahead of the Novice Master. He puts my case down near the door.

I have chosen death.

In my suitcase are just two shirts, so convinced am I that I can't stay more than a week: they'll get me out again; it can't last...

It lasted twenty-one years.

Part One

Can do better

1

The vestiges of a childhood are of interest only if they clarify what is to follow: there is little remaining to me from those early years that might explain the strangeness of my life.

When Chancellor Hitler decided on war, my grandfather, sensible man, sent his barely married daughter off overseas. My father had a family in the French colony of Madagascar: those youngsters would be safe there, more so than in Paris. They were put onboard ship at Toulon a few hours after the wedding. My mother was in tears. It must have been in the Suez Canal that I was conceived. A good start.

Madagascar afforded me an infancy of aromas and affection. My grandfather there, a genuine count from old Bordeaux nobility, was a bank manager at Tamatave on the coast. We often used to visit him, for the holidays – was I three, or four? Well, one memorable day my countess-grandmother took me onto a sun-drenched station platform. We boarded a small local train; the only people in the carriage were whites. The blacks were on the platform – you could see little caps and frizzy hair. My grandmother leant out of the window and reappeared with some lychees, warm and well rounded, which she cut open with a small penknife. There was no forgetting it: a spurt of juice, and then a sweetness in the mouth, soft and firm, like a tongue that rested on my tongue and fondled it. And a flavour, a penetrating flavour that spread right into my head. There were several opportunities to repeat the experience, as the train jolted from side to side, but I remained conscious only of that sensation, the first to teach me what pleasure might be.

Madagascar – it meant, first, the joy of being alive. My parents were young and dependent on their family, but it did not cost much to live well, and my mother had the services of three or four "boys". Each of them had his function and would have felt demeaned to perform another. Every day I used to see the boy who did the floors scrubbing them with a half-coconut strapped to his right foot: he hummed to himself as he hopped along on his left leg, burnishing the floorboards to a fine sheen with his nut. Then there was the cook, who treasured up the handkerchiefs that my mother gave him and went on blowing his nose with his fingers as he cooked.

I was the first baby of the family: so I was king, and made the most of it. I was put in the care of a "*nénêne*", who might elsewhere have been called my governess, but who was first and foremost all my own, just as I became more than her child: her little blond idol. She enveloped me in a love that matched herself: generous, buxom, overpowering, full of laughter and kisses. My mother was just a young girl: Razanne, older than her, was my African mummy, anxious, protective, life bursting from her at every moment. When it was time to go out, it was she who checked that the red lining of my straw hat was properly tucked inside:

"You must un'stand, Missel dear, zat ze red, it ssades you better from ze sun; zat's what your gran'mozer said."

Whenever I achieved something for the first time she went into raptures, exploding with laughter: she would move away from me clapping her hands, then turn round and do a little dance on her bare feet before covering me with kisses.

It was you, my Razanne, who used to take me to Tamatave beach. We would go along paths bordered with clove trees, their strong scent mingling with that of the sea-spray, for the surf was close by, the waves as high as houses, the sound deafening. There you took off my clothes, and we would lie down on the wet sand where the tongues of foaming water would come to caress us. You never took off your dress; it clung to your body, to its heavy contours. *For the Negro, to be naked is neither good nor bad; it's a matter of convenience. But the Whites have taught us that it's shameful, something to hide like a deformity.* So, in the presence of her little blond idol on the empty beach, Razanne kept her dress well wrapped round her and then dashed with him into the ocean foam. If I ran away, she would run after me raising ramparts of water:

"Missel, Missel, Missel!"

I think she relished my first name: she had only to use it for me to belong to her completely.

The day would come for us to leave the island of aromas and return home to France. A photograph taken a little while before our departure shows Razanne hugging in her arms a child already big, blond and good-looking. But her eyes show a kind of wild despair, a sadness beyond measure.

A year and a half after our return to France, a letter informed us that Razanne had just died. She was perhaps between thirty and forty and had a family, I suppose. But I knew nothing of her outside my home.

For the present it was war. Madagascar having remained loyal to the Vichy government, our number-one enemies were the British, who had told themselves that the big island would make a useful addition to their staging posts to India.

Well, the British landed one day, at the time when I was just beginning to speak. So it was that my first words were uttered from a pram pushed by Razanne, as I passed three of His Majesty's soldiers crossing the road, baton beneath the arm:

"You British pigs!"

This did not actually change the course of the war; but Razanne spent the whole evening touring the town:

"And zen 'e looked zem full in ze face, my Missel, and zen 'e said to zem you know what? 'E said to zem: 'You Britiss pigs' – zat's what 'e said!"

And there were hoots of laughter and dancing.

My father, having nothing else to do, joined the forces – never mind which forces or what they were fighting for. What was for sure was that the army took up his time and he was often away. And already my mother's voice was becoming hollow with an

15

anxiety that would never leave her. She began to keep me close to her to exorcize those ever-lengthening absences, and stifle those rumours that reached her of pretty half-castes and planters' wives.

Never having received affection from her own father, my mother had transferred her whole capacity, her whole need for love to the man of her life. And that capacity, that need was huge, never to be satisfied. Love was her religion, and she only had one god: that man so handsome, so charming, so accomplished, so ineffectual. She would support him to the end; beyond him nothing, no one, would ever really exist.

He – I think he loved her, just as he loved so many other women. Many men can love two or more beings at the same time, with a love that is sometimes different, often heartfelt, but never closed to fresh opportunities. That attitude was poison to my mother: she could only love one man at a time; all she would know was one man, all she would love was what came from him and what related back to him.

And as for me – I did not realize it, but I was already beginning to count the score.

2

"The war's won! The war's won!"

I careered down the steep, sunlit street, shouting and waving. The locals stood still in astonishment to see me making such an uproar. The news meant little to them, as indeed to me: that distant war – what of it? – had changed nothing in our dreary colonial lives. But I had sensed great excitement in the house, and I amplified it, with little idea why.

There followed a frantic period: wooden crates being nailed together with great hammer blows, trunks being strapped, and finally suitcases being packed. My grandmother the countess bustled about to hide her sorrow: the little king was about to leave, to go all the way back to France. It was December: they kitted me out with what seemed like tubes that fastened around one, stiff and heavy, like the turtle shells that were sometimes washed up on the beach. My Razanne kept passing them to me as she wiped her cheeks, cheeks ever moist since the declaration that the war was over and our departure near:

"Zat, Missel dear, is 'n ove'coat, it's to wear in France where it's so cold, you'll see m' darling..."

And she turned her head away in tears.

We left in a military aircraft: two rows of benches on each side, with a hole for the parachute where the back-rest should have been – five days' travelling without leaning back, and stopovers with strange names: Nairobi, Khartoum, Djibouti, Cairo. We stopped at each for a sleep. I didn't know that it was the white colonists' empire that I was travelling through like that, for the last time before it disintegrated: from London to Madagascar the earth belonged to us, the Whites were at home everywhere...

What I did observe was that it was always very hot, and that in Cairo the dense crowd in the torrid streets was all in white. It was there that I was given an unforgettable experience: in the hotel a military-looking man full of gold braid ushered us into a sort of cupboard in the side of a wall. Then the wall began to move before my eyes, and when we emerged again, it was a different corridor, a different floor! In our wooden colonial-style houses I had never seen a lift, and I decided that day that our resonant, gleaming staircases were much better.

After Cairo it was Paris. I was made to wear the overcoat, and exposed to a series of painful impressions: a biting cold; a frozen, dirty-white mud that made you slip; thin people, pale people, who none of them laughed, who made impatient gestures and who seemed not to notice me, or almost not...

My grandparents in France were awaiting their young folk and their first grandson with the utmost eagerness. But they were strait-laced people, who were emerging from the war. My grandfather, a labourer's son, had managed to secure a foothold in the middle class by dint of intelligence and hard work. He still

17

owned the business that he had created between the wars, plus an enormous apartment on the Place de l'Alma by the Seine. It was there that we were to be put up to start with, while we looked for accommodation in Paris.

My new grandmother was not like the other one: you had to be careful of everything, stay in a corner without misbehaving, observe a heap of unfamiliar rules... Above all, I was the little king no more. Razanne, my Razanne, was no longer there to protect me with her intense love. So I turned back towards my parents: they seemed as much in a state of shock as I was.

My father had no aptitude for anything but to be good-looking and a nice talker. So they put him in the family business, and made him well aware of how lucky he was to have married an heiress. Gradually he became for me no more than a façade, an outward aspect, of a father: his life was elsewhere, with the multiple women and the dreams that he indulged in parallel.

My mother began to tread the long path of suffering that would be hers. In Paris she had come back to a father who did not love her and who crushed her with an authority that was daunting and incontestable. So she fled for refuge to the one being that existed for her, the one being who had taken notice of her, who to a degree had loved her, who had treated her with kindness and who had given her a son.

We had just moved into a little flat near Auteuil. The crates had arrived from Madagascar, and we used to keep ourselves warm by burning their wooden boards in the fireplace of the little living room, where I had my bed. Every morning of that dark, cold January I would open my eyes on the same picture: my father and mother huddled near the fire that lit up the ceiling with its sporadic bursts, talking in an undertone, their voices lowered at the prospect of a life for which they were so little suited and before which they felt so immature.

As I watched them, snuggled away in my corner, its chill shadows momentarily pierced by the blaze of our boards, I unconsciously began to learn who it was that would be my companion for so long: loneliness.

3

My little world slowly took shape, put together by me as I picked my way through the absence of grown-ups. The winter passed, then a whole year.

The big novelty was school. A few months before our departure from Madagascar I had indeed been put in the care of the good White Sisters; but all I remember of that is the smell of chalk and the rustle of their starched veils. It was my aunts who taught me to read, and I lost no time in devouring whatever material came to hand.

Otherwise I knew nothing. Truly, nothing. The children of the nursery school seemed used to dictations, sums, lessons... while I could hardly write.

So that first year I was given detentions every Thursday, every Thursday with one exception. Why, by what miracle I had escaped detention that Thursday I do not know. But I can still see the school headmaster, a thin little man with bulging eyes, hammering into me every Wednesday, when he handed me my notice of detention:

"Michel, you are a dunce, a DUNCE!"

He would lean towards me, transfix me with his large eyes and, with all the force at his command, knock into me this awesome truth:

"You are a dunce, a DUNCE!"

What had become of the little king? To whom could I turn to regain my footing when everything was giving way beneath me, when everything was closing in around me?

My parents had ceased to exist. Wholly preoccupied with the Parisian environment to which they had come, lacking bearings themselves, they were to me less than shadows: they were transparent objects.

I was already getting used to sitting at the back of classes, those cosy refuges that were the instinctive gathering-place of all those who exploited remoteness from the teacher's desk to indulge their fantasies. There I used to sit next to a very fair, very pale boy who spent the greatest part of his time pulling from his flies a penis just as pale and rubbing it with his fingers. To begin with, I just stared at him in astonishment. In Madagascar I had never seen such a thing. And at eight I had never used my penis except for passing water.

For his part, he seemed to find pleasure in it, and one day he said to me:

"Feel it!"

But the mistress was coming in our direction: hands returned beneath desks, and heads looked down studiously.

That same evening maybe, or another one, I tried the fair boy's action out on myself, and I discovered pleasure and above all solace. The business went no further, because the fair boy was caught masturbating in the middle of a lesson and expelled forthwith – as good order required.

But from then on I was aware that there was another use for the penis, and that I could draw comfort from it at any time for the rest of my life.

Then there was the catechism class that I went to soon afterwards, without any involvement from my parents. We used to watch a "magic lantern" projecting transparencies painted on glass plates, while beams of raw light escaped from it in all directions into the dark hall of the presbytery. For the first time I gazed at pictures of Christ carrying his cross, then crucified, bearing his suffering alone in the midst of an uncaring crowd. At that point something decisive took place: I emerged from the session in turmoil. What a strange power an image can have! Who was he, then, this guiltless man surrendered to a mob? He too was quite alone, with no one to talk to; and, though I could not tell how, he was interested in me, he understood me and loved me...

So it was with eagerness that I applied myself to the catechism course – right through to my first confession, from which I re-emerged full of assurance, announcing to all and sundry:

"The Devil can come now; I've strength enough for him!"

The others scoffed. But I had discovered a pattern in the world: evil, identified, brought to light; and to protect one from it, Christ, who was strong, and for whom I was sure I existed – even if I did not know how.

Paris at that period was slowly reawakening from the years of darkness. I tasted my first liquorice, black strips rolled together with a bead of sugar in the centre, the ultimate in scarce sweetmeats. There were the first imports of condensed milk, white honey, sweet as sweet, the cartons of which I licked to the last drop. And the first grapes, and the first steaming cup of Bovril, which warmed you in autumn down to the soles of your feet...

It was the year of –

"*Douce France,*
cher pays de mon enfance..."

which my father used to hum in our flat. There were still buildings camouflaged against bombing raids with great brown patches; but the metro was running, and I thought the passers-by less pale.

I had spent that Thursday afternoon, like every Thursday afternoon, in an empty classroom next to the headmaster's office. And in the evening, by the wan glow of the gaslights, enveloped in the smell of dead leaves that they were burning in piles on the corner of the avenue, I was on my way home by myself in the night, carrying my dunce's satchel, carrying the burden of my non-existence, and the desire to have a life somewhere, and light, and warmth, and good order.

4

Something had to happen, something had to turn up, to get us out of that all-too-obvious inertia in which I was growing up at the time. My father, still just as ineffectual, did not have the situation or the prestige that would allow him to hold his own in society: he was only his father-in-law's employee and, even with plenty of imagination, that did not have a good ring. As for my mother, she fed on her jealousy – not for herself (poor woman, she hardly existed), but for *him*, her husband, the being of such distinction who had been denied his deserts, who lacked the wherewithal to have himself appreciated, to take pride of place in the world, *her* man...

That "something" was the death of my grandfather. True founder of the family that he was, he had worn himself out preserving it through the war. One day, realizing that he had contracted tuberculosis, he called my father to him:

"It's the business that brings us all comfort and security; I'll give you two years to prepare yourself to take it over. In two years I will be dead."

My father, whose only idea at that time was to write screenplays for the cinema or for the new medium of television, must have thought that he had a good line there, worth remembering. Two years later my grandfather did die as he had lived, without repeating himself.

He left behind the magnificent apartment on the Place de l'Alma, which for him was the material manifestation of his success.

We used to go there every Sunday for lunch, leaving our dim and drab little two-roomed place to go and breathe the air of the mountain summits. First a marble staircase; then a huge vestibule that led on the right to the double salon (grand salon with formal furniture, small salon for taking coffee) and to my grandparents' suite, bedroom and dressing-room. Outside ran a balcony overlooking the Seine, and you could see the Champs-Élysées too.

On the courtyard side – a large, well-lit courtyard – there was also an internal balcony onto which opened the dining room, the mosaic-panelled bathroom, the children's bedrooms and the servants' quarters.

We realized that this style of living appertained to the sovereign: we ordinary subjects used to attend in order to play our part each in our own way. I was rather bored, more at ease in kitchens than in the salon, and angry to observe that my grandmother distinguished between the bread of the master and mistress and that of the servants and set them apart. My father had finally found a backdrop to match his self-esteem, but his failure to learn his lines produced a strained performance. My mother was home at last, but pained each moment to see her husband denied the one pedestal that might befit him: was not that his due?

The Sunday meal brought us together in the dining room, its walls decorated with huge mirrors in the *style moderne* in which my father might have had the opportunity to practise his delivery. I had no right to speak, but my attention was sufficiently held by the aristocratic bearing, the natural presence, of my grandfather, still handsome, but showing his age, and coughing every moment.

He was the only one with no illusion as to the situation he would be leaving behind. That son-in-law of his would take over from him, not because he had the ability, but to ensure that the business remained within the family. When he died, in his oxygen tent, one of the last names he uttered was mine:

"Michel... tell Michel..."

Tell him that he'd better be quick to pick up the torch, or in the meantime everything will have vanished.

But I was only ten at that time: my father could be sure of a reign, not just of a regency.

So we installed ourselves in the state rooms of the grand ocean liner. I had my bedroom there at the end of a succession of corridors, my father took possession of the managing director's office, and life was turned on its head.

At last we had arrived; at last our circumstances matched the notion that my parents had of themselves. Money began to flow in torrents, and the apartment became the scene of another comedy, entitled "the allure of success". To their delight my parents discovered a host of new friends, who enjoyed drinking

23

our champagne and inviting themselves to the constant receptions that my mother gave.

After the war a whole generation had profited from the rebuilding of the country to make more money than they had ever had before and to use this quickly to erase the mediocrity of their origins. These *nouveaux riches*, while staying only too true to themselves, had achieved the outward appearance of a glittering social position. There remained a few signs that pointed back to where they had come from, above all their surnames. As it cost too much to change them, there was a rich crop of composite names. Our friends were not called Durand, but Durand-Darnis, Lefèvre-Boisset or Lombardo-Klein. Their cigars were a little too fat, their wives were a little too made up, their private chaplains were all Jesuits and they preferred playing poker to bridge. But never mind: my mother went to enormous trouble to entertain them in that fine apartment, and as they moved between the salons, friendships sprang up that they vowed would be firm, true, enduring, eternal.

We had three domestic staff in our service, and my mother spent the best part of her time in the dining room making them shopping lists or in her dressing room doing her nails. The reception rooms were immaculately kept, but the areas out of view – the service rooms, my bedroom – were left to the whim of our staff. And here and there, little by little, trickles of water appeared in the ship: balls of fluff pushed under a bed, objects crammed higgledy-piggledy into a wardrobe, linen that was not always of the cleanest.

My father's high managerial responsibilities did not seem to overwhelm him. Wholesale trade was not an occupation truly worthy of him, and the periods he spent in the office were a concession he made to the family, who worried about our joint income. My grandmother often returned to her old apartment, invited as her turn came round. After the meal my father would sip his coffee in the salon, expatiating at length – too much "at length" for my grandmother, who was concerned for her dividends. She called him to order:

"Well, my lad! Off we go! It's time to go to the office. Come along, don't stay sitting there doing nothing!"

"Yes, mother; of course, mother…"

His true vocation, though, was surely to write screenplays: he spent a lot of effort thinking about them while he listened to classical music with my mother in the salon.

It was only right that my education should follow the pattern: I was taken out of the state school to be enrolled in a smart academy, not because it was run by priests, but because all the best people sent their sons there.

One day in October I was accordingly summoned with my mother to see the Principal. Pretty and well-dressed, she glided smoothly over the waxed parquet of the vast oak-panelled study. Facing us sat a rather plump man in a cassock, with a soft voice and elegant movements.

"Alas! madame, the academic year begins in a few days; all our fifth-year classes are full, ab-sol-ute-ly full. But maybe" – he nodded in my direction with an ingratiating smile – "maybe, in view of the circumstances, and for people like you…"

"The fact is, Michel is very backward, you see, coming back from the colonies; and your academy, Father…"

"Of course, of course. Well, we'll try our best; I'll deal personally" – a bow of the head, a smile – "personally with his application."

He walked with us to the door, his hand on my back, while my mother thanked him effusively. For people like us the fathers always had room…

This is how things were arranged: the worthy fathers busied themselves with my education, and at home the servants took care of my daily existence. So for all those years I was supervised by priests and brought up by housemaids – which gave my mother the spare time to get on with her mysterious tasks and my father to forget completely that he had a son.

* * *

The school's first concern was to do an academic assessment of me, which proved disastrous. Since no one had ever bothered with me, it could hardly have been otherwise. My mother was summoned a second time and found herself in the presence of the old moustachioed schoolmaster who was in charge of my class. With him my mother turned back into a helpless little girl, and he took pity on her:

"But my poor girl, he knows nothing, nothing at all!"

She could only sob... It was accordingly agreed that I would have private tuition while the others were in the playground.

"And the main thing is that the Principal, who's so good and who's very fond of you, has told me that he'll keep an eye on your progress."

So from time to time, not so often at first, I found myself alone in the Principal's study. He would call for me when we came in from a break, and I would turn up dripping with sweat, my shirt tail hanging out of my shorts. He would spread my exercise books out on his desk, sit me near him and give me comments on what I had written while his hand found its way under my shirt, then moved up my back to the neck, and returned gently to the waist. It never went further, and I took it as no more than the token of an affection that gave me back some confidence. For I had returned to my old position in the class rankings – the bottom. This protection was a guarantee of safety.

All my school reports bore the following remark, which was to dog me for a long, long time:

"Performance unsatisfactory. Can do better."

5

The cyclone that was to engulf the ship developed at great speed. My father was elated to see his qualities recognized at last, and went absent more and more. I often encountered him in the early hours wearing a dinner jacket and trailing perfumes behind him. It was not just one but several mistresses he drew in his wake. And I often heard talk of gaming, of the casino.

It seemed that, the more time he spent away, the more my mother loved him and clung to him. So there were long scenes, always semi-public – the script was better when played before the stalls – and the apartment became the backdrop for Act III of a recurrent melodrama.

Instinctively I used to take refuge in my bedroom at the end of the corridor. There I spent long hours in self-absorption, accompanied sometimes by the lonely pleasure, my one comfort. That den of mine was more and more unkempt, and now it was the dirty washing that accumulated under the bed. At school my chums called me "Messy Mickey", and it is true that I hardly ever washed.

During those dismal years I have no memory of having learnt a lesson or of having done a single piece of homework. My monitoring sessions in the Principal's study proved essential. Since I had grown, he would now stand up at his desk and squeeze me against his cassock, kissing me on the corner of my lips. While he was holding me tight against him, I noticed that his belly was hard as wood. I was not the only one at the academy to be pursued in this way, for sure, and we pupils talked about it a bit among ourselves. But I went up into the higher classes despite my zero grades: so all was going well.

From now on the ship was letting water on all sides. To explain away his multiple lives, my father used to tell the most implausible tales, which my mother swallowed one after the other, in tears.

The dining room had become the stage set where lines were declaimed in front of embarrassed domestic servants and a dwindling number of friends. But I myself was the favoured spectator of the grown-ups' folly; I was my mother's confidant, and soon her only support.

At twelve, lonely as I was, I had become my mother's father-figure.

The long evenings and nights that I spent with her waiting up for my father became more and more frequent. I recall the winter's night when, fast asleep, I was woken up by the insistent ringing of the entrance bell. Almost naked in the huge, dark apartment, I went to open up: it was a woman, well-dressed and well-perfumed, asking if my father was there. I ushered her into the salon, where my mother, looking pale, joined her. Then my father arrived, smiling, in evening dress. While I was trying to get back to sleep, I could hear from my bedroom the Act III dialogue and the sounds of hysterical fainting fits and, probably, some face slapping.

Early in the morning, shattered, I picked up my satchel to go and doze at the back of the good fathers' classes.

The time came for first communions and the week's retreat in preparation. Eight welcome days away from home. The aim was to engender some religious feeling in these upper-class youngsters, but the priest who led the retreat did not need much skill to deal with my distress. Away from the group, often alone, I used to find my way to the chapel. There, in the silence and tranquillity, I would talk to God, and God talked to me, at least I thought he did. Up there I had a family, my true family. "God loves the poor," the priest kept repeating; if that was true, there was no one poorer, more lost, than me.

Prayer became a more enduring relief than masturbation, and I took up the practice of attending mass of my own free will.

Then matters came to a head. While away on holiday I heard by letter that my father had seduced my mother's youngest sister, one of my aunts. Shortly afterwards she died in an accident, which seemed to me a sort of ruthless judgement on the part of God.

I was physically nauseated, and I began to vomit up the world of spineless, disloyal adults, surrendering themselves unrestrainedly to primordial passions. Everything was untrustworthy, just lies, lies.

It was at that time that I chanced upon a series of articles in *Paris Match* that described the life of monks in various contemplative orders. The writing was sympathetic, the photography stunning, the monastic buildings idyllic in their mountain fastnesses. The monks had handsome, tranquil faces and appeared to live a life of timeless harmony. It was a world of order and beauty... I shut the magazine in a daydream. These men, had they not found a way out of chaos? I wanted to know more about that window opening onto another existence.

But there were plenty of other matters demanding attention.

Money was finally running short. One night, towards two o'clock in the morning, my mother burst into my bedroom:

"Michel, quick, my darling, go to the casino and look for your father: he's in the process of losing everything, go quickly!"

For a moment I imagined myself running alone through the night towards a casino of which I knew nothing, to ward off the downfall and shipwreck of the whole family. Then my father came in and embraced my mother with a noisy laugh, while I retreated to my bedroom, crushed.

An inexorable logic governed what happened next. My father was found to have accumulated large debts. The board of directors of the business finally relieved him of his directorship, which left him of course a lot more time for writing screenplays. As though by magic, the fine-weather friends abandoned the apartment, telling themselves, presumably, that the splendid parties, the generous hospitality and the vows of eternal allegiance had never taken place. Hardly a single one could be found to lend my mother a small sum of money.

That was the moment that the good fathers chose to take notice that, in spite of everything, my academic progress was not proceeding at a desirable tempo. In any case our credit was running out, and rumours were circulating. The Principal's "monitoring" sessions and personal protection were no longer enough. In academies like this a pupil of good social standing is not expelled: it is sufficient to let it be known that next year "all our fourth-year places are full, ab-sol-ute-ly full" and that there will – alas! – no longer be room for him.

The grand apartment, the lovely apartment, had become a derelict wreck. No maintenance for years, no housework for months. The purchaser who came to look at it grimaced in our presence:

"But, madame, it's a pigsty!"

That allowed him to give peanuts for it, and this went to pay off the main creditors. As for my father, he had disappeared to Africa – a land conducive, as is well known, to the drafting of literary screenplays. My mother and my two young sisters were taken in by my grandmother. Urgent decisions had to be taken on what to do with me.

6

In the end I landed up with my uncle. There was no blood tie between us, as he was the husband of my remaining aunt. Our family regarded him with a touch of condescension, for he was a long way beneath us: his mother had begun life as an assistant in a dressmaker's shop in the inner suburbs. And even if she now administered – with an iron fist – her own shop in the Boulevard de Strasbourg, she nonetheless remained a working-class woman, with blunt and colourful speech to match.

Her whole life had revolved around her only son: he at least would make it good. Hem by hem, she had made it possible for him to receive a higher education. And it was in the corridors of the university that he had met my aunt, as she happened to be passing.

Why had that young girl of good middle-class background, from all the suitors that her flirtatiousness drew around her, picked out that rather pale, shy and stubborn lad? In the end they got married, without real love. It was the end of the war, and she must have recognized in him my grandfather's pedigree – the pedigree of builders and money-makers. With him she would progress further, and maybe she would relive the saga of success-out-of-nothing, that lullaby from her own childhood.

"I've chosen a good horse," she liked to say.

Unfortunately the horse had a stable, and they had to go and live for a time with the dressmaker, next to the shop. Leaving the Place de l'Alma for the Porte Saint-Denis – the great ocean liner for the noises and smells of the inner suburb – that was a lot to stomach. Very soon they became a partnership of convenience, each with their own parallel escapades that they did not even try to conceal from each other. For her it was some childhood friend, for him his secretaries. They were, in the language of the day, a "modern couple", and society saw nothing to find fault with, since appearances were preserved and success followed.

My uncle had a relentless craving to enter his wife's world. He began by delivering his first cases of medicines himself; but fifteen years later he was one of the young captains of the re-emergent pharmaceutical industry. His fine apartment in the 16th arrondissement, his car, his position in society – he had won it all by his intelligence, hard work and strength of character.

Uncle was small of stature, but quite good-looking. Fine features, unblinking eyes, square chin, a manner dry and abrupt. He would not, could not, be other than the first. Thus his dealings with my grandfather caused sparks to fly: those two stallions could never share the same stable. It was soon obvious that Uncle would not take over the family business, but would go his own way.

His generation had witnessed the German army, confident and proud, sweeping across a land vanquished and humiliated. It had then supported the Americans, complete with chewing gum and bebop, in their lightning conquest. Its wish was to live and to build. Uncle would never allow himself to gamble with capital. He only had his salary, a high one, and his wits: his ambition was to create an industry, develop it and exercise authority over men. He had never wished me to come beneath his roof, and when he saw me arrive he put me under watch.

So I turned up in this superbly organized household, where everything was clean, tidy and quiet. I was given my bedroom, and informed that breakfast would be taken together at 7.30.

Next morning at the stated hour I was of course still in bed. I pulled on some trousers and rushed dishevelled into the dining room. My uncle, sitting with his cup of tea in front of him, was buttering a slice of bread. He was dressed in suit and tie, his working day already beginning. He raised an eye in my direction, and by a movement of the finger sent me back without a word. I returned a bit later, fully dressed, hair combed, in a temper, to find the table empty. That day I left for high school hungry. And I realized that the years of gloom were about to be followed by the years of iron.

It was double or quit. Either I submitted, or I must go and slouch around elsewhere. Uncle very soon gave me to understand this: I would only stay with him if I accepted his authority. I had never been subjected to any regime, nor to any rule of life. I had just used to follow my idle imagination and live out my dreams. Suddenly another world was revealed to me, a world of rigour and precision. I remember having deliberated for several days, before deciding to play the game – it was my last chance. But I would sell my skin dear: the struggle commenced.

Nothing could have pleased Uncle more than this challenge – to turn a wild horse into a mount for riding, walking quietly, well groomed, harnessed for life. Day by day, inch by inch, I lost ground. I had been enrolled in the Janson-de-Sailly high school. I was there every day on time, at all the classes, even at gym where no one had seen me for years. On return from school I would find my tea laid on the table; I no longer had anything to do but work. Dinner was served at a set time: there was talking, but never with raised voices.

On Sundays Uncle fetched fat files and settled himself at his desk. I watched him work in silence, a vein beginning to stand out, then throb, on his temple. There was only one thing for me to do: go to my room and do likewise.

In the third month the miracle happened: I came top of the class for a French essay. Never in my life had I come first in anything at all. My usual position was bottom – a matter of habit. The event took me unawares. I got ready to shout the extraordinary news from the rooftops, but Uncle said nothing, not one word of praise. Then I suddenly understood that, for him, coming first was normality. The struggle was rejoined, but something had changed: I was no longer struggling against him, against his unyielding regime; I was beginning to struggle against myself. Uncle was still just as demanding, but I was gradually becoming a partner in his demands. He was hard on everyone, and finally I became hard on myself: he had won. He no longer had to drive me: I drove myself, and the respect that I occasionally saw dawning in his grey eyes became my most precious prize.

Uncle had inherited my grandfather's library, and the books now lined his study. I began to read everything I could lay hands on: I discovered the world of the mind, of culture. Uncle had never had time to read, but he approved of the gaps I was making in his bookshelves: afterwards he had me talk to him about what I had read. His only interest was paintings, and on Saturdays we used to scour the Left Bank galleries. He had money, and he bought pictures. The apartment gradually became covered with leading artists of the Paris School. On Sundays, in the hour of rest between two files, we used to rearrange Brayers and Chapelain-Midys on the walls. A sort of intimacy developed at those times: I discovered another man, sensitive and enthusiastic. Then on the Monday work began again, precise, organized.

This austere life created a structure in which I recovered my equilibrium. To live was to work, and the goal was to succeed. There was room for nothing else, not even for affection. If Uncle began to be fond of me, he never showed it.

What is more, I never noticed any display of affection between him and his wife either. But if they were not the couple they used to be, if they were maybe drifting apart – that was something I could not, did not want, to see. My life was still reshaping itself around them; it was all still too fragile. And could he, a man so strong, experience anything but success?

My mother, for her part, had said goodbye to life, for good and all. She had only ever loved one man, and she would not marry again. She devoted herself to my two little sisters; and though I might see her regularly it was as though she were transparent: she personified failure, while I had discovered the appetizing taste of success.

* * *

So it was skiing in winter, seaside in summer.

That July, the last of my childhood, I was fifteen; *she* was fourteen, with delightful little breasts. We went into the water together by chance, and we came out holding hands. It was my first love affair, and that is something you do not forget. For the whole month we lived looking into each other's eyes, while my hands explored her body. Kisses, caresses – in those days one hardly went further, even if my penis became wooden… We exchanged letters for a few months: the romance lasted as long as holiday romances last. My overpowering hunger for pleasure found nourishment there for a twelvemonth.

Time came for the first *baccalauréat*: in two years I had had to catch up on six years of truancy, and I just passed. But with one more year of frenzied work, I passed the second *baccalauréat* with merit. I had chosen a scientific path, despite my literary predilections.

"Why this unnecessary work and risk?" Uncle had asked.

"Because later I want to work in the same field as you."

He said nothing, but I had hit the mark. From that day on I began to feel a little more at home. In truth, he had never made me feel the poor relation, taken into his house for charity. Ever since I had played the game, he treated me on a par with his only son, my young cousin, with whom I lived as a brother. Well clothed and clean, I was living rather comfortably. But, if I was refused nothing, it is also true that I asked for very little. For well I knew that I was still no more than a guest: nothing was owed me as a son of the family; everything was granted me as a favour. I had an overpowering sense of the insecurity of things, and the awareness of owning nothing for myself.

In addition, I continued to attend mass at a neighbouring monastery, partly out of habit, and Uncle was prepared to overlook this little abnormality. As long as it did not hinder me from working, I was allowed to indulge my religion – on condition that it was early on a Sunday morning so that I was on time for breakfast. He was as tolerant of religion as of sex – though the first seemed to him totally useless, while the second made for a healthy lifestyle and, practised in moderation, had nothing but advantages for a man. I was of course a virgin, like all boys of my age: there would be time for that later.

7

To my great surprise Uncle accompanied me to my university enrolment. It was the first time that he had taken care of me in person. It was at that period that I realized that the man who seemed so strong, so firm and solid, bore within himself a dreadful trauma. As I found out afterwards, he was unable to have any more children, and his wife, my aunt, wanted more at any price. The breach between them became apparent even in everyday life. One day I came upon him as he was taking her hand, but she withdrew it hurriedly, as though she had received an electric shock.

There was never a scene. One November day she simply announced to us that she was going on holiday. My cousin and I took the remark at face value. But from then on there were only three of us in that apartment; without a woman it felt suddenly empty; and Uncle was particularly glum.

One evening in his office he said to me:

"Michel, I've something to tell you."

I was taken aback and wondered what could have prompted such a preamble. He sat down at his desk. Suddenly I saw before me a man shrunken, devastated, his eyes swimming with tears.

"Michel, your aunt won't be coming back. She's left us. We're going to get a divorce."

The ceiling was crumbling; fire and lightning descended; everything reeled once again; again chaos and rupture deep within... I took several steps into the drawing room, racked with dry sobs. Uncle got up and came after me, shaken by my distress, speechless. I turned to face him:

"Listen... she's gone... but I'm still here... if you want..."

Then spontaneously – something that I could never have imagined till then – in an impulse of affection I leant down towards him (I was taller by a head) and kissed him on the temple.

Never had there been the least physical contact between us, and I would never kiss him again. Then he pulled himself together, and in a voice that was at once flat and kindly:

"Michel, I've got used to you now; you're at home here; you can stay if you want."

His look pleaded for a response. I said nothing, just:

"Fine. And would anyone be going to the cinema this evening?"

We had just chosen each other, for ever. From then on I had a father whom I loved and respected. And I believe that from that day he regarded me as a son.

We went to see a popular western on the Champs-Élysées, with a restaurant afterwards. And, truly, I don't know which of us was taking the other out.

The next day we were confronted with harsh reality. A child of ten, an adolescent of seventeen, a businessman eaten up with his work, a large apartment with no one in charge, left to the servants. Uncle had to do the accounts, and busy himself with looking after my cousin and seeing to his ears and nails. Gloom settled on the apartment. He would hand me a banknote:

"Oh, go and buy us some flowers."

I would bring back a load of white flowers – you would have thought yourself at a first communion! He would give me more notes:

"Go and buy some records, some music…"

And I suddenly became close friends with the record dealer, who was able to offload his stocks of light music.

"You see, it's for an invalid who's bedridden…"

There was no story I would not make up to hide my own distress. So wasn't there anything solid, anything that held firm? Hadn't those adults anything to offer me that would make life worth living? It was all just falsehood, just betrayal: what was there to rely on?

I went to mass again the following Sunday, no longer out of habit, but to find an answer to my agony, something to cling to, and maybe also something, or someone, to fill in small measure my need for understanding, for love.

As I walked alone along the smart thoroughfare, I kept saying over and over again:

"Loneliness, my closest friend,
loneliness, my fellow-traveller,
here you are again beside me,
you will never let me go.
You stand by me, no one else does,
loneliness, my closest friend…"

There were few people in the church for that early mass. The officiating priest was a new one. At first my only view of him was from behind, as he bent down, intoning the prayers at the foot of the altar. Then he faced us, and I discovered a broad forehead wreathed in white hair and beneath it penetrating eyes, lively and gentle at the same time, and a melodious voice. For a brief moment our eyes met, and I felt as though his gaze fixed on me, pierced me through and through.

As I went out, I asked the nun on duty at the door, who was deaf and a bit dim:

"Sister, who's the new chaplain from the community?"

"Oh! That's the Reverend Canon. Well educated he is, and modern: just imagine, he preaches to us on texts from the Holy Bible!"

So that was what it was to be modern. I walked back, reflectively.

It was the start of the university year, the baptism of fire. The first thing I discovered was friendship. Till then I had had nothing but classmates. Very quickly groups got together according to common interests. I found myself encircled by the warmth of a band of friends who were at once both serious and happy-go-lucky, both mischievous and good-natured. We helped each other out; we filled the corridors with our laughter; and we came to understand the comfort of belonging to the group – that little cocoon amid the mass of students, our point of reference, our mooring, our refuge.

The second discovery, so eagerly awaited, was the opposite sex. None of the lads had experienced mixed-sex high schools: and suddenly there we were, day after day, living side by side with numbers of girls. The students from the provinces usually stayed in a rented room: they could invite in whoever they fancied, indeed they could even lend it to a less fortunate pal.

But in those days we eighteen-year-olds thirsted above all for sentiment, for romance. If close attachments developed, they were confined to the university corridors or to the paths of the Luxembourg gardens. Love seemed a rarity, and its physical realization even more so.

It remained a matter of language: especially among lads bawdiness was the rule, and seemed unbounded. We were all the cruder in what we said for being, in fact, chaste in what we did. This outlet provided us with an equilibrium that for the present seemed to satisfy our student existence.

I learnt very quickly to have a tongue livelier than a hand.

Learning about bodies took place primarily through dancing. We danced a lot, and one Saturday evening I felt the need to grope a girl rather enthusiastically – and she was thrilled. But the next day there was mass. Seized by a vaguely uneasy conscience – *maybe it's wicked; I think that's what they say* – I made my way towards the confessional. To my surprise I found there the white-haired priest they had referred to as the Canon. As soon as he saw me entering the box, he said to me:

"No, not here; let's go to my office."

Slightly taken aback, as though caught red-handed, I followed him. He took me to an interview room in the monastery and sat me down.

"Well, what's the trouble?"

His voice had a marked warmth that wrapped itself around me. The man emanated an air of intelligence and distinction:

"OK, you squeezed her a bit tight. Come along now! – that's no sin; next time you'll be more careful, that's all. You can take communion. Come and help me by serving at mass for the nuns – now."

I found myself launched into the complicated ritual of a convent mass, swinging a censer on a diabolical chain that I kept presenting too early or too late – objects that seemed to work without a hitch for the priest, but with which I, silly chap, was all fingers and thumbs. The nuns present pulled their veils across to have a good laugh...

I emerged sweating and panting. But in an absolutely level voice the Canon said to me:

"So next time you want to make your confession come to my place. I live a couple of steps from here, in Rue de la Faisanderie. I'm always there Saturday afternoons."

I mumbled some reply and went out, bumping into the doors.

Life resumed in our great, dismal, bachelor apartment. Uncle often went out, leaving us alone. One day when I was with him in the car, a convertible pulled up beside us at the lights and a stunning creature with brown hair streaming in the wind made signs at him with her hand. Embarrassed, he forced a grin and pulled away. I suddenly realized that Uncle had become a desirable prey for unattached women: money, a large apartment, youthful, good-looking, unattached, without inhibitions... Whenever I saw this swarm buzzing round the hive, I would say to him:

"'Father, watch your right; father, watch your left!'"*

He would give me a wan smile:

"Never, you hear me, never would I have wished for this divorce. We'd created a balance at home..."

These confidences brought the two of us together, but they worried me. So everything was just prey; we had to make our way amid sharks, both male and female; there was nothing pure, nothing decent, nothing reliable.

"Loneliness, my closest friend..."

Shortly after the beginning of the next university term, we had to undergo a compulsory health check in the Boulevard Jourdan. I went along with the others. But as I emerged from the chest x-ray, a red light lit up:

"You have a shadow on your lung, sir; we have to make additional tests of a serious nature."

I was bombarded with further x-rays, and the diagnosis was delivered, with no right of appeal:

"Tuberculosis."

My grandfather, such a fine, determined man, who coughed up the lungs the war had undermined... I overheard the consultants say that infection did not explain everything; that the unleashing of the illness was almost always a reaction to repeated emotional shocks, badly coped with, badly borne.

I knew the source of this illness – the private war that I had waged all alone, the war for survival among irresponsible grown-ups, as immature as they were wealthy, lacking nothing but balance, inner peace, calm and contentment.

The treatment was straightforward: for six months I could not leave my bed, and for six more months I was forbidden to go out after nine.

At the age when lucky students enjoy themselves and get to grips with life, I was confined to my lonely bedroom, with only books for company. My pals brought me the lecture notes, and I read up the library.

Then one Saturday, on one of my first outings, I made my way to the Rue de la Faisanderie.

8

The building was plain and dark. I hesitated a moment before ringing. Uncle was unaware of my venture: so what was my purpose in coming?

The door opened to reveal the Canon haloed in his white hair, and wearing a black cassock.

"Oh, so you've turned up? Come in."

We walked down a long corridor flanked with bookshelves up to the ceiling, packed with books free of dust, their bindings often well-worn; then into an unremarkable room, with a desk at the end. There too, books everywhere, a table strewn with files, a typewriter, and in one corner the simplest of beds.

"Sit down."

I was face to face with him once more; he had ensconced himself in a revolving chair. The place smelt a bit musty, but one got used to it.

He placed his elbows on the armrests, the tips of his fingers meeting on mouth and nose, head a little to one side: he was watching me. His face was round, indeed chubby; his lip sensuous. He radiated intelligence, but also something indefinable, perhaps a little sly, perhaps a little crafty, but at once both gentle and authoritative. The man inhabited another world from that of my infantile relations: he was possessed of certainties; he did not waver, he *knew*.

I was surprised at the interest he took in me. Bit by bit, everything had to be told. It was the first time someone had examined the condition of my soul, had seemed to find it significant and had asked me searching questions that illuminated me to myself.

That day I took away with me a huge book, the *History of Thought*, by Jacques Chevalier:

"You can come back when you like: I'm always here on Saturday afternoons."

I read and read, and I discovered a continent, a planet. All through the ages men had posed the same questions as I had, and they had responded to them in their lives and their writings. Those men were not all Christians, but they all seemed to point towards Christianity; Christianity was drawing to itself all sound thinking, in order to locate it within a broader, more coherent, more homogeneous whole.

I read during my long hours in bed; and every Saturday, at the end of the long corridor lined with knowledge, I once again met the Canon with the fine and gentle features beneath the crown of white hair. He seemed to expect my visit as a matter of course. I used to talk to him of what I had read, and he would relocate each item in a different perspective, wider, more complete: and at every moment there were new insights that I vowed to myself I would explore later, without fail...

But above all he made me talk about myself. And after such hardship, such lonely exertions, such groping along walls that were either impenetrable or immaterial, I came to realize that I was significant in myself, and that I had a desperate thirst for loving.

With great empathy the Canon had sensed this total lack of emotion, of human warmth: without my realizing, he was playing his rod and line deftly behind the bait of our intellectual conversations.

Our Saturdays became a ritual, the secret of which I guarded absolutely. Who could have understood what I was searching for there? My mother, locked up in her misery? Uncle, who lived so intensely, constantly out, constantly at work? Not of deliberate purpose, but through a kind of defiance of the iron world that surrounded me, I kept my secret garden to myself. And I began, without knowing it, to lead a double life.

That first year did not put a stop to my university career: the serious stuff would come the following year. I sat my examination without trouble and left for the mountains to finish my convalescence.

On my return a woman came to the house more and more frequently. Very young, pretty and vivacious, Francine was like a child, and Uncle allowed himself to play up to her a little. He needed a woman above all to manage the house. He determined to marry her, not out of deep feeling, but from good sense. So we recovered a semblance of our normal routine; Uncle began to smile again and to be around a bit more.

He was approaching the summit he had so much coveted. Chairman and Managing Director of one of the leading French pharmaceutical companies, he had been accepted into the world of what the English call "self-made men" searching for legitimacy and roots. These were no longer the paltry upstarts of the post-war years; they were men of substance who had achieved their elevation over a pile of corpses, eliminating their predecessors one by one. They had no difficulty recognising each other: long fangs, sharp claws, they had succeeded because they were the best and often the least scrupulous. They used to live between Trocadéro and Avenue Foch; they met on the golf course; they endeavoured to be seen at receptions given by the old aristocracy, who were in decline, but whose pedigrees still had drawing power. Once it might be "a hunt at the Duke of R's – a real duke, well worth the cost of a complete hunting outfit"; or another time "a cocktail party at Count B's, where I met the Soviet ambassador Vinogradov – a hell of a lad, old friend... takes his drink neat; and he tapped me on the shoulder..."

No one used to miss the obligatory concerts of the season; and even if one was bored stiff there, one could still comment afterwards:

"Rubinstein, especially in the... you know, yes... the softest passages, that's where he's the un-riv-alled master!"

Then they would buy themselves the latest hi-fi system, so that they could make little exclamations after the harpsichord solo in the Fifth Brandenburg Concerto:

"Ah! it's the whole of Beethoven there, don't you think?"

Uncle tagged along, amused and sceptical. His life was his factories – and, on the side, the young colt he was giving shelter to at home.

When I was almost cured, I had thrown myself into my studies. Chemistry fascinated me, as did everything that touched on the life sciences. I rejoined my old pals, and they provided a world of companionship. A dream-existence began, composed of quiet study, endless discussions on the Boulevard Saint-Michel, a few dates and occasional evenings out.

"Not too late, please; don't forget that you're convalescing!"

I was in fact very careful, partly by necessity, and partly because of the work ethic that prevailed at home. Everything was allowed, provided that work was done first.

Life was hardly erotic, but I needed to think about normalizing things. Uncle encouraged me in this direction, and this was something in which he had sound experience:

"With women it's like hunting: you have to have handled the gun a lot before you catch one."

Yes, but how? The girls at university were OK for dating, but they were careful to stop at the point where I wanted to begin. There was no pill: it wasn't so easy to go to bed together in those circumstances, and I really could not dive in with one of Uncle's lady friends. So I chose the solution that was both simplest and most widely acknowledged: armed with a twenty-franc note I went on a tour of the Rue Saint-Denis.

Her name, her trade name at least, was Barbara, I think. It was quickly done, and did not leave me with the memory of any special pleasure. It seemed to me I was the same person as before, except that I had definitely lost my virginity.

My conscience and I reached agreement that we would not mention this to the Canon. After all, nothing had happened, nothing in the least significant. This kind of thing, all too crude as it was, had to be beyond his ken.

In any case Uncle's advice had been followed: sex would remain for the moment a matter of healthy living. Of love there was no question: on the path we were taking, that could only be a hindrance. Emotion, the evidence suggested, would only weaken a man, impede him in his struggles.

At eighteen I was learning how to fight, not how to pine.

9

The important things were the university and science. Free of all other concerns, I studied voraciously, like a hungry eater. Most of my pals did what they had to do, but nothing more. But I wanted to get right inside that world of scientific studies, which was after all no more than a new language. And in a few months I achieved, in a small way, a depth of scientific knowledge that amazed my friends. My approach was simple: I learnt everything indiscriminately, and a bit more too. Uncle, who observed me both working hard and having a reasonable social life, said nothing. He was still in his honeymoon, and the stability that Francine brought us freed up our lives. I sensed well enough that the young woman was not up to her role, but she loved him. As for him, he played along with her, still a little bewitched, but deep down unconvinced.

It was time for the end-of-year examination. It was a serious business, this: 700 students had entered; and there were 250 places in the faculty the following year. I approached the exam in the manner of a bulldozer, adopting a rigid schedule that would allow me systematically to complete all my revision by D-Day.

Uncle was a little anxious, even so: it was his colt's first race, and he had taken certain precautions. Without my knowledge university teachers had been contacted, to give a little helping hand, just in case – a privilege afforded by his social position... With a tight feeling in my stomach, I went off to see the results, which were posted in the main ground-floor corridor. A crowd of students was jostling in front of the noticeboards, amid shouts and tears. My name did not appear among the passes: I turned pale. But a chum caught me by the sleeve:

"Michel! Look over there, on the exam board's special list!"

There, in red, were shown separately the names of the first ten of the year, who were to undergo an extra test for the title of laureate. My name appeared there, for all to see. In a daze I telephoned Uncle at the office. He pretended to scold me:

"So how will I look now? I go to the lengths of intervening on your behalf to get someone to pass you, and you end up a candidate for laureate!"

Never had telephone line transmitted more joy and pride. I passed the exam and so became laureate of the faculty.

Success achieved, I was a completely free agent. So I could resume my regular visits to the Rue de la Faisanderie.

* * *

There I felt myself understood, and I lived in a realm that transcended all else. Book after book, I devoured everything. I had never read the Gospels or the Bible, but the Canon gave me Pascal's *Pensées*, Valensin's *Letters* and the sermons of St Bernard. I was enthralled by the consistency of Christian thought; and I began to discover religious fervour by way of the mystics.

At the beginning of that year he must have felt, I suppose, that the fruit was ripe. One day on his desk I came across the *Paris Match* articles on monastic life, bound in hard covers.

"Yes, read that. And this summer you should go on a retreat in a monastery. It's easy, there's accommodation, I'll give you an introduction."

During our long conversations he began to talk to me about himself. He worked for the Holy Office in Rome, the unit of the Vatican formerly called the Inquisition. That age had passed, of course; but they were still responsible for maintaining the purity of the faith and of religious practice in the Church. That all seemed to me quite strange. I was actually a young pagan, attracted by "something other", but without any Christian background or orientation. I also learnt from him that he had already packed some ten individuals off behind the grilles of religious houses, most of them women – and a few men.

I had happened on an effective recruiting officer.

He often talked to me of "his" nuns, with whom he remained on terms. But he seemed to have quickly broken with the men, from the moment they had crossed the monastery threshold. It was as though they had in a way betrayed him, had ceased to belong to him, by taking to their own wings. It was different with the women: deep inside their convents they remained dependent. On the rare occasions when he mentioned the Carmelite or Trappist that he had "created", it was almost with resentment, a kind of disappointed jealousy. What ties of affection were there between him and his "children"? What was going on within the mind and heart of this solitary man, dedicated as he was to case files and chastity?

At the time I did not ask myself any of these questions. The world was mine; I was once again the little king, and I even had the satisfaction of not being anyone's property, because unbeknown to all I was leading an utterly successful double existence: outwardly, the young student, brilliant and lionized; within, enmeshed unawares by a churchman who was leading me stealthily towards what I most lacked: an ability to love, a motive for living and, perhaps, for dreaming of vast horizons. God was not my first goal, but behind it all the mystery of him was beginning to interest me. So I decided to go on the proposed retreat.

But I had to reckon with Uncle. Like a mechanic, he was assembling an engine. And he had decided that each year I would go to serve an apprenticeship in a European country, both to learn the language there and to gain work experience.

That summer it was England: a month and a half in a chemical products factory. I already spoke English very well, but I needed to graduate from books to laboratory, from office to workshop. And so it happened, without setbacks. The university vacations were long, and I had the end of the summer free.

"I advise you to go to the Abbey of P—," the Canon had said to me. "It's a very strict order" – he pronounced "strict" in the tone of a gourmet – "and I'll write on your behalf."

Go on a retreat in an abbey! It was a big step to take, to make a public admission of my quest: I did not feel up to it. The Canon was sympathetic: he advised me to mask my stay under the guise of a cultural trip. His authority overrode my scruples: was he not for me a moral reference point beyond questioning?

An obliging friend provided my alibi; and one fine September day, unbeknown to all, I set off for Morvan.

The monastery was buried in the forest, eight kilometres from any habitation. That distance had to be traversed on foot. The scenery was superb, stark and majestic. Gradually, as the road led deeper into the wilderness of trees, I felt myself entranced, bewitched. Then I emerged in front of a huge building of pink granite. I came to a great door of carved wood: I rang the bell.

The Father Guest Master had been forewarned by the Canon and was expecting me. Dusk was falling.

"Listen, we have a service now. You wait for me there; I'll take you to your room straight after."

He spoke in a dull, almost toneless voice. He was entirely covered in a black habit, with a long flap of material in front – the scapular – that hid his hands, so that one never saw them. He was just a face, and a voice. He seemed outgoing and aloof at the same time, as if he was performing an act of charity by coming out of himself momentarily to speak to you. Truly weird. And then, after a brief communication – a minimum of the necessary words – he would recede like a wave, and there would be nothing to look at but an effigy, an engraving, that smiled. But where did he go at that point? Was he still there?

He took me round and led me in the direction of a neo-Gothic church, narrow and dark. In the nave were some seats for the congregation, then, further on, filling the dim chancel, a kind of large wooden structure on several levels: the choir stalls for the monks.

Utter silence. A sweet smell of old incense hangs in the air. On the seats are a few men in lay attire, transfixed, like a still from a film. They wait, leaning forwards, heads in their hands or kneeling low. I sit down at the end of the row: my legs ache, and I'm very hungry.

Silence.

A bell rings sharply, and I see a line of monks approaching two by two; they pass in front of us, turn to the right, bow before the altar and gradually fill the tiers of stalls. They move without any sound whatever, their gaze fixed, in unending procession. How many are there? Sixty, eighty? Then, in close formation, come youngsters, skipping a little as they walk: these must be the novices.

In less than two minutes the choir stalls are filled with a host of black shadows, their tonsures gleaming in the half-light. They turn their backs on us to face the altar. The laymen beside me have risen to their feet, as if to attention, expressions intent.

Then suddenly, in the enveloping silence, *just one* voice, made up of all those men's voices blended to perfection. It's the first time that I've heard Gregorian chant. The tune rises up, floats a second, then sinks, timelessly. How do all those men – there are almost a hundred of them – manage to give the physical impression of a *single* voice unfolding the melodic contours of a chant that remains supple, melancholy and perfectly controlled?

Overwhelmed, I forget my weariness and hunger. Every now and then they turn, bow low and rise again as though one; there's no clumsiness; there is even grace. You'd say that all those bodies formed a single body surging and living as though stirred from within. I watch those who are nearest to us: their eyes are open but their gaze is fixed far into the distance or sometimes lowered, their looks expressionless, their faces frozen. And from that assembly there goes on rising a chant that's solemn and captivating, a melody simple and spare and sometimes moving, so that one feels it issues from stones that are alive.

After my tramp through the forest without food, this experience hits me like a punch in the face.

Suddenly it all dies away. They're on their knees or bent low in the renewed silence. Someone touches my arm: the Father Guest Master – he seems to have appeared from nowhere – is smiling to me out of the top of his black habit:

"Come," he whispers without opening his mouth.

A scrap of bread and cheese, and then I find myself in a small room that's totally bare, with rough grey walls, a bed, a table and a washbasin.

"This is the cell that you'll occupy during your stay among us."

"Cell": the word is well chosen. Left to myself, I sit down on the edge of the bed. Within me there's coming into being the conviction – commanding, overpowering, inexplicable – that I want... well, I should like... yes, I should like to live a life similar to this. It's "something other". It attracts me.

* * *

The six days of the retreat unfolded themselves on a little pink cloud. Between long walks in the forest and services that were always as inspiring, the Father Guest Master granted me all his time. The weather was fine, and our conversations took place on the bench of a little garden that looked out over the valley. Without my suspecting it at the time, I was the object of a sort of highly successful seduction. He remained distant and out of reach, just enough for me to want to know more. And at the same time he stressed the human side – "very human, you know" – of the monastic life. A special life led by special individuals, who were wholly detached from the vicissitudes of everyday existence so as to dedicate themselves to living in the spirit and experiencing God. On this last phrase he remained quite unspecific – "It's indescribable, you see." And as I did not in fact see much, I dressed the quest up in all the allure of mystery.

And I prayed – or at least I spent long periods alone in the church.

But I had to get back, to resume my university place. I did not go to see the Canon straight away, and he wisely left me to digest the discoveries I had made.

10

This second year was the one with the heaviest load of subjects, and it was staked out with exams like a combat course. By common consent our group went out less and worked determinedly. Even so it did not escape me that the atmosphere between Uncle and his new wife was deteriorating. The marriage of convenience had not resulted, for him, in any love.

Anyhow, was there such a thing as love?

The difference in attitudes and characters became more and more apparent. Little by little I once again became the confidant of one and of the other, the impotent spectator of my elders' inability to manage their lives.

To be sure, Uncle had achieved brilliant success both socially and professionally. But in the end it had all proved empty, in my view at least. The forward momentum was not self-justifying. There had to be another reason for fighting than the struggle itself.

A reason for *living* – but what reason? To be first to reach the top rung of the ladder, so as to find another ladder to climb? No, thank you. To have a companion, so as not to be alone? No, thank you. To make love without love, to keep healthy? No, thank you.

A crestfallen Cyrano, I went back to the Rue de la Faisanderie.

As the months passed, my relationship with the Canon underwent a subtle change. For my part, I remained wholly confident, committed, full of life. *He* seemed to be letting himself become more and more attached to me. He would call me his "baby", his child; and, if this sometimes made me smile, it was with grateful indulgence. After all, it is true that since my Razanne I had never been anybody's "child": so I let myself be mothered without protest. If none of this was very clear to me, it was even less clear to him. I failed to register the gradual slide towards something slightly ambiguous, the more so because he was guiding me towards heights that were too pure, too idealistic. Certainly, there was no action, no word, out of place. But when the times came for my confession and I surrendered my soul to God, the Canon was its recipient. As I knelt at the foot of his armchair, he would take my arm, put it around his neck and give his six-foot baby the absolution with an emotion that choked him.

That only lasted a second. Straight after we each resumed our place, and sailed smoothly on over the crystalline waters of Christian mysticism. As far as I was concerned, I was receiving my share of affection and allowing myself to be led: I was much too naive to be able to imagine what else it might be.

I had told him of the impact that the monastery of P— had had on me; and gradually my monastic vocation became something that was acknowledged, then taken for granted, between us. He had no trouble contrasting the harsh world through which I would have to pick my way with the framework, perfect, timeless and pure, of monastic life. He was the only being to whom I could open my heart: he filled it with the radiance of a unique call to a life that was different, where success could be called fulfilment. Who could have resisted that?

It was a subtle game: I understand it now. At the time I was incapable of seeing it for what it was. I recall now no more than a dim feeling of unease: if I had followed up on that momentary sensation, I should have slammed shut the only door that might have opened onto "something other". To pass through that door, to enter that promised land beyond, I needed – and I would need more and more – to become blind.

It goes without saying that from then on I was lost to the girls of the faculty and elsewhere. As I was to all appearances quite "normal", actually a handsome lad and a good catch, they would flutter around me, without managing to settle. One of the girls in our set used to look at me with eyes large as saucers and would regularly dissolve into tears at my coldness. But I could not explain to them that I was engaged to Christian philosophy and in love with Cistercian mysticism. There are things that do not go down well, even in the most open-minded quarters. And if I had told the lads – and we used to talk very freely – that, following the advice of a priest, I wore pants at night to avoid any "uncleanness", they would have taken me off to the nearest doctor. But I was good company, I enjoyed dancing, and that sufficed.

Week by week the Canon initiated me into the byways of chastity. He would speak to me about it in long monologues interrupted by silences, his eyes lowered or suddenly fixed on mine: the ultimate goal was the purification of one's thoughts, the uprooting to their hidden depths of all sexual urges.

How did I understand this at the time? A reckless nineteen-year-old, in a confused way I identified the world that surrounded me – that jungle where human contact was guided by instinct more than by love – with evil. Sex was a dark impulse demanding satisfaction, and its opposite – light – was purity.

Incapable of half-measures, I launched myself into purity like an athlete into the disciplines of the running track. Confining all human relations to friendship was not too hard. There remained my own body:

"There are certain areas of the body, are there not..."

The Canon said no more about it; but from then on my hands found themselves condemned to banishment from myself.

The world of thoughts was harder to channel: it wasn't so much the girls I knew at the faculty that filled that world; it was my dreams as an enthusiastic dancer. The uneasiness that dancing generated in me was the subject of my weekly confessions:

"You must keep yourself safe, you must keep yourself safe and whole for God..."

Why "must", I did not know. But because I found no satisfaction in the life-models that I observed around me, I felt at least that I was doing better than *them*, I was escaping from *their* world, I was discovering – alone of them all – the king's highway to a perfection beyond their ken.

I am astonished now at the obvious delight that the Canon took in organizing and checking my progress along this path that was so abnormal for a lively young man. Did he just want to safeguard me for God, or rather – also – to keep me, body and soul, for himself? Did he want to have me share the vocation that was his, and that he was fulfilling perhaps less than fully?

With no answer to the question, Canon, I leave you the benefit of the doubt. But, with your permission, I do doubt.

And because the spoken word escaped any criticism, my reputation for bawdiness became firmly established on the faculty corridors.

The difficult second year at university went well, and I garnered in exam successes one after the other. I was even a laureate once more: it was becoming routine.

The following summer it was Spain, a factory in Barcelona. I came back speaking Spanish, and unchallengeable on amino acids. But there was still the end of summer left... I had told the Canon that the austere regime and huge size of the community intimidated me a bit at P—. I should have liked to see another monastery, on a more human scale, one with more of a smile.

"Well then, go on a retreat to B—! It's quite a recent foundation; the community's small. Of course" – pouting slightly – "the Gregorian chant isn't as fine as at P—, but anyway it's the same order."

At the cost of another subterfuge and another lie – the Canon's conscience was remarkably elastic in a good cause – I found myself one day in front of the abbey.

11

I was captivated from the start. The small monastery was in the final stage of construction at the side of a huge old church. The community was congenial and homely. Tucked in a bend of the great River, it was a delightful spot, exuding an air that was at once energizing and soothing.

My dealings with the monastic authorities were painless enough: my decision had already been taken. They did not give themselves a lot of trouble checking the authenticity of my monastic vocation. I was applying for entry; that was enough. I was an exceptional candidate, of good middle-class stock, an unlooked-for recruit: this kind did not need too much discussion.

I could have joined immediately. But, prompted by some kind of anxious premonition, I informed them of my wish to finish my studies and receive a degree. This seemed reasonable, and since I had already kept up a double life for two years, it was natural to assume that I would keep it up to the end.

So now the next two years had to be sorted out. A triangular consultation took place with the Canon and the Superior of the abbey, men of the Church, men of God. The outcome was that, as far as my family were concerned, I should maintain the pretence for as long as possible and continue to lead the double life that had succeeded so well up to then. Evidently the family circle was an incarnation of evil: it was important to avoid a premature confrontation, which I might not have withstood. To conceal my true life from my people was not immoral, because it was for my salvation: and later, from within the cloister, I would secure theirs.

Gradually, in the Superior's office that looked out over the valley, the arguments were pressed upon me. It was not my personal decision that worried me, but the consequences that I foresaw for those around me.

"My mother has no one but me to rely on; Uncle has given me a new life and his support..."

None of that counted. "Service to God comes first" – this justified the sacrifice that I was forcing them to make.

And if they saw it as a betrayal of their affection?... Let them. They would understand, later.

It was the Church authorities at the highest level that were talking to me, that were pointing out to me what was true, that were pointing out to me the road that I must follow in God's name. If I listened to them – and how could I not have listened? – I was leading a personal crusade against a depraved and fraudulent society. Truth was on their side, and on mine.

Besides, in two years I would come of age and would no longer be accountable to anyone.

I listened to all this with a certain tightness in my heart. Uncle, my real father, who trusted me completely, who had staked everything on me... My mother, poor woman, already betrayed once in her love, who was watching her big son grow up apart from her with so much pride and hope for the future... But God demanded everything, and my choice was God's everything.

"Once more, it's a matter of the salvation of souls, yours and, through you, theirs. A redemption is on offer to them through the mediation of yourself. It comes by way of a death, for sure, but with the purpose of a resurrection that's beyond their imagining, the resurrection of Christ on Easter morning."

So what was at stake was placed at its proper level: death and life. Death was passing, transitory, unavoidable and contemptible. It was the key to life, a life that would come thereafter, the quality of which would match the quality and unconditionality of the sacrifice freely offered.

I sensed that the death that I was choosing was also that of my near ones – especially theirs, because through my initiation I, at least, would be having a foretaste of the joys of the new life. I sensed that that death was going to be imposed on them without their having asked for it. I sensed that resurrection was the last of their concerns: they were simply trying to live, and were looking to me for a renewal of life. I even sensed that they were probably quite incapable of taking pleasure in the outcome, but would most likely be crushed by my desertion and by the suffering that I would be inflicting on them... None of this seemed to make any impression on my instructors, sure as they were of being the trustees of higher truths, to which it was not after all to be expected that I could have access.

Reassured, I watched the door I so much wanted to pass through swinging open. Without too much questioning, without too much consideration of it all, I submitted. God requested it, God wished it, the Church backed it. So...

I resumed my studies.

12

That year commenced calmly, compared with the one before. It was the opportunity for a spectacular success. So simultaneously I enrolled at the Sorbonne for a master's degree in biochemistry. For that to be in any way possible a special arrangement needed to be made at the faculty. Stunned, my supervisors agreed and devised a tailor-made course of study for me. I would do my practicals alone, so that I could be sure of fitting in the biochemistry ones too. Friends would attend lectures on my behalf, while I attended those at the Sorbonne. All this was unheard of, but they were not going to refuse to let one of their best students attempt a brave gamble. Everything was put in place, and the engine started to turn at full throttle. I swapped from one faculty to the other without mishap, and without even neglecting my pals and my evenings out.

At the Sorbonne the teaching was at doctorate level. Biochemistry was a new science, the domain of pioneers. It was a life science *par excellence*, and life was what I loved. At the end of the year there was a special course of lectures by Jacques Monod, director of the Pasteur Institute, and I went along, my mouth watering.

Monod was in the process of discovering the mechanisms for the transfer of DNA, which won him the Nobel Prize shortly afterwards. His lectures were straightforward: he told us, step by step, of the progress of his work and his research.

At this level the students were fewer – around sixty – and well informed. The prevailing atmosphere in the little lecture hall on the Boulevard Raspail was like that of a small church. Monod came in, a fine-looking man with a perpetual tan, sparkling with intelligence. He spoke without microphone and with few notes. Behind him on the board was a large drawing of a DNA double helix: he held us spellbound at what he had discovered.

On one occasion, a rare occurrence in those days, he addressed himself directly to us:

"Right. Look at where we've got to. Now, at this stage of the work, what would you have done? In which direction should we go?"

The audience stayed dumb, as though turned to stone. I raised my hand.

"Yes?"

In a few hesitant words I went on to say what I thought I had understood.

"Yes, that's not stupid, but you see…"

And he explained – which surprised no one – that my grasp of it was incomplete, that there was this, and also that…

On the way out of the lecture I met him in a corridor. He stopped me:

"What stage are you at? What are you doing?"

Monod had us utterly bewitched, and I do not know now what I replied.

"Good. There's a research unit being formed, at Villejuif, under the direction of Professor Jean Bernard. We're working together. We have to set up a molecular biology lab: I should love you to make contact with us at the end of the year, after the exams. Don't let me down."

I made no reply and told no one. Monod had taken note of my name and details.

At the close of the lecture series he took a loftier standpoint. In front of us, on the board, there was written the most exact knowledge that man had of the origin of life. That – Monod pointed his finger – is where existence came into being. The rest – what came between the molecule of DNA and the fully formed human being – the rest was the work of chance and the product of a kind of necessity. Chance and necessity… so was the miracle of humanity just that? And was existence the product of a sort of blind fate?

I held out against Monod's conclusions. As I listened to him there were ringing within me the opening phrases of St John's Gospel, which I had just read:

In the beginning was the Word,
and the Word was with God,
and the Word was God.

To be sure, I kept saying to myself, great scientists do not know everything. At the very point where *he* stops everything begins, and I know the key of a science that he rejects: the science of God, which allows us to go further.

In any case, for me the one did not contradict the other.

Uncle had grown used to my success, and now he watched me succeed in both arenas; a close thing at the Sorbonne, but even so… Delighted, he made arrangements for the summer: it was to be Italy.

The factory was situated in open country, ten kilometres from Naples. They manufactured vitamins there, and I was assigned to the laboratory. The fact was, they had a synthesis problem that was costing the business a lot of money, because the chemical reaction was working badly. They entrusted me with this job: I had four weeks available, and they gave me carte blanche.

On the specified day, the eve of my departure, I submitted my report identifying what was happening and what needed to be done to improve the output from the reaction process. As a precaution the director, without telling me, had sent a sample to England to duplicate my research: my findings matched theirs, and Uncle received an appreciative letter. The summer ended without a monastic retreat, since everything was already arranged. There remained one more year, the last with a clear line of sight ahead. I realized that the ordeal could not be put off any longer, and that I should, I must soon, launch the confrontation: I had just reached my long awaited majority. How far away Naples seemed already, with its light, its smells and the explosive joy of the local folk!...

The last university year brought quite a workload, but that bothered none of us. We all knew that I had to make a success of it as before. Truth to tell, Uncle was totally preoccupied with his emotional entanglements. Nothing was going right now with Francine, who was wasting away in misery. Additionally, his attention had been caught by his sister-in-law, a pretty brunette, clever and sophisticated. A third woman was looming on the horizon; and I was more and more everyone's confidant. In short, life carried on; there was nothing new.

I needed to bring my secret, my hidden life, out into the open. I needed to interrupt that stage performance in which all the characters were known, where the words gave the impression of having been already learned, already spoken. But I did not manage it and kept putting the moment off from week to week.

13

That first Sunday of November, very early as usual, I went to serve at mass for the Canon. The Gospel for the day, read in Latin, told of the calming of the storm and recorded the cry of the apostles:

"*Domine, salva nos, perimus!* Lord, save us, we perish!"*

It was like a sign for me: it would be today, then, this morning. I went back to the house repeating to myself, as though to avert the impact:

"*Salva nos, perimus, salva nos...*"

After breakfast I accosted Uncle:

"Will you come into my bedroom? I've something to tell you."

Suspecting nothing, he followed me in and sat on the bed, smiling. Often recently he had come there to talk to me about himself, to seek the support of my sympathetic ear. He looked at me with affection.

"You see, I..."

I steeled myself, and stared him in the eye.

"You see, I've decided... I want to enter a monastery. I want to become a Catholic monk."

No reaction. He doesn't stir, doesn't blink; he sits motionless and dumb. The smile has left him, that's all. I've the impression that he's not fully understood.

"I want to be a monk in due course, at the monastery of B—. I'm intending to enter once and for all when I've finished at university."

I watch him. He seems to have become one with the bed. His eyes are enlarged, as from a huge shock. He knows me well enough to realize that I'm not joking. He says nothing.

Move, Uncle; do something; don't sit there like that looking at me; I can't bear that look; react; explode; don't stay stock still, with those eyes empty and staring...

Did it last for long, or only a short moment? I do not know. He just got up and went from my room, leaving me on my own.

One hour, perhaps... I came out myself and joined them in the drawing room. He was sitting opposite Francine; they both turned in my direction when I entered.

It was Francine who spoke:

"Do you really understand?"

Then I repeated my decision; I told them that it had long been coming to fruition in secret, that it wasn't just a whim, that everything was arranged...

"So" – Uncle spoke slowly, as though unwilling to understand, and then unwilling to say what he said – "so, for all this time you've been lying? You've lived with us, bringing to fruition this... thing; and all that we've achieved together, it's just so that you can go and end up 'there'?"

He could not pronounce the monastery's name: it made him choke.

For two hours I reaffirmed everything; I rejected all the arguments; I refused to budge an inch. My instructors could have been proud of me: I held my ground.

Finally Uncle stood up quickly and struck me on the breast with his hand:

"Michel, you've nothing there. You've nothing where your heart should be."

And it was as though he fled from the room.

We did not see each other again until breakfast the next day. When I entered, he was motionless in front of his full cup of tea, which was going cold. Hunched and gloomy, he had clearly not had much sleep.

With unprecedented vehemence he adjured me, ordered me, commanded me to give up my plan, not to do it, not to do it to him... He was beating on a block of wood. Then, deadly pale, he seized his cup and smashed it against the wall opposite him:

"Get out. I don't want to see you here again. Off with you!"

I got up, went to my room – as though in a dream. I took down from the top of a cupboard the suitcase I had used for my holidays. I placed it on the bed. Then he came in and saw the open suitcase. He slumped down on the edge of a chair, tears in his eyes.

"Michel... why, why are you doing this? Michel, Michel... stay. But why, why?"

Uncle, Father, you who've made me what I am, you're not really going to cry, are you?

He stood up.

"Michel... you're the greatest disappointment of my life."

There was no need for us to talk of it much more. But I knew that he would not give in just like that. I waited for the warfare.

For several days we avoided each other: he came home late, I left early. And then all at once I had the whole family on my back. He had told them – and I was almost grateful for it. I had to face up to my mother, assault her in cold blood, without painkillers, this woman who now had nothing – I had to watch her suffer, watch her beg, then abandon herself to misery like a child, grow old within a few days, float off downstream like a boat that one pushes out into the current with a foot...

Notified of these dramas, the Canon had in turn informed the abbey. I received my first letter with the order's letterhead, beneath a simple black cross:

My dear child,

  You are living Christ's struggle in agony in the garden of Gethsemane. Like him, raise your eyes towards the Father from whom you draw your strength. And do not forget that your dear ones will, later, be the first beneficiaries of your decision. Hold firm.

In truth, I do not know from where I drew my strength, for I needed it to beat the others into the ground as I did. But above all I do not know whether it was indeed myself that was acting. One look, with eyes no longer raised aloft but simply resting on my family, was all that should have been enough. But I was not looking. I was moving onwards, beyond, elsewhere...

And the Canon gave his blessing to my steadfastness:

"You've been of age for several months now: they can no longer do anything against you."

62

He was mistaken: Uncle would fight with every means he had.

Ever since my father's departure my mother and sisters had lived off the income paid by the family business. The board – that is, the family – met and decided that for the current year there would be no dividends. They all did without their money to put me in touch with this other reality: my mother would have nothing to live on any more, what would become of her without me? Uncle was playing his last card.

A second letter arrived from the abbey:

> But that is all to the good. Find some employment quickly that will allow you to fund your mother's needs while you finish your studies. In this way, like the apostles, you will work with your hands for the Lord.

All this seemed obvious from the monastery. No one imagined the apostles having exams to sit in June and warfare at home. So I found a night job in a factory, for a meagre wage. Returning in the small hours, I used to get a few hours' sleep before going to the faculty.

Silently Uncle watched my struggle. At bottom he was not sorry that I was facing up to things: good blood could not lie. In any case, this was a trial that he was making me undergo, to test my determination. As time went by, he realized too that one cannot oppose a life choice; one can only wait and see.

He waited and saw. I held my course. At the end of the month the money I earned went to my mother, and I was studying as well as could be expected. Busy day and night, I met no one. I had memorized the monastic evening office, and I repeated it on my way home in the car after midnight, on the empty boulevards of outer Paris.

What Uncle had not foreseen was that the warfare would confirm me in the attitude of one who had seen the light: the last thing one should do is to provide a crusading cause to a warrior of Christ who is prepared to fight it out for God.

"Service to God comes first": the family had to submit to what they saw before their eyes. You cannot fight on equal terms with an ideology. Neither sentiment nor coercion can prevail over a mindset founded on dogma. The Catholic Church, with the daunting weight of its certainties and traditions, had the power unilaterally to determine questions of ethics: what was good, what was not good, what was right. Since I had chosen God, I was in the right: no obstacle, no impediment, would hold me back. As for human suffering – my own, my family's – that was of little account where God was concerned. And besides, I was convinced that, if there was suffering, it was only more of what Christ had endured: he had led the way. These things were beyond discussion.

I could no longer speak to Uncle, but sometimes we passed each other in the house. One day he stopped me:

"You know, I feel like someone who's assembled a racing car, and it's now going to be used to do the shopping."

He was admitting defeat: I was beyond retrieval. And, as my conduct in battle had been pretty honourable, the final months went by in a kind of truce, sad and quiet.

I passed my final exams, for the first time without distinction. A few days later I received a letter from Villejuif: there was a position, a tempting one, on offer from Monod for the young graduate. Then came another letter, from Naples: they would be glad to employ me, the laboratory would soon be in need of a competent manager…

"Present a thank-offering to God": I put the letters in the waste-paper basket. They had come too late; I was committed elsewhere.

My departure was stealthy, almost secret. I put my things in a maid's room above my mother's place, where I was going to live for a few more days. I made a last visit to the Rue de la Faisanderie:

"You have given everything, sacrificed everything, for God. God will pay it back to you, from now on. Have confidence: you are not abandoning your people, you are going to serve them elsewhere, and they will receive you back in another way. We'll see each other again soon, at the abbey."

Then he gave me his blessing, standing in the office for dramatic effect. I went out into a street that was already dark, and I burst out sobbing amid the traffic.

That evening I went to say goodbye to Uncle. He was reading his newspaper and put on a detached look:

"Michel, we'll never see each other again."

"You know very well that there are two words that a person cannot say – 'always' and 'never'."

That was all. There was too much between us, and too much love, for any words to be worthwhile.

That night I got out of bed and turned on the light in the silent apartment. They were all there on the walls, my colourful, beautiful friends: Brayer, Oudot, Pasquin, Jansem, Chapelain-Midy, my favourite pictures... And the gramophone records, the books, the old furniture... *Come on, Michel, since you're giving everything to God, it's right that your sacrifice should be one of value.*

I turned the light off and went back to bed.

Part Two

The abbey

1

The cell, where I find myself alone again once the Novice Master has left ("I'm called Father Master"), measures three square metres. In front of me a window looks out onto the valley and a few village houses. Behind me the large pane of rough glass in the door will allow anyone to find out if I'm there and what I'm doing. On my right a plump straw mattress, of real straw, is laid out on a pallet. Two coarse sheets, one khaki blanket, one bolster. In the corner, a washbasin with no mirror, and a single tap for cold water.

On the left a large cupboard-like structure, fixed high on the wall, and closed with a white curtain; in the other corner, a table of raw wood, a lamp, a stool, a bookcase with shelves – and, conspicuously, a thick Bible.

That's all. The walls are white, the floor's of polished wood. There's nothing to hold the eye, but a large red wooden cross above the bed. "If the cross is empty," the Father Master told me, "it's because it's meant for you. Your place is on that cross, and you will learn here how to stay on it."

I sit down on the bed, which doesn't give under my weight. All around me, silence: a silence such as I've never heard before, complete and impenetrable. Yet there are in that section, I know, five other novices, five young men like me, who are at that very time in their cells, only a few metres away. Have they all turned to glass? I cannot hear a single human sound. The village that I can see from the window seems itself to be wrapped in cotton-wool. Oh for movement, for something to do...!

My suitcase: the only link I have with the outside world – have I already covered such a distance in such a short time that there's now both an "outside world" – the world of humanity – and here?

My suitcase is still in the spot where the Father Master put it down. *Pick it up, open it: but where to stow my things? There must be a place... The large cupboard, that's it!* I quickly pull open the white curtain, then back away involuntarily. At eye level there's a shelf of coarse, bare wood; on the underside several hooks, and from one of them, right in the middle, hangs a thin cord with a ball of bright red material halfway along. Out of this acorn dangle six plaited strings with three tight little knots at the end of each.

The "discipline", the scourge of cords with which, stripped to the waist, I'll have to lash my back every Friday for as long as it takes to recite Psalm 51. I'll learn later that, though you can find shorter psalms, this is not the longest of the 150 in the Bible. But some Fridays it will seem quite long enough.

The red of the ball that binds the strings together stands out against the wall. It's the only touch of cheerfulness in the cell. I slowly close the curtain: I have arrived in the monastery, for sure.

The morning must have passed, I don't know how. Just before midday that first day the bell rings in the silence: time for the office – that is, an act of worship in the church. So I'm finally going to see some people; I step out into the corridor.

A rustling, swishing sound, like sliding doors make at airports: fifteen or twenty billows of black serge are descending the stairs, apparently without touching them.

I know that every service is preceded by a "station", a time of waiting motionless in a dark corridor that leads into the church. At the end, starkly illuminated, a great baroque crucifix, streaked with blood. The monks line up against each wall, facing the patch of light, in order of seniority: the Superior in front, the novices right at the back, each in his precise spot, which would never vary.

I arrive at the place, arms swinging loose. A shadow emerges from the wall and leads me to my exact position. I find myself pressed tight against a stained glass window of abstract design: directly in front of me a shaven scalp shows slightly from out of the broad hood that is drawn down over the head. Let's keep a sense of humour: I suppose that in ten years, at the same hour, I'll be enjoying the same view of the same scalp...

A double black line, upright, motionless, reaching all the way to the crucifix. Now and then a shadow emerges from a side door and, gliding on a cushion of air, goes to find its place in the formation. They brush by me and pass on without seeing me: I must myself have become part of the wall; things like that happen without one realizing.

Then nothing moves any more, everyone is present. Are they really there, inside their habits? Presumably.

"My brothers," I say to myself, stunned.

2

I retain no clear memory of those first days. Although I had taken up residence in the monastery, I was still regarded as a visitor, and I still wore my lay clothes. One afternoon the Superior – the Father Abbot – received me in his office. Above an alert face his shorn scalp was covered with a black skullcap; a metal cross hung from a chain on his breast; all the while he spoke he kept mechanically twisting the silver ring that encircled the ring-finger of his left hand: the emblems of power.

The Father Abbot was a shrewd and intelligent man. Product of one of the *grandes écoles*, he had taken his monastic vows late on, and he carried out his responsibilities with the efficiency of an engineer. In a certain way he had recognized in me an equal, different from the young high-school leavers that made up the bulk of the noviciate. He chose to speak to me as man to man:

"My dear brother, tell yourself that you are going back in some ways into medieval times. Plenty of things are going to change: a Council has just assembled that carries within it every hope for renewal of the Church. For a period that I cannot estimate you're going to have to live as in the Dark Ages. You will accept that for love of the Lord."

I only truly entered the Dark Ages at the end of the first week: it was then that I would take my habit, it was then that I would lose my name and my hair; it was then that my time as novice would really begin. For the moment I was on a full retreat, along with two companions who had arrived at the same time as me, and whom I kept close to without addressing them.

For the rule of silence was absolute: human speech was an evil, or at least it was forbidden. So people never spoke to each other, save in very particular circumstances, in unobtrusive and well-defined places, with a distant formality. Anyone wanting to speak would signal to the other by putting a forefinger to his lips. They would then withdraw to one of the places designated for speech – cubbyhole, broom store, toilet area – and the older would say "*benedicite*", to which the younger would reply "*dominus*". Once these outpourings were finished, one said what one had to say; the very delights of the location served to limit discourse.

Otherwise we used sign language, like deaf mutes. But I had not reached that stage yet, and I contented myself with keeping mum. They seemed nice chaps, though, the two lads who had chosen the king's highway at the same time as I had...

A "full retreat" meant no post. All at once the tangle of tensions, difficulties and confrontations that was snagging me had unravelled itself. The total break with everything that had hitherto made up my daily life gave me a sort of peace that I relished, even though I dreaded finding out all too soon what had been happening on the other side. From the day after I took the habit I would be allowed to read my letters. The artificial and impermeable cocoon that enveloped me would then be broken. I was almost enjoying it, like a holiday.

Truth to tell, I had become anaesthetized: the time of anguished partings was over: I wanted peace, I wanted tranquillity. I had made my choice: it had to come out right.

So I entered into what was offered me with unbounded zeal. If the details of everyday life struck me as odd, incomprehensible, I simply took note of them.

But the penetrating gaze of the mocking student had not been quenched. Michel watched, forcing himself not to pass judgement. The adult I have now become is able to assume a distance that might have been fatal at that juncture.

There were periods of instruction, hours of meditation in the icy chapel, long services chanted in Latin, in which, as I was swept along, I tried to clutch at some passage I recognized, as at a life-buoy.

Then came the day: I find myself in the chapter room, seated on a stool in lonely state at the centre of a rectangle of fathers in great black habits. The Father Abbot speaks immediately before the ceremony: I then take off my right shoe and sock, and each of the monks kneels low before me to kiss my bare foot – a token of humility and a gesture of welcome that I savour for its high-mindedness – the joints of the most senior creaking as they crouch.

The great moment arrives: still at the centre, I go down on my knees. Strangely, I feel nothing. The Father Abbot comes up, helps me off with my jacket, undoes my tie and pulls over my head and arms a gown of black serge. It's clean and smells of mothballs. There's a leather belt, and then on top of it all a broad scapular with hood. None of it fits well, and beneath their shaven scalps the fathers let show some kindly smiles. I swear they think they're attending the presentation of a newborn child.

And that's very much what it is. From now on I'm no longer myself; I'm someone else. And even my name – those syllables by which I had identified myself since birth, the name that Razanne used to shout on Tamatave beach when I ran away from her – that name is going to be taken from me.

The Father Abbot looks at me gravely, and in complete silence he lets fall the Latin phrase of the ritual:

"Michel, *amodo vocaberis frater Irenaeus*. From henceforth you will be called Brother Irenaeus."

He hasn't asked me my opinion, but a wicked gleam in his eye seems to say: "Do you like it? Nice surprise?"

73

Brother Irenaeus rises and goes to join the shadows along the wall – from now on indistinguishable from them.

Well, not completely: as I leave the chapter house, the Father Master grabs me by the sleeve. A small room on the first floor, a swaying electric light bulb, a stool, a grubby cloth around my neck, the sound of an electric razor, and my hair falling to right and left, any old how – *we must hurry: the bell's ringing, we're going to be late at the refectory, off with it quickly, we're hungry.*

I do not remember the flavour of my first broth as Brother Irenaeus – just that my scalp had joined the line of the others at table, and the top of my head felt cold.

* * *

So that evening, in the abbey cloister, you could see one more shadow rushing down the stairs, lifting his gown with one hand at the front, then bending in the half-light to receive the Father Master's benediction. You could see him in his cell, taking off his rough new habit, fumbling over buttons and loops. After a pause, he kept his shirt on and put over it a small scapular that reached down to the buttocks, with a small hood at the top that only just fitted his shaven scalp: this was the "night scapular", the purpose of which was to bring to mind the jolly time when monks used to go to sleep fully dressed in the day's sweaty clothes, but preserved from the Devil's nocturnal wiles by the holy habit's meritorious power.

Finally he could be seen forgetting to scrub his teeth, sure proof of distress that evening; then putting the light out and groping with his hand for the top of the bedclothes; sliding between damp sheets that were smooth like wet cement, and searching for a position between the corn stalks that poked out from his new straw mattress; realizing that his scalp was decidedly cold and pulling the sacred hood down over his eyes; then, stretched at full length like a recumbent effigy – with a corn husk pricking his thigh – pleased to be playing his role of reckless monk so well, falling at last into the easy sleep of youth.

3

The next day I was admitted to the "noviciate room", which resembled the classroom of a village school. Raw wooden desks were arranged in rows, with benches facing the Father Master's lectern. There was a blackboard, and shelves on the walls full of devotional books carefully selected for the novices.

Every morning, after the service that marked the end of the great nocturnal silence (no talking except in cases of grave emergency), the sharp ringing of a bell summoned us together there. The novices positioned themselves in order of the date they entered the monastery, most senior at the back, newest arrivals in front.

Standing in our places, eyes looking straight forwards, we waited for the ritual *benedicite* of the Father Master:

"*Dominus ...*" came the murmured response.

After a sign of the cross everyone sat down, slid their hands beneath their scapulars, and the Father Master started speaking.

It was there that I received, every day that year, the teaching provided specially for the novices, with no communication with neighbours, even though our elbows touched.

Times have changed, and minds have opened. But those who were trained in those distant Dark Ages – this was the beginning of the Sixties – retain the indelible imprint of it.

The first god I would learn to worship here was to be the timetable, and his herald, the bell. Brother Bellringer was an important personage. A good monk having no wristwatch, he kept a huge timepiece buried in his bosom: he would hold it in the open palm of his left hand, eyes fixed on it, his right hand clutching the bell rope, so as to sound the bell at the precise second. For long years I watched him at it, seven or eight times a day. On two occasions, I think, he missed the wake-up bell – and they still talk about it. Then one day he heard that his mother had died of old age. This man, uncouth and extremely ugly, never put a single sentence together again. His mother was the only one, I think, ever to have loved him for himself: once she had gone, he rapidly went mad. They buried him with some relief: his attacks were becoming harder and harder to match with the decor. I was very fond of him.

So, wake-up bell, six o'clock; then twenty minutes later, after a quick wash at the basin, bell for chapel; bell for the morning chapter meeting, bells for meals or for work... bells till night-time, and even during the night.

For we used to hold night prayers – wake-up at 2.25, chapel five minutes later. We would chant psalms in a monotone for an hour, a little longer on feast days. Then I would make my way back to my straw mattress through dark corridors, chilled to the bone, and try to get some precarious sleep before the second wake-up bell of the morning.

The superiors were careful to look after our health. I only went to night prayers every other day, and I noticed then that more than half the community were absent – certainly not through slackness – a serious offence – but with the Father Abbot's permission, since bodies and nerves wore themselves out quickly under that regime. They relied on us, the young, to keep it up.

The Father Master taught that of all the modes of monasticism then practised ours was closest to the perfect ideal – that is, it was the most *observant*. And in this way I discovered one of the keystones of the monastic edifice.

"Observance" – he spoke very softly – "is a certain way of conducting oneself, a particular manner of carrying out each of the most humdrum actions – so that nothing, absolutely nothing, should ever be humdrum any more. You are to give each of your actions its eternal significance."

From then on I would do everything *differently*, in order to erase the memory of a previous existence: I would be taught this in the tiniest detail, and I had the privilege of "observance classes" three times a week. For example, one morning the Father Master came in with a complete table setting – napkin, earthenware bowl, knife, fork, plate – which he solemnly set out on his desktop in the classroom. "At the Father Abbot's signal the cloth is unfolded like *this*" – the left hand undid the napkin that was held in the right – "we drink holding the bowl *in both hands* – certainly not in one hand, the way the 'world' does – like *that*; and at the end of the meal we rinse the implements in a little water at the bottom of the bowl – like *this* – the dirty water being swallowed in one quick gulp so that nothing is wasted. Then the crumbs have to be collected by gathering them up with the right hand into the left palm, and – hup! – we swallow it all down with a rapid movement as we toss back the head. The hands are then folded and placed against the edge of the table, and we wait for the end of the meal, keeping our eyes fixed on the ground about two metres in front." The rows of tables actually faced each other across the great refectory, but it was out of the question to stare at one's opposite number during the meal. With everyone acting in this way, it was a meal of hermits, taken communally.

I thought I knew how to walk: my Razanne had burst into roars of laughter at my first steps, so proud she was at my progress… Well, no! there was a monastic way of walking, hands under the scapular, eyes fixed to the ground, foot sliding forwards. And there was an "observant" manner of noiselessly opening and closing doors, of going down a staircase quickly without hurrying, gathering up the serge gown in one's right hand so that it did not wear out on the stairs… Our lessons even specified a way of putting on one's shirt in the morning in the privacy of one's cell, but I am not sure I was always "observant" on this point.

I learnt how to be "observantly" poor in everyday things: not to let oneself get attached at all to any article. Periodically each novice would leave his watch and pen at the door of his neighbour to the right, and would find outside his own door the watch and pen of his neighbour to the left, which he would then use as his own. What is more, I was never to say "my" book or "my" handkerchief any more, but "our" book, "our" shirt, "our" watch. It was only (if I remember) the toilets that escaped "observance": there I could perform "my" needs, without being told how.

77

Nothing was unavailable. But since money did not exist, we had to go and request each article, each object we needed, from the community member responsible – who would give it with the usual smile.

There was, in fact, a real joyousness indwelling that unreal environment. We had given up everything; we were the last adventurers to leave a rotten world, and the recognition of this singularity in ourselves afforded us a kind of childish delight. It was all so simple, because we have nothing left – nothing but our individual surrender to the freely accepted tyranny of "observance".

Mornings were spent in devotional reading, minor household tasks and "noviciate classes". The Father Master did most of the teaching himself: his lectures on the meaning of monasticism were of no value whatever, but that did not matter, as we absorbed the "meaning of monasticism" – the new person that we had to become – at every moment of the day through the countless details of "observance".

The classes in sign language, on the other hand, were pure entertainment. Because the spoken word was in principle outlawed, we usually expressed ourselves through a system of signs, like deaf mutes. A small roneoed dictionary gave the basic vocabulary of signs, and we used to learn one letter of the alphabet a day:

"Parsnip": the forefinger and middle finger, extended, are placed on the right cheekbone.

"Pope": the forefinger, extended, traces three circles around the head – to represent the three tiers of diamonds in the papal tiara.

"Potato": the forefinger, on the right cheek, makes a screwing motion as if boring into the cheek.

As each sign was explained, a novice mounted the platform in front of the blackboard. There were then exercises in composition and translation:

"Well, Brother, say to us: 'The pope ate parsnips'…"

The attempts at mimicry unleashed great peals of laughter from the lads, three of whom had come straight from university.

* * *

The oddest thing was the total seriousness with which the "observance" lessons were delivered and received; no distinction was made between what was important, what was ancillary and what was useless. It is true, though, that nothing is useless, nothing is excessive, when you are having to stake all your chances on reaching your goal...

Two of my fellow-novices were from Paris: one had done a business course in the USA; the other was a professional organist and musician. In the silence there was a playful complicity between us. "All this is certainly Dark Ages stuff, but since God is so other-worldly, it's not so surprising that we have to submit to these other-worldly procedures. Besides they can be amusing, and one gets used to them."

We rapidly became very proficient in sign language, and we were even able – discreetly – to make plays on words (plays on signs) that were hilariously funny. It was even said that at the end of the last world war the reverend fathers used to give news of the advance of the Allied armies in sign language.

A paradox had come about: effectively, the pattern of life in the monastery was steeped in a silence that was all-pervading, almost total. Not a sentence, not a word, not a sound. Amid the tumults that I had just been through I had dreamt of this silence: I needed it to sink into my being, so that passion and imagination would fall quiet and God's soft voice make itself heard. But now the monks themselves had invented a system of speech that did without sound: there was no talking, but they communicated freely. Speech had never in fact ceased to take place, with all that it conveyed: but "observance" was safeguarded.

So my head continued to be full of wheeling birds – memories, anxieties, aspirations – loud and disorderly. When, then, would I know silence – the silence that I had come to seek?

Among us no word was spoken. But during the morning each of us could go and see the Father Master. There too everything was done *differently*. I would knock discreetly on the door: behind the glass pane a black shadow was seated at the table. He did not reply "come in", but made a dull tap on the table with the flat of his hand. Then I would enter, close the door and kneel down. It was on my knees that I had to traverse the two metres that separated me from the desk. From his chair the Father Master towered over me, but he welcomed me with a kindly smile:

"*Benedicite.*"

"*Dominus.*"

"Well, Brother, what is it?"

Then I was at liberty to speak, though the wooden floor was crushing my kneecaps.

I was trying to get this man to understand who I was and what I had left behind. He listened with kindly attention. But I had the feeling that nothing I could tell him of myself really got through to him. The pain that kept tormenting me was for the family I had abandoned: as far as he was concerned, the matter had been settled once and for all. Every time he asked me:

"Well then, is everything going fine?"

Of course, Father, everything is going fine. Ever since I had been there and had got into the rhythm, everything was going fine. After a few minutes he would stretch out his hand towards a pontifical mitre and would proceed to embroider it intricately in my presence till the end of the interview: I was talking to an amiable absentee.

He was completely at one with the system that I, for my part, was trying to find my way into, and he was simply incapable of grasping problems other than those that were already resolved. So I smothered my questionings at source: was it not better that way?

I used to go out again into the long corridor, silent and dark, a bit disappointed not to have said anything, a bit surprised not to have heard anything, dimly relieved perhaps not to have initiated anything.

Then, every Saturday afternoon, there was the walk.

Formed up in a group, we used to leave the abbey walls and take a walk along the valley; once the signal was given, we could talk freely. Strangely enough, there was no torrent, no flood of words.

Having lived all week without verbal exchange – but not without communication – we had to make a return to spoken language, and it came rather slow and measured. Then, as we approached the River, tongues loosened, and we began to learn a little about who was hiding behind the sign language, the hoods and the functions. With the young monks there was often little to learn: the influence of the "observance" was such that it seemed to have extinguished at source the natural ebullience that makes a living man. Conversation, laughter, everything was stilted. Moreover, even if discourse was free, there were exclusions: politics, food, critical remarks. With such burning topics eliminated, all that was left was the theologians, who each week brought a hair to split four ways, or the manual workers, who would comment at length on the growth of vegetables and salads in the garden.

Only the youngsters knew how to laugh at a bit of nonsense, marvel at everything and bring freshness to the walk; and a few old ones, more subdued, who recounted their memories.

On our return, after a breath of fresh air and a couple of good laughs, we recrossed the threshold: hands under scapulars, eyes lowered – it was all over for another week.

4

My taking of the habit had made me an official denizen of the Dark Ages. From then on I had a status – novice monk – and an identity. So I was allowed to communicate with the outside, subject to very strict rules to safeguard our withdrawal from the "world".

There were only one or two telephones, reserved for the authorities. But there was the post: to write a letter you had first to request the materials from the Father Master, who would hand you without comment a half-sheet of headed notepaper. Whatever I had to write, it all had to fit onto this scrap of paper. The letter was slipped into an envelope that remained unsealed, and I would drop it into a box in the common room.

The mail, outgoing as well as incoming, was read by the Father Abbot. The letters I received were passed to me opened. Did he read everything? Certainly not, if only for lack of time. But he used to sample them, and this allowed the father the better to know his children, and the better to keep an eye on them.

My mother was unaware of this detail. I received in quick succession two melodramatic letters:

It's not possible, your abandoning us; the family is in a state of shock; first your father, now you; and your little sisters...

The truce had been short-lived. I had no need to inform the Father Abbot: he read the letters before I did. It was agreed, exceptionally, that Mother would come to see me the following week.

Mother here!... Kneeling in the Father Master's office, I took delivery of the armoury of arguments that would protect me from my family:

"Remember that anyone who loves his father or his mother more than Christ is not worthy of him. You have left them, but you have not abandoned them: in immersing yourself in the solitude of the cloister, you are actually, in a deeper and more real sense, present with your dear ones, in the mystery of God. One day they will realize it; it's for them to make their way towards you, their source of riches."

Mother... I go forwards, heart pounding, into the corridor where the audience rooms are. How cold, how bare it is, for her who has lost everything!

"Brother Irenaeus, there's someone waiting for you in number 2."

I open the door of room 2: I don't see her at first, shrivelled up as she is on a chair, but I do feel the impact of her glance. Those eyes that look away, that spasm of revulsion, that head bent sideways as though it has received a slap – it's me she has just seen, large black object with shaven scalp and other-worldly smile... *Is this you, my child, my big baby, the boy on whom I'd pinned so many hopes, the life that's been torn from me?*

I've said nothing. None of the sentences I've learnt, none of the words I've prepared – nothing comes. None of my contrived defences hold firm against that traumatized woman. How did I fail to understand at that moment that she was the human one, she was the one possessed of the love that I had come here to seek?

We go out into the garden. *We're walking, we're moving: Mother, I'm alive, I'm with you.*

"The Father Master is going to come and see you. He's the one, you know, who deals with the novices, who's responsible for our training. He's very kind."

There's only one thing she has heard: he's the one who deals with her son, he's the one who's responsible for him, who'll take care of me...

My practised ear has already picked up the rustle behind the nearby hedge. The Father Master is gliding in our direction, his habit brushing against his feet.

My mother sees him, smiles and, with a sudden impulse of her whole body, advances towards him, holding out her hand.

"Good day, Father, I'm Michel's mother."

But no hand emerges from the great black scapular to grasp the hand extended. The Father Master bows slightly with a wan smile, and doesn't move. The rule is explicit: a woman is not to be touched; women are unclean.

"Good day, Madame. Let's sit, if you'd be so kind," he says, looking down at my mother, who no longer knows what to do with her hand...

...and remains standing there, stupefied.

5

The next day I had my work assignment: ground-floor toilets in the morning, and manual work in the garden in the afternoon.

"Manual work" was aptly named. Recreation and relaxation did not exist, so the whole of life was work of some sort. But *manual* work played a special part in the formation of *homo monasticus*.

At the start of the afternoon, on the bell, we took off our great black habits and pulled on a lighter gown of grey material; and we put on a pair of clogs picked out from the heap at the bottom of the stairs. Then we made our way to the noticeboard in the common room where the list of teams was pinned up, with their jobs for the day. The teams were never the same, and from one day to the next the jobs were always different – no gaining stability, no observing the outcome of yesterday's work...

In solemn silence everyone went to pick up a tool in the garden shed. And then, hood pulled down over eyes, tool held tight under left arm, we proceeded in single file towards the end of the plot. ("If provision is made for every tiniest action, the soul is freer to stay in God's presence," the Father Master had explained.)

So that day, with vacant gaze and feet rubbed sore by the hard clogs, I went with my two fellow-extras from Paris towards the far end of the vegetable patch. The garden was within the monastery walls, so we were well protected. One end of the plot had been freshly dug, and on the side there were crates full of gleaming shallots. The father in charge of the work was waiting for us ("I'm called 'Father Cellarer', it's an ancient title from the monks' Rule"):

"*Benedicite.*"

"*Dominus.*"

"Brothers, you're to plant shallots the whole length. Take one row each."

And these city lads, who've only ever seen shallots on their dinner plates, find themselves squatting down, grey patches in the middle of the plot. With the left hand we dig a hole, with the right we thrust in a shallot: it's not difficult. The weather's fine, the silence pleasant; heads look up to exchange knowing smiles; we race to see who can get to the end of the plot quickest; we exchange innocent signs...

After half an hour the Cellarer comes to see how the novices are getting on. One glance at the furrows and he leans towards us with a twinkle in his eyes:

"*Benedicite.*"

"*Dominus.*"

"Hey, Brothers! If you want to have shallots for eating this winter, you'd do better to plant them *roots* down, not heads down..."

Stunned, we look at our rows: right from the edge of the plot the shallots are neatly spaced out, the roots pointing proudly to heaven.

The following day I found myself with a floor-cloth and sponge in front of the entrance to "my" toilets – four urinals, four cubicles with shutting doors. I had been entrusted with keeping the place clean for a whole year. At Uncle's, it goes without saying, the toilets were always spotless; but it had never occurred to me how that outcome might have been achieved. *Oh well, a wipe of the cloth over the ground, that's easy. I must just see that I don't get my feet caught in the gown. But the seat, and there inside, the brown marks, how to deal with those?*

Most fortunately a father happens to be passing and notices my dilemma. Without batting an eyelid he stands facing me and performs the action of rolling up his sleeves and thrusting his hands into the basin and rubbing.

You see? Yes, got it. It's obvious, of course. So, with my soul still in God's presence, I manfully thrust the sponge to the bottom of the first toilet bowl.

This community was in fact made up of three quite separate groups. First there were the fathers, men of middle-class background who had completed their studies before joining. These were priests, and they formed the backbone of the community.

Then there were the lay brothers, from a lower social background – peasants, manual workers: they would never be priests. It was they that provided most of the services necessary for community life.

Finally there were us, the novices, whom no one could speak to except through the Father Master, protected for the moment, like shoots beneath a garden frame. It occurred to nobody that we were reinventing here the division into social classes that was such a prominent feature of the world we had shunned.

At the time of our first discussion the Father Abbot had simply remarked to me, as if stating the obvious:

"And... of course, you'll become a father, won't you?"

Of course.

6

"Brother Irenaeus, someone's waiting for you in the reception room!"

Again the bare corridors, again the small, echoing cubicle. This time it's the Canon. He has come after a few weeks, as promised, to spend the day here. He is to take lunch with us at the guest table.

I push the door open and find him seated, in his spotless black cassock, his head slightly bowed. We embrace, we chat. But very soon I notice a difference in him: the man before me is no longer the friend, the confidant, the spiritual father. He has withdrawn behind a sort of reticence that is remote, exaggerated even. He scarcely seems pleased to see me again.

As the day progresses I understand why: I am no longer his child, his "baby", I no longer belong to him. He no longer holds me in his hands; I have in a way escaped him. Very simply, it's the reaction of an abandoned lover. Ever since I stopped being his property, I've ceased to be of any real interest to him.

After the monastery mass, lunch. As often on a Sunday, the passage to be read aloud is taken from a journal; today it's an article about Africa from the *International Catholic Newsletter*. After the meal, over coffee, I find him turned in on himself, like a block of wood.

"Do they often read extracts here from *that* journal?"

"No; well... I don't know; why?"

"It's a left-wing journal, the standard-bearer for progressive Catholics in France. Truly I didn't expect that *here*. And then next to me I had some sort of worker-priest, dirty chap, in a mildewed cassock. No, really, no..."

The fact is that parish priests from the surrounding countryside sometimes came in of a Sunday to spend a few hours at the abbey. This one was a good fellow, poor as his country parish, a fair reflection of his wardrobe.

At the door of the guest quarters you made your parting from me without warmth, without feeling almost. I was no longer on your side: I'd been indoctrinated by unsound people, and my life could henceforth take its course without you.

I never saw him again.

7

"Nine, ten, eleven, twelve, thirteen, fourteen."

The nuts make a rattling sound as they drop into the bowl. I still have the whole of the left-hand row to fill: today I'm on refectory duty.

"One, two, three, four..."

In the vast high-ceilinged hall two rows of tables face inwards. All the tables have a shelf underneath into which each monk slides his three pieces of cutlery rolled up in his napkin, and his earthenware bowl with handles. The tables seat two or three. When the monks come in they find at their place a flat dish on the stool side, and on the opposite side a bowl in which the dessert is served.

"Three, four, five, six..."

My duties: go and get the dishes from the kitchen, where they're drying after washing up; first, arrange the two rows of tables, dishes on one side, bowls on the other; check to see that they are precisely aligned; then, put out each monk's dessert ration.

"Brother Irenaeus, you won't forget Father Maurus's Gruyère and Father Anthony's dry toast. Today it's nuts. Fourteen per person."

In a corner of the kitchen the Father Caterer is muttering the instructions for the day. He's a large, florid man, always moving about. He bears an ancient aristocratic surname; and he's never been able to keep his voice really low. His muttering must be audible from the far end of the refectory, and I have the feeling that I'm receiving orders before a battle in Flanders, where his forebears distinguished themselves.

Fourteen per person. Why not fifteen, or thirteen? That's how it is – and all the more arbitrary as some nuts are smaller than others. I try not to put these on the younger monks' dishes; the older ones won't mind.

The evening meal will be quickly over. A soup tureen is doing the rounds of the tables; each person helps himself and passes it on to his neighbour without looking at him. The soup is always made from the vegetables left over from the previous day: they're emptied into a saucepan and given a dash of water and a dash of the blender. It's given the name "commemorial soup" – liturgical-sounding, and therefore uplifting.

While the tureens are going the rounds, a trolley comes by and everyone has a metal pot placed in front of him; it has two flat handles and is three-quarters full of vegetables.

"You are earnestly advised to finish off your pot," the Father Master had warned us. "To know how to find contentment in what is given you, and to finish it all up, is a sign of vocation."

My monastic vocation received reassuring testimony from my healthy appetite. Sometimes I even cast a hungry eye on the pot of my neighbour the musician, who didn't always manage to get to the end, but second helpings were out of the question.

"If you're still hungry, there's plenty of bread available on the tables."

Portion of soup, pot of vegetables, fruit in the bowl... *This evening, after my fourteenth nut, I'll dig into the bread; that's all there is for it.*

Good, almost done: I just have to fill the water jugs, one per table, and then get the herbal tea ready.

This was an innovation of the Father Abbot. There were three great lime-trees in the garden, and each July we used to fill three large sacks with the sweet-smelling flowers. So at each meal the Brother Waiter passed along the tables and poured into the bowls held out to him a dark, sweet liquid that was above all hot, very hot. We sipped this with a gourmet's relish, and the warmth reached right down to our heels.

Last thing: the reader's place setting... At one end of the refectory is the Father Abbot's table, visible to all beneath the great bare wooden cross. And right at the opposite end, the reader's rostrum. Ten minutes before the bell he'll come and swallow his meal down, then take his stand up there. When all the brothers are in position by the tables and grace has been chanted, he'll bow before the microphone:

"*Jube, domine, benedicere.*" ("Father, please bless me")

The Father Abbot chants the Latin formula for a blessing, and everyone sits down. Stools scrape. Hands are folded on the table edge. Then, all is still. The Father Abbot reaches out for his wooden gavel and gives a resounding knock. That marks the start.

"In the list of martyrs, this Thursday 24 November..."

The reading is performed *recto tono* – that is, the text is intoned to a single note, in an expressionless voice. Otherwise the reader might manage to put an interpretation on the text, give it meaning, and in so doing maybe thrust himself into prominence.

So the list of the saints for the day flows over our heads like smooth water, while the aroma of the "memorial soup" wafts our way. A moment later the Father Abbot slips his hand into the cavity under his table and undoes his place setting. No head has moved; but everyone has observed from the corner of their eye: it's the signal: forty right hands grope beneath the table, bring out the napkin, unfold it with the left hand; the soup does its rounds, and so does life.

After the reading of the Rule or of the list of saints, the reader up on his rostrum sits down and resumes the reading of the current book, in the ritual manner:

"There follows the *History of the Church* by Daniel-Rops-of-the-Académie-Française, chapter 15 ..."

The choice of book for everyone to listen to during meals was so serious a matter that it was entrusted to the Father Prior, the Father Abbot's right-hand man and number two in the hierarchy. For the present, Daniel-Rops, with his fourteen volumes, had disposed of the issue. This Christian author of prodigious literary output was the salvation of monastery refectories.

"The whole of our life is centred on listening to God," the Father Master had remarked. "Nothing must distract us from concentrating on his presence. Eating is a necessary activity, but we come to the refectory also to feed the soul. We take our food primarily by the ear; what is served to us must not concern us. Let us be content always to have something on our plates."

So it was that for the whole of that winter I tried to ignore the regular cycle of potatoes – noodles – potatoes, while my soul drew its nourishment from the Academician's prose.

The midday meal followed the same ritual, but was more substantial. In summer salads from the garden replaced soup. The pot of vegetables was accompanied by a main course of fish or eggs that did its round of the tables. There was never meat, of course.

"This is prescribed in the Rule," the Father Master stated, "and the Rule makes this unceasing abstinence into one of the pivots of monastic life. Tradition adds that meat overheats the blood."

The Rule and tradition had spoken: no further explanation was required. The notion of a balanced diet did not figure in the regime, so I swallowed back my scientific knowledge.

There was no freezer in the monastery. One day we were served a dish of skate that let off a smell of ammonia familiar to my chemist's nose. In consternation I looked up – something that one did *not* do – and tried to catch the Father Caterer's eye: he was seated exactly opposite. He noticed my gestures and understood the silent message: *Withdraw the dish; it's poisonous!*

He gave me a fierce look, and with a bold movement, without lowering his gaze, he stuffed a huge lump of skate into his mouth and swallowed it down without a blink.

That evening in church everyone was still there, myself included. *Oh, man of little faith…*

* * *

That's it; the refectory's sorted. There's a short time left before the bell. I emerge into the deserted cloister and go to get changed in my cell. The sky's heavy; it's a grey November. This evening it's to be turnip-and-potato soup – and the vicissitudes of the Carolingian Church, as viewed by Daniel-Rops-of-the-Académie-Française.

8

But the place that seemed to be the focus of all the community's energies, its pivotal point, was the church. There perhaps I would find the key to the quest I had embarked upon, there I would surely draw near to God, there I would encounter the Inexpressible.

As with everything else, I was pitched in without explanation. After we had stood motionless in the long, dark corridor for the "station", the bell began tolling insistently. At the first stroke the Father Abbot stepped forwards with his right foot, and the two parallel lines moved off towards the church.

There's a stoup full of holy water on the left as we enter. With the same movement each monk throws back onto his shoulders the hood that covers his head, and the monk on the left dips his hand in the holy water and holds out three wet fingers to his immediate neighbour.

Everyone crosses themselves, with a broad sign. We turn, to reach the entrance to the chancel. To our left the huge nave is empty. Just a few lay-folk have got to their feet and stand stiffly, watching us pass. Instructions are not to look at them, never to turn the head towards the nave, towards the outside world. They do not exist; the service is not for them: they are there under sufferance, and they know it. They are lucky to be there, as though at the edge of the beach, to inhale the sea air – and the monks' worship.

We turn again, and I face the altar. There I bend myself in two at the waist, and swivel on my heels: I end up standing in a stall at the end of the row, my back to the congregation.

Just before the station the Father Master has presented me with two thick black books the size of dictionaries:

"Your service books – one for the daily office, the other for the monastery mass. You'll get used to handling them; I've placed markers at the key points. Inscribe each book on the flyleaf in pencil: '*ad usum f. Irenaei*' – 'for the use of Brother Irenaeus'. You have no private property any more, but these books are for your personal use."

I open one of the books: four-line staves with square notes that rise and fall above the Latin text: Gregorian chant! In a flashback I see the Canon and his connoisseur's lips:

"And then, you'll have a fe-e-east of Gregorian chant…"

Except that within the chancel the effect is not at all the same as from the nave. First, one has to find the right page (I glance over the shoulder in front: luckily I'm tall); then my neighbour to the left is singing out of tune, like a boiling saucepan. I'm ready for all this. But there's another awful factor to contend with: my neighbour to the right, who's singing his heart out, has foul breath. And just at that moment a mischievous draught is wafting his nauseous stomach odours into my face. *Am I, year in year out, to seek an encounter with the Inexpressible amid these sewer-like exhalations? Come, take courage! – after all, the draught must sometimes change direction.*

Now it's I who have the fixed gaze, standing up, bowing, kneeling low with the others – trying all the while not to slip on the damnably well-waxed floor. Suddenly, a moment of panic: I want to pee! I omitted to go to the toilet before the service with everyone else. Will I be able to hold out to the end? And what will happen if the need becomes overpowering?

The divine service follows its majestic and impersonal course, while I do battle with my pages that need finding, my nose that's too good at smelling and my bladder that wants controlling, all the way to the final *Deo gratias*.*

No initiation, no specific training in the forms of service. I keep telling myself that things would come clear of their own accord, progressively, by dint of practice. All we had, every other day, was a lesson in "rubrics": how to place the hands, how to bow, how to stand up straight again, what to do with a candlestick and censer, how to give the "kiss of peace"…

"It's the ritual kiss that believers exchange during mass. The one that gives the kiss turns towards you and puts his hands together. You bow. He places his hands on your shoulders, you place yours beneath his elbows. You lean forwards in such a manner as to bring your heads to the same level. But on no account are they to touch! He says: '*pax tecum*'; and you reply: '*et cum spiritu tuo*';* again, a greeting with hands together, and you proceed to your neighbour on the right."

If I had understood properly, the essence of it all was to kiss without touching. Well, of course, we were in church, and the brothers were ill-shaven, so for one reason or another our cheeks avoided contact, and the liturgy proceeded in good order.

Nonetheless, my longings remained unsatisfied. What of God, what of the experience of God, of which we had talked so long in the sunny garden above the forest of Morvan?

Patience! For the present the task was to find one's bearings in this other forest and gain the outward demeanour of a seasoned monk. The training had no other aim. But how did this lead to God? Indeed, could it lead to God?... *No untimely questions, my lad! Get on with it!*

I got on with it. Four or five hours of offices each day, not counting the various masses.

Each morning there was a sung monastery mass celebrated on behalf of the community by one of its priests. The rest attended as ordinary congregation. But, yes, they were also expected to say their own mass each day; this one did not count. So at sunrise, after getting up, there was a flitting of white shadows, with chalices in one hand, bound for the innumerable little altars scattered around the church.

Mass is celebrated for the people: that is Church law. So a priest could never celebrate on his own; he had to have an attendant to play the role of the congregation and to give the monologue the guise of a dialogue. So each white shadow was followed by a black shadow – a brother, a novice – and in all the recesses there was a mumbling of Latin formulae delivered, uncharacteristically, in all haste, because someone else needed the place.

As there were fewer brothers than priests, it fell to me to serve at two masses in a row between the morning office and the main monastery mass. During that time the spirit was busy.

But what of God? But what of the experience I so much sought after?

I went on responding: "*et cum spiritu tuo*"; I went on changing service books; I went on going and coming, bowing, offering holy water... Time passed smoothly by.

9

Gradually, without really noticing it, I was being brought within an extraordinarily effective regime, the aim of which was to train up the *new man*. At the end of that training I would be a "real monk", worthy of my superiors' confidence, someone to look up to.

For me this process was to last several years. It was during this period that Michel became Brother Irenaeus.

How did he live, day after day, through this slow transformation? I examine my memory, and I find a sort of blank. That is something I have to accept: the mature man I now am is no longer capable of identifying himself with the novice of that time. Is this a defensive reaction, dismissing a painful experience into the depths of the unconscious?

I do not know. But from now on he is beyond my reach, that young man hazarding his life. It is only from the outside that I can rediscover him, a bit like a voyeur.

The first phase of the discipline I was submitting myself to was this: one had to *destructure* – that is, cut away one by one the roots of the former man.

Each morning of the course I would listen to a jargon that disguised unsettling realities. The Father Master talked to us about "escape from the world": the "world" was everything we were coming from, all the values instilled into us from childhood by the society that had created us.

In opposition to the "world" was the monastic outlook, monastic reactions. Some things were monastic, others were not – and a true monk instinctively knew the difference.

"Escape from the world is Christianity lived in its absolute purity..."

For the Father Master this statement seemed self-evident. But for me it was a seething mass of questions: what was the source of all this? how? why?

I began to explore the "fathers of monasticism" shelf in the library, and I read the old texts avidly: monks from Egypt and Palestine in the fourth century; Irish hermits of the tenth century; Cistercians of the Middle Ages... Luckily most of these writings had been translated into French.

I discovered that the foremost ideal of these pioneer fathers was the "desert". The desert became in my eyes what the American West must have been for immigrants from old Europe: a goal accessible only with difficulty. It was something I directed all my energies towards; it merited every sacrifice.

I should very much have liked to discuss what I discovered. But it was clear that the Father Master was not familiar with this source material. He limited himself to repeating dutifully the lessons that he had himself received during his noviciate. Through living day and night with the "trained" monks, I would one day acquire the proper – that is the *monastic* – way of looking and reacting.

So I endeavoured to provide my own answers to my questions.

And I learnt how to escape from the world to establish myself in the desert.

The starting point was the complete absence of external news. No radio or television, of course. But the periodicals room was also out of bounds for several years.

A room at the end of the main corridor, the fathers' corridor – a room I veered away from, as from hell. Sometimes the door had been left ajar. I noticed then a wooden table on which the authorized publications appeared each day: the *Catholic Gazette*, a compendium of the pope's speeches and every least statement; the diocesan journal; and a few weeklies from Catholic Aid or other charitable organisations. Then, of course, there was monastic literature coming in from everywhere, small pamphlets about the worldwide brotherhood of New Men.

At that period the French daily *La Croix* was banned. If nothing else, was it not rather too left-wing, infiltrated as it was by worker-priests?

The fathers had free access to that room. But it was not the done thing to be seen there too often, and the best of them made it a point of honour not to slide their foot there at all. And they would take advantage of one of the walks to mention this to the youngsters and dazzle them with such remarkable "observance" and dedication.

I don't know by which channel I learnt, six months after the event, of the death of the great Édith Piaf, the Sparrow Kid I used to idolize. She had been given what was almost a state funeral. But it would take six months for the rumour to find its way, by a reprehensible gaffe, inside the abbey walls. I was struck by this incident, which also demonstrated to me that that I was well and truly on the desert road.

There remained the reception rooms as a unique place of contact with the world outside.

During the noviciate year no visit was allowed. That of my mother had been a compassionate measure; the Canon had taken a dim view of it, seeing it as proof of our dangerous permissiveness. Enclosure was effective in creating a vacuum that demanded to be filled with something else.

I came gradually to realize that conflict was seemingly excluded from community life. Provision had been made in the "observance" for every action; I witnessed individual human beings circling round without strains or clashes.

It was during the walks – the only chance we had for contact with the fathers – that I grasped the source of this apparent serenity:

"I spoke to the Father Abbot about it... I went to see the Father Abbot... That's up to the Father Abbot..."

The Abbot's authority was omnipresent, permeating every happening, cushioning every impact. Passion had been the engine of my existence: it seemed that, from now on, it had to be utterly eradicated.

Later I was to learn under what guise this passion would express itself. For the moment I would be entering a world without conflict, without passion, without any of the stimuli that had till now driven me to face up to things, to be a man.

If the desert is the place of no desire, that is to enable the desire for God, for him alone, to occupy the whole space. But this, this was another matter.

So, item by item, I absorbed my lessons in "destructuring" – that is to say, the putting to death of everything that had till then caused me to live.

10

Reading was the primary means for "restructuring" the new man. I thought I knew how to read. I learnt that, for a monk, reading is not an effortless pastime; it is hard work, to which everyone would devote several hours a day. The Rule even prescribed that for the month of Lent everyone had to choose one book, which was publicly presented to him in the chapter house on Ash Wednesday. The announcement of titles provided a pulse that measured the abbey's health as a monastic community. The Church Fathers took up a large share, followed far behind by a few works of modern spirituality. In our minds Christian Antiquity and the Christian Middle Ages took on a tangible reality and filled the vacuum of the desert.

In the early mornings, then, during the long silence, I used to digest avidly the biographies and confessions of monks who had been dead for more than a thousand years. Little by little they became as familiar as the people around me.

The Father Master used to insist:

"You're not reading out of curiosity, but to identify yourselves with these models, to think like them, to live like them. Your reading is nourishment. Distrust 'intellectual gastronomy', which is a sin. You are not conducting a study of history, sociology or culture: perhaps later, if obedience demands it of you... You are taking in the experience of the past, not to analyse it, but to make it your own."

But I was too fond of these long periods of reading. The library became a place of encounters: I only had to reach out to bring a new friend to my side and converse with him. I knew well that I was yielding to "intellectual gastronomy": I took rather too many notes... and rather too many books – a minor sin, for which I never charged myself.

The public readings in the refectory were a supplement to this personal reading: the titles were chosen carefully, often to accord with the time of year and the liturgical calendar.

Liturgical worship: the great event of our lives, from which I expected much. For several hours each day we turned up in church to hear together, and read aloud together, texts that had been carefully selected and arranged to create a collective awareness – to make of these individuals a unity that would simultaneously experience the same feelings, move towards the same ends and progress together over time.

For the liturgy followed the seasons, and transformed them. In the desert where I spent my life, the cycle of days and seasons occupied a dominant place. It was in some ways the only persistent element of novelty. For the townsman that I was, the unfolding of the seasons had never held great importance, apart from the eagerly awaited arrival of the holidays. But here I had the leisure to watch the leaves fall and the buds burst.

Our church was splendid, finely and simply decorated. Vestments, colours, fragrances gave each festival a unique character.

I do not believe that it was primarily God that I encountered in the course of those long celebrations, but there was certainly an inner feeling of beauty and gratification. I confused the one with the other, and the pleasure that I felt took the place of religious experience for me.

Yet they were not very gifted performers, those brothers of mine who brought the rich framework of our services to life. Their gestures were a bit cramped, their voices faltering, their expressions strained by overattention to detail. Be that as it may, the festival services filled me with joy. I was still too much of a novice to play an active role; I was more often spectator than actor, but a rapt spectator.

The first of these festivals was Christmas, a Christmas away from my people. The country around us was in the grip of a severe cold spell, and the temperature within the church hovered around zero. To avoid the holy water at the entrance freezing over, the Father Sacristan kept adding, with a smile, a few pinches of salt. The midnight mass always saw several coachloads of tourists join us to do penance for the sumptuous Christmas Eve dinner organized for them by a tour operator in the neighbouring town. Nothing was done to welcome them or make them warm; the mass used to last nearly two hours.

Since morning there had been great activity in the sacristy. The Father Abbot would be officiating at what was called a pontifical mass, and every wardrobe and drawer had been opened for the occasion. Mitres, crozier, dalmatics, censers, embroidered and bejewelled vestments were spread out on the tables.

For the past week, despite the preparatory fast, the novices had been working at the music. As in all monasteries there was a choirmaster responsible for the singing. Every morning he took us into a room – unheated – to extract from our voices and bodies all that they had to give.

"Come along, sing this for me! You can put all your energies into this; this is the moment to be forceful: you won't have any others!"

He had undergone no musical training – natural gifts had to make do for technique. But he had the soul of a musician, and he startled me a little: he showed enthusiasm, and urged us to do the same: it ruffled the smooth and oily surface of the surrounding lake.

From 6 o'clock in the evening the abbey fell totally silent. The Advent fast had been in force for a month: evenings, a soup and a vegetable; and in the morning ten grams of bread, and a coffee made from roast barley and chicory, without milk and only slightly sweetened. Now we were gathering our strength for the coming night.

The office of matins took place before midnight mass: two hours of chants and readings in a stuffy crypt. Then a half-hour break, in which we could go and have a warm tisane. At midnight precisely the procession moved off to enter the church. About a hundred people were waiting for us, imprisoned in the nave as in a block of ice. The first chants rose with the mist our breath made. Then, while Father Maurus sang the epistle in his inaudible little voice, a group of novices left the choir to go outdoors to ring the Christmas bells.

The church was not warm, but outside an icy blast swept down beneath a sky of black crystal. We were going in the direction of the porch to unfasten the four bell ropes: they were frozen solid, as stiff as tree branches. At a nod of the head we grasped them high up and had to pull on them hard, while our bare hands seemed to freeze to the rope. Then the joyous bells began to ring out, carrying the news way beyond the half-frozen River: Christmas, Christmas!

Christmas, Uncle; Christmas, Mother; Christmas, all you that have given me so many Merry Christmases enfolded in your love!

Christmas in the night; Christmas in the wind; Christmas, alone beneath the stars...

Come on! Only a few seconds more and we'll be going back into the church – which now seemed like a haven of well-being. It was too cold to feel sorry for ourselves.

Towards two o'clock in the morning the mass was drawing to

an end. The Father Abbot had several times solemnly changed mitres, chasubles, copes...

But there was plenty more to come: each priest now had to say three Christmas masses by himself.

By himself? Actually not. Each one had to have an attendant. And there were not enough brothers. So I had to be attendant at two series of three masses, one after the other, in the icy side-chapels. In all that must have amounted to five or six hours of services in the middle of the night on an empty stomach. And if I was a little light-headed when I got back to my cell in the small hours, it was certainly not from champagne.

In this shared life of isolation words spoken in public assumed a special prominence. They issued from one source only: the Father Abbot. So the community took on the appearance of a strange organism, possessing one mouth and eighty ears. Even so, words were only uttered sparingly and in a formal setting, that of the abbey chapter. At the end of the rectangular hall where I had taken my habit stood a little wooden throne, well-lit, while the benches along the walls were left in semi-shadow.

Each morning, at the sound of the bell, the monks line up in order of seniority. As the latest arrival, I am right at the back near the door. The Father Abbot makes his entrance, takes his stand in the pool of light, and sits down after making a sign of the cross. He opens the Rule, reads a short passage, then expounds it for several minutes in the silence.

The monks' Rule is not very long: there were three cycles of exposition a year, *ad infinitum*. I observed early on that the text was no more than a pretext. If the Father Abbot had something to say – a point of doctrine or observance to underline – then drop by drop, day after day, he could ram it in like a nail. And if he did not have anything to say... then he spoke nonetheless.

I used to listen with all my attention to this unusual exercise in communication. One man gradually let himself be taken over by what he was saying, in order to bring a group into conformity with his words and tirelessly lead it back to the straight path of "observance". He let show nothing of the personal relations that might also link him to each of his monks.

Sometimes he ascended to the sort of spoken meditation that is the preserve of the hermit. At those times it was as if I was being allowed an inside glimpse of a solitary existence that had been chosen and fashioned, and which would fashion my own.

In the evening there was a less formal chapter meeting. We were given the day's news – if there was any – and sometimes a few news items from outside. But then too it was only the Father Abbot who could speak. So he was in total control of the community's information. If he decided to question a monk, then the monk would stand up, say a few words, and take his seat again in the shadows.

The essentials of the process were well established – to empty at one end, completely; to refill at the other, efficaciously. We wanted this training, we were volunteers, and each monk believed it to be to his good.

By the end of the year I had very nearly entered into character. I had acquired the appropriate reflexes: if I happened to meet a layman in the church and needed to answer a question from him, he would certainly believe he was addressing a monk – eyes vacant and downcast, speech brief and expressionless, language formal. I knew that I ought not to be there, that I must cut short this contact with the outside world. For my part I would recoil like a wave; or I would be there without being there; or I would stand inscrutably like an effigy.

The trainee could be pleased with himself: this exam had been entered and passed, like the others.

11

I cannot now think back to that young novice – me – on the riverbank, without asking myself: What made it all possible? What economic and social arrangements enabled such an elaborate organization to develop and prosper?

We occupied a huge building, with all the expense that entails. We owned several tracts of land, plant and equipment, two cars and a van. At the individual level the life of poverty was lived in earnest; but the community lacked nothing, and there was even a surplus that allowed some large sums to be invested. The sick were cared for, and cared for well. What was the source of the funds that allowed us to enjoy such comprehensive security?

I knew what it was to work; in laboratories and factories I had toiled hard. In comparison the abbey's activities gave me the initial impression of an undemanding amateurism.

The novices were of course supported by the community. What about the fathers? Yes, like all monasteries we had our workshops and took pride in them. In the afternoons I used to see my seniors go off there, at a gentle pace, for several hours. Their actions were unhurried, and their harmonious placidity seemed to rub off onto the machines themselves.

Clearly our daily livelihoods did not depend on this work; it was rather the work that depended on a loftier way of life. "Whatever was not done today would always be done tomorrow": I ended up believing this myself.

All this was far from turning in a profit, but there were some less evident activities that supplemented this "official" work. One of these activities I had found out about during our walks.

Father Du Bellay de Saint-Pons came from a fine French noble family. He was one of the first that I had met in the cloister on the day of my arrival, and I had been struck by the aquiline nose and the bushy eyebrows crowning a lordly gaze. He looked a bit like the politician Chaban-Delmas, particularly in his masterful gait. And when, transfigured by ceremonial vestments, he censed the monks' chancel at vespers, it was just as if a member of the *ancien régime* were wafting wreaths of fragrance heavenwards.

This father also had connections, among them a professor at the School of Political Sciences in Paris. Students at the "*Sciences-po*" were, as part of their course, given practical assignments, which normally ended with their submitting analyses of economic conditions in France and worldwide. Nothing unusual about all that.

But, instead of putting these exercises away in a file, the professor sent the best ones to his friend the monk. The latter then had them duplicated with an attractive cover, thus producing a journal, the *Economic Newsletter*.

The second stage was simple. His tonsure visible for all to see, and wearing his long habit – "never in mufti, that doesn't work as well" – the Father would turn up at the commercial department of a large company; he would invite the company to subscribe for the journal ("put it down to general expenses…"); and he would nearly always receive a subscription that would be renewed the following year among the rest.

There were no grounds for criticism: some of the articles were interesting, and the *Sciences-po* students were glad to have their course-work published. So the funds accrued in good faith, and the businesses hardly ever refused to subsidize the abbey – the cost was small.

At the end of one walk Father Du Bellay told how one commercial manager – less impressed, it seems, by the habit – had said to him one day:

"But, Father, we already have so many journals, we haven't time to read them…"

"Dear sir," the Father had replied urbanely, "I'm not asking you to read this one but to subscribe to it!"

The cheque arrived by the next post.

Other activities of this kind enabled the "monastery brand" to earn harmless profits. There were in addition several generous donors, and several legacies converted into stock-market portfolios: I was certainly going to be poor, but I would never want for anything.

Economic subvention was not enough: to exist the monks also needed support of a social nature.

So we had the assistance of a small group of technical experts and consultants from the laity: their goodwill, though we could rely on it, showed itself in unobtrusive ways – a free consultation from a financial adviser, a helping hand from a highly placed contact.

But most evident to me was the women's brigade.

In our eyes Woman was a being dangerous beyond all others, the origin of evil. As described in the works of our authors, she was the main obstacle to be surmounted on the desert road.

Because of this women ran no risks with us, and they knew it.

I used to witness a swarm of forlorn women circling around our reception rooms, coming primarily to gain an attentive hearing. Drawn by that throng of available and slightly helpless men, they were both motherly and expectant of reassurance. At interview time they at last had a man at their disposal, without antagonism, without danger. Hearts could be opened without fear of rebuff.

On the other hand, they were unshakeably loyal and were happy to get feminine solidarity to work in our favour.

Curiously, then, this group of men vowed to absolute chastity was upheld by a considerably greater number of women, per head, than the national average.

12

But, for the moment, women were the last of my concerns. With all our energies dedicated to mastering "observance", there was no room for sexual impulses, which lay still, to some extent of their own accord.

I knew that I possessed a susceptibility to bodily pleasure: it had been demonstrated very early, then quickly repressed, but it had not disappeared. I was sure that, sooner or later, I should have to compromise again with a force that was liable to erupt – but this time it would be within the constraints of monastery life.

Though I went along with being restructured to a new design, I was expecting that this re-formation would extend to those deep and dark regions within me. What I had been promised was an ideal of perfection, and for me perfection meant oneness of being – the whole in its entirety. Nothing should escape God, because everything belonged to him.

But as weeks, then months, passed, I was struck by a huge lacuna. Never in the Father Abbot's morning chapter meetings, never in the Father Master's daily lessons – never was there any talk of "this".

Nor did it come up in private conversations. This was, I suppose, entirely my own fault: because sexuality was not in the forefront of my current concerns, I did not raise it. But another reason was that those men seemed to me so sexless themselves that I did not expect a response relevant to any questions of mine that might have surfaced.

Truth to tell, life was so much simpler without this goad of humanity! It was finally by denial that I dealt with the problem – the one problem that troubled the life of the people I had left behind. Let sleeping dogs lie.

I was also expecting a lot from the "preached retreat" that was to take place in the spring. Each year a celebrity of the Catholic Church – an eminent theologian or a bishop – used to join us for a week. All activities were suspended. We had two, sometimes three, lectures a day, and a huge amount of free time in which to digest this abundance of nourishment.

The intention of the practice was that it should be a kind of general review: our way of life, its values, its structure, everything was submitted for reappraisal. The extremely varied personalities of our speakers guaranteed a variety of instruction that should have been all-inclusive.

Neither that year nor in the years that followed was the subject broached: the speaker talked away about everything – except our sexuality. Could it be that, along with their newcomer's suitcase, my colleagues had put something else away in the linen cupboard – something essential to their physical wholeness?

Of course not! But from that time sex apparently ceased to exist.

This surprised me a little, without troubling me too much. It would take me much more time to realize that a human being does not split up into slices, some of which might be consigned to the dungeon.

I would make this realization only at a painful cost to myself.

I was capable of living, temporarily, without sex – but certainly not without friendship. I had broken ruthlessly with my warm-hearted group of friends: they respected my decision and kept their peace.

Would there be, one day, among those men in the midst of whom I now moved, something beyond conventional "monastic" relationships?

"Brother Irenaeus, you will take Father Nicolas his tray after mass."

I had already noticed this father, who was not yet priest and so must still have been finishing his years of study. What had struck me was his exceptional corpulence – at least 110 kilos, which moved with agility and almost grace. He had a large round face pierced by lively eyes, always alert and keenly involved. Strange stories were told about him.

He came from the canton of Vaud and had retained the sing-song intonation of French-speaking Switzerland. One day, well before the existence of the hippy movement, he had knocked on the door of the abbey, hair reaching down to his shoulders and pipe constantly alight.

They had paused a bit before admitting him. But the race for recruits was such that it would have been worse not to open the door. The authorities were gripped by an obsession with numbers, and this impressive hulk would certainly constitute a number. So he had been down to the River to throw his pipes solemnly into it, before having his head shaved. From then on he had put himself within the mould, though certain bursts of originality used to raise an indulgent smile.

Father Nicolas was highly intelligent and, while adapting to monastic life, had found a way to remain to some extent himself. He was the only one, when intervening at an evening chapter meeting, who managed to raise an unforced laugh among the community. So we excused Father Nicolas a lot.

The cell that I came to with my tray – soup, vegetable, piece of fruit – was at once both totally bare and utterly disordered. It was the den of a tramp that had kept nothing, or almost nothing. There was a very thin mattress on a pallet, and random objects scattered in every direction: sock, radio condenser, airgun, small clock, hat, tricycle wheel, the other sock... And then, on the table, a book.

"It's Maritain. You know Maritain? French philosopher. He writes well, actually, but he's missed the whole point. You'll read him, later."

Father Nicolas was lying fully clothed, half-covered by a grubby sheet that emphasized his impressive bulk. He was flushed with a fever, but the window was wide open and it was freezing outside.

"Your tray..."

"Thank you; put it there. So, you're Brother Irenaeus? How's it going, Irenaeus?"

I stood speechless, mouth open. Orders were strict: a monk was never addressed by name alone. It was *Brother* Irenaeus, full stop. But there was so much mischievous kindness in Father Nicolas's eyes...

So when at the bend of a corridor I came face to face with this breezy bison of a man, and when, instead of just bowing his head and lowering his eyes, he looked me straight in the face and whispered, "Hello, Irenaeus! How are you?" – horror-stricken, I felt a surge of new cheerfulness.

13

There was still God. God was the point of all this, God had been the justification for all the suffering imposed on my family; God was the reward for putting myself through all this. I did not in fact know much about him – he remained a big question mark.

I wanted to meet him, to *experience* him – this word came up frequently during our lessons. The *experience of God*, so much sought after, was the only thing that could validate the life we led, the sacrifices we had made.

The Father Master talked of it a lot, but only as something to be taken for granted. The "escape from the world" was regarded as leading to this end automatically, or nearly so. The impressive monastic tradition, tried and tested for centuries, could only lead to God. "Do all this," the Rule said, "and you will arrive there."

"*You will arrive*" were the last words of the Rule.

In fact, what I arrived at mainly was "doing all this" – that is to say, adopting a compliant attitude. But God, where was he, then?

I read the Bible diligently, without understanding any of it. Evidently my teachers considered it enough to read in order to appreciate, to appreciate in order to experience. But to me the Bible was mainly a hotchpotch of stories of wars that had racked the Near East.

Liturgical worship? We used to spend hours each day reciting psalms in the church, in Latin. The Rule itself had set the objective – quantity: in good time something would be achieved. But nothing was achieved in me beyond the sensation of a mill wheel turning, of a steamroller going on its way. It seemed to be the fathers' central concern that the prescribed quantity of psalms should be well performed – then all was well, we were men of prayer. So I became a professional choral performer.

But what of God? Once the service was over, I was left with a vague hunger deep at heart.

Then there was what they called "private prayer", or silent meditation. At the end of every afternoon the entire community devoted a good half hour to this, gathered together in the chancel. Everyone remained in their place in silence and could watch everyone else. The favoured posture was kneeling, eyes closed, hands hidden under the habit, head bowed. Thirty minutes of complete motionlessness under the eye of the seniors: their eyelids couldn't stay hermetically sealed the whole time...

Beware of cramps: sitting was tolerated, though it signified weakness. But the true ones, the virtuous ones, sitting? Never!

The most obvious foe was sleep: in case of need you could take a devotional book from your pocket and draw a little help from it. But drowsiness was treacherous, and came on you without warning. The book, after several fumbles by weary hands, would fall to the floor with a crash – with the effect of making everyone jump and awakening the other sleepers – who were overjoyed not to be the ones it had happened to.

Father Nicolas had a bad back: he would sit down early on and doze off just as quickly. The inevitable tragicomedy with him was a mighty snore, which everyone dreaded, proclaiming as it did loud and clear that someone was not at prayer. His neighbour had received instructions to give him a discreet nudge in the ribs. Nicolas would wake up with a start and mutter:

"What is it then? I'm not asleep!"

People smiled into their hoods, and meditations were resumed until the bell rang.

But what of God? When and how would I have the encounter I had so long been waiting for?

I refused to see all the pretence that there was in our lives. A comfortable poverty, an anaemic chastity, a bulldozer of a prayer routine... To admit it, or just to consider it, would have been to call everything into question. "You will arrive": I based my life on that promise in the Rule.

Meanwhile I committed myself to do everything to perfection, to play my role of professional monk faultlessly.

One of our women in the nave had noticed this commitment – those eyes piously lowered, those unyielding postures, and my wan complexion. She had whispered to a neighbour (who later reported it to me):

"Brother Irenaeus... Oh! he's the angel of the abbey!"

But what of God?

14

At the end of those twelve months – I was twenty-four – I was invited to complete my noviciate. An examination was held for this purpose, involving an appearance, before the Council of senior members of the abbey. I was to be questioned on the Rule in the presence of the Father Master. I was supposed then to repeat back the pious sentiments I had listened to each morning in the classroom.

Unquestionably guilty as I was of "intellectual gastronomy", I had, while ferreting round the library, come across the ancient text of a then unknown Latin work *The Rule of the Master*. I had seen somewhere that this was the source St Benedict had drawn on in the sixth century when drafting our Rule, and I had started reading it with interest. Then I had the idea, without telling anyone, of comparing these two texts. This allowed me to go behind the traditions about St Benedict and find out how much of his work was original, which parts he had borrowed, and which represented his own true contribution – a scientific study of the texts that was made possible by the leisurely novices' timetable. It seemed to me the obvious approach.

When I entered the Father Abbot's office on the set day, I found myself face to face with a row of venerable seniors of the abbey with gaunt cheeks and expressionless eyes, gathered there to assess the spiritual fruit of this young tree. I answered the question put to me by citing from memory the Latin texts and giving a brief comparison of them. Amazement. The Father Abbot was the only one to have heard of the *Rule of the Master*, and he interrupted me in the middle of my brilliant exposition. It was not this, not this at all, that was expected from a novice. They required evidence of my piety: but, as I had given evidence of this elsewhere, and in view of the pressure to recruit, I was nonetheless approved for the next stage.

So starting the following autumn I was to take a two-year course in philosophy.

* * *

For a scientist philosophy is on the face of it something artificial, a bundle of arbitrary theories founded on nothing. My education had been in matter, and I could not envisage any branch of study that was not based on matter and could not be validated by it. Nonetheless, that was the way I had to go: two years of philosophy were an obligatory introduction to the study of God, to theology.

Since my studies had to take place within the monastery, my teacher was to be one of our own people. So one day I was summoned to the cell of Father Joseph.

The cell of a perfect monk. Books lined up on the wooden floor are a signal to everyone of his role as an intellectual. The place is spotlessly clean. He has a round face in a square head that's slightly hunched into his shoulders, and a stubborn brow. He speaks with a lisp, in a staccato rhythm:

"Thit down, Brother. I've prepared a programme for your introduction to philothophy. You'll begin by reading the workth of Maritain and Gilson, and you'll do a critique of them."

Fetch Maritain, then. True, it was very well written, and easy to understand. He claimed to be no more than a disciple of St Thomas Aquinas and to be passing on nothing beyond the medieval philosopher's ideas.

Well then, why stop at the disciple? I went to find an edition of the *Summa Theologiæ*, and immersed myself in its fourteenth-century Latin.

Father Joseph was surprised, but let me get on with it. He had not foreseen that I would cut the normal circuit short and depart from his plan. So I confronted St Thomas Aquinas head on.

But here was a new challenge. In the first place the language was a technical Latin, where the simplest words took on a meaning that escaped me. I went to see my instructor, who frowned and opened a dictionary – which is what I had already done just before, without his help.

Gradually I sensed that in my reading I was coming face to face with something new to me – an approach to the real world that I had been completely ignorant of till then, but towards which all my studies were leading. It was metaphysics, queen of the sciences. And as a scientist I had to master this.

I pressed Father Joseph over his fixed positions, I jostled his inflexibilities and I soon discovered the pathetic truth.

He had entered the abbey at the age of fourteen and had never been out again. A yellowed photograph of the time – it was just after the war – showed him in short trousers in the middle of a group of zombie-like monks, his eyes already agleam with confidence.

He was the only one of his generation to have done his studies at the Catholic Institute in Paris. So he had been dubbed a philosopher, and an authority in this sovereign among the sciences. He was in fact barely a logician. Having grasped once and for all that two and two make four, he had used this unchallengeable proposition as the basis of his system of thought, of his philosophical convictions and of his process of reasoning.

One day, when I was questioning him about metaphysics, he tilted his head, and gave me a sidelong glance:

"Er... d'you see, it's a very, er... abstruse point."

I could never get any more out of him.

As I understand it, St Thomas put forward doubt as a means of exploring all aspects of being. But the wing of doubt had never brushed against Father Joseph's square head. Sure of having chosen the side of truth, he doubted nothing, least of all himself.

He was in fact in the grip of an appetite for power and of a thirst for honours that he was the only one not to recognize.

Since there were only a limited number of men in the community, the young turks always ended up by climbing the staircase of power. So one fine day the Father Abbot, who was now getting ready to retire, appointed Father Joseph prior. Having come so near his goal, Father Joseph from then on signed even the most minor letters with his title *Prior of the Abbey*, which was quite unusual. At chapter meetings pronouncements poured from his lips: he forbade what no one had dreamt of doing, and authorized initiatives that had already been taken. It all seemed to me a bit childish, nothing more; but, to cut a long story short, he did so much of this that the Father Abbot removed him from office. Sensible man that he was, had he perhaps simply wanted to open the community's eyes before they came to choose his successor?

Later on Father Joseph was appointed Master of Novices, a post that he occupied for a long time. As his only responsibility there was a spiritual one, the damage would be less apparent. And it was appropriate perhaps that the youngsters should have someone to lean on who did not know how to step backwards. So he lapsed into silence, which was clearly his strongest act.

But none of this was yet on the horizon, and there was an immediate problem that needed to be dealt with urgently – Father Joseph's evident inability to fulfil his engagement to me.

The Father Abbot took his decision: I would continue my studies at the abbey, but under the supervision of a professor in Paris, whom I would visit from time to time.

15

The train was the same as when I had come, but the journey felt shorter. Paris had not changed, and yet everything now seemed to me frenzied, chaotic. Passers-by looked with astonishment at this great black shadow with shaven scalp and lowered head.

It had been agreed that I could take the opportunity to make unrestricted visits to my family. How would Uncle react? I took my first meal with him, at home. I was back in the same familiar surroundings – fine furniture, paintings:

"Well, Michel, is it OK?"

Uncle smiled, and I sensed a continuing affection. But there was a kind of vague distance, as if I no longer really belonged to them. And was not that actually the case? Life, their life, was going on without me. Since that was what I had wanted, they would live on in my absence, and henceforward our two worlds were utterly foreign to each other.

Uncle found a way of giving me his opinion, and perfectly logical it was:

"I would just about have understood your becoming a priest, because that could lead on to bishop one day. But a monk, really, a monk..."

So no one was shifting their position.

With my mother, it was a kind of sorrowful resignation. Her son was there; he seemed happy: for her that was all that mattered. So I thought I had won the match and wanted nothing more. The terrible myopia of self-centredness that must have afflicted my eyes! But was I focusing on her at all, on the life that she was bravely trying to live in silence?

My philosophy professor was at the right level. Did I want to tackle St Thomas Aquinas? Very well. He advised me to confine myself to a few of the opening chapters of the *Summa Theologiæ*, and supplied me with a list of useful commentaries. In short, he gave me free rein, which suited me. I was to report back to him every couple of months, visiting Paris for the purpose. And this too, such as it was, suited me: I would see my mother regularly, which would make her happy. All was well, and my conscience was lulled. Metaphysics for us both! I set my sights on ten chapters of the several hundred that comprised the *Summa*, and I picked them apart line by line, word by word.

I found that St Thomas was a remarkable teacher. From that central point he encouraged me to go on to other sections of his work, and to his main source, Aristotle. So little by little I extended my field of exploration, and little by little there emerged before my eyes a cathedral of thought, disciplined and coherent.

Being and its categories, matter and its innermost structure, language and its ability to describe the universe – it all seemed to me a logical, inevitable consummation of Jacques Monod's lectures. But at the point where the Nobel prize winner seemed to me to have been brought to a halt, as though at the outer edge of knowledge, from there St Thomas had pressed on much further, right to the very origin of things. And yet his understanding of matter was virtually insignificant next to mine. But starting from some unpromising examples, with a simplicity that was almost childish, he went behind matter to reach its very heart.

I was overjoyed, unconscious of the passage of time. At the abbey they reached the view that I had made a little glass bubble for myself. During the walks I tried to share what I had discovered, but in vain. Study was allowed, on condition that it produced a good monk, observant and pious. But finding pleasure in it, that was suspect: did not the Rule affirm emphatically that "death begins at the very point where pleasure begins"? Without my realizing it, I began to come under a certain suspicion: an intellectual could not be an observant monk.

Undaunted, I continued on my way. What St Thomas offered me was the possibility I had yearned for of integrating my view of the world around a few stable, simple and clear reference points. Certainly, I was straying into abstractions, but can one blame a student for that?

The two years of philosophy passed like this, smoothly and straightforwardly. To finish off, my professor gave me a copy of Sartre's *Being and Nothingness*. Very few people, I imagine, have read the whole of this huge indigestible tome: I made do with a few chapters, then took an excursion to Hegel and Heidegger, the German masters of modern metaphysics.

16

I realized that I had become a denizen of the Dark Ages from the fact that time passed over me now without leaving any imprint. A new year was beginning; and my lonely evenings, the heavy tedium of Sunday afternoons without visits or work, the excitement that came with the approach of the great liturgical festivals – I greeted them now like old acquaintances.

Life seemed to have become as unchanging as the River that enfolded us in one of its bends and to which our steps took us unfailingly on every walk. The waters, sluggish yet flowing, were a perfect reflection of that central French sky with its innumerable permutations. I do not think I ever saw in them, from one week to the next, from one walk to the next, precisely the same combination of colours. They seemed to shift from grey to blue in a range of infinite tints. And when near the beginning of March the walk was drawing to an end at sunset, the waters managed to reflect both the purple and the indigo. For that brief moment they were a stream of molten lava that flowed by at our feet.

On those days too it was easier for us to re-engage with the silence when we were back within the walls – as though the River would continue to lull us protectively, even within the monastery.

Was that happiness? I do not know. Is the absence of suffering enough to create happiness? Yet I was no longer numb, but rather fossilized, solidified, so to speak, into my role as fully trained monk.

Perhaps, if nothing had changed in that stationary universe, I might have been able to tell whether or not one might talk of happiness, or of success. Another few years would have been enough for me to have stopped feeling and become like the friendly River, superseding time in its indomitable flow. Then I should have had the leisure to contemplate my navel, and I am sure that this constant study of the centre of myself would have given me a vaguely mature assurance, source of peace perhaps, and certainly of celebrity. People would have come to consult the man who had resolved his inner conflicts, the stone figure that looked like an oracle. But I was not granted time for that.

The Father Abbot was observing all this with interest. He had been following very closely the proceedings of the Vatican Council that had opened in 1962, though very few echoes of it had reached us in the abbey. He sensed that a great upheaval was about to take place in the Church and that the monastery would need some well-educated men to handle it. So one day he summoned me with a note – in that world of silence we often used to communicate through these terse little notes, slipped under a cell door or into a pigeonhole in the common room.

"Brother, your professor is pleased with your philosophy studies. It seems that you have the potential to develop a little further. I have therefore decided to send you next year to take a degree in theology at our order's university in Rome."

Consternation. Like all the large orders, ours ran what was effectively its own university in the Eternal City. But here it was mentioned as a laboratory for dangerous experiments, a place where observance was non-existent, or where a monk – a true monk – could be sure only of losing his soul. It was fine for the Americans or the Germans, second-rate monks with huge colleges within their abbeys. It was only the French who were depositaries of monastic orthodoxy; in those other countries they were reception-room monks, every one of them educated in Rome. Would I not come to grief there?

The Father Abbot listened gravely to my objections:

"You'll find a way of remaining observant in your heart. But I have to prepare for the future. Anyhow, you're not the only one to be leaving: I've also decided to grant Father Gerard a sabbatical year; he'll spend it at the Catholic Institute of Paris. A little study will do him a huge amount of good."

Father Gerard was the cellarer, the man with the shallot patch when I started. Because he talked very little, even on walks, he was considered a deep thinker. The truth is, he seemed to be forever listening, then adopting unreservedly the views of his interlocutors. A round, almost chubby face, slightly slanting eyes that puckered up at the least smile. Quiet though he was, he smiled a lot, and everyone around him felt himself to be understood, indeed unmasked.

The surprising thing about him was that – although he knew himself to be intelligent – he had never studied. He had ended up by turning his lack of education into something of a point of honour: he limited himself strictly to the Bible, which he pored over every day without the help of any commentary or guidance.

At the end of the war he had been just old enough to climb on board a tank (presumably an American one) and liberate some kilometres of French territory. As the years passed this outing had assumed epic proportions; and if people whispered in awed tones that he had been with the US Second Armoured Division, he never contradicted them. And if, going on from there, some concluded that he could well have planted the French flag on Strasbourg Cathedral, that was up to them.

These innocent silences, together with his resemblance to a man from the cultural backwoods, made him an intriguing and slightly enigmatic figure. In a life without the spoken word real silences exercise other people's imagination. No one knew for certain what lay hidden behind Father Gerard's puckered eyes, but people thought – they were even sure of it – that there was plenty to discover beneath that evasive smile – and that he was assured, one day, of a great future in the community.

There remained, however, one formality before my departure. It was certainly nothing more than a formality, since I had surmounted every hurdle and had as good as won a certificate of compliance by my diligence at the abbey. The formality was that I should make my solemn vows – that is to say, my definitive pledge, given in public, that a breach between me and the community would come with death alone.

If I was binding myself for ever, the community too was binding itself to me. I was entrusting my life to the community, and through it to God alone. But the community were accepting this life; they were taking on administrative and moral responsibility for it before the same God. The Rule specified that the abbot would be held accountable for each of his monks. It was a reciprocal commitment, which implied on my side an application, and on the community's part a vote of acceptance.

My application was a matter of course. How could it have been otherwise? Certainly, I had no feeling yet of having reached fullness of life, but I knew that only time would allow me to reach that goal, and I was committing myself to take the time: "You will arrive…" I had not sacrificed such a promising future, and with it a little of my family's future too, just to cut the project short for no good reason.

And I had no reason: the vague unease that I felt was not one. I had not arrived, that was all; that did not justify calling into question the life's aim that I had chosen, and that I had forced my family to accept.

The community voted. Meeting in chapter, it listened to the address in which the Father Abbot declared me fitted. No more was needed; the abbot's verdict carried with it the acquiescence of his sons.

One morning, then, in the middle of the chancel, I held out my arms in the form of a cross facing the crucified Christ, as though to identify myself with him; and I chanted the sentence that made a monk of me for life and for eternity:

"*Suscipe me, Domine…* Receive me, Lord, and do not fail me…"

It was done. Nevermore would I be able to go back. I was scarcely aware of it – any more than the community seemed to reckon that it was taking *me* on, such as I was, to carry me, come what may, to the very end, and beyond. It was the logical next step, that was all. People were a little surprised that no member of my family was present; but it had been my wish to spare them a pointless ordeal.

Truth to tell, I was already focused on the future: Rome… And my vows sank into the background, as something obvious and well understood.

So one fine September day I went to fetch a suitcase from the linen store. On our final walk to the riverbank the abbey seemed to me from a distance both awesome and at the same time vulnerable. Little did I know that this universe, my universe of unruffled calm, would soon explode.

The next day I boarded the train for the south.

Part Three

Revolution

1

At the beginning of that autumn the *Palatino* Paris-Rome express became a microcosm of the Catholic Church. A good part of the train was occupied by churchmen of all complexions travelling to commence, or continue, their work beside the Tiber.

But most of them were dressed in clerical suits or as laymen: I was witnessing for the first time one of the Vatican Council's most visible effects. In fact, lay attire fooled no one: in grey or coal-black, the ill-cut clothes betrayed the churchman twenty paces off – and emphasized the paunch and impressive buttocks that a cassock would earlier have covered in a more modest and certainly more elegant manner.

I was the only one in a great black habit, and everyone was amused to see me caught in a carriage door by a flap of gown as I tried in vain to gather up decently all those billowing folds that the French Railways had not catered for. Sympathetic smiles: *you see? – monks don't live in this world any more...*

"The only one"? Not entirely. In the compartment next to mine there was another monk, freshly tonsured, spotless scapular hanging just so, glasses unobtrusively rimmed with gold, delicate hands with brushed nails holding a leather-bound book.

"Good day, Brother. You're bound for Rome? I'm Father Jean Claire, from Solesmes."

With its trace of condescension, this introduction was meant to set matters in place. I remembered instantly that he was the choirmaster of the famous abbey, Dom Gageard's successor, and therefore repository of the authentic Gregorian tradition. I suddenly felt a bit of a bumpkin.

Solesmes earned a very comfortable living from the Gregorian chant. The abbey charged a royalty on each disc, each public performance, each printing of a service book. The publisher

Desclée de Brouwer had made a quiet fortune from this goldmine; and the nickname that people laughingly gave his business, "investment in vestments", was not unjustified.

Father Jean Claire gives me the look of an entomologist examining a specimen and turns over a page.

"It'll soon be time for dinner. I'm going to the restaurant car; if you like I'll take you along: Solesmes can well afford you that."

"No thank you; it's really too kind, but I've got sandwiches."

A monk in the restaurant car: can't be true – am I dreaming?

So while the Solesmes choirmaster is on his way to dinner without once getting hitched up in the lurching corridors, I'm tucking in to my cheese roll (no meat!) and gazing out of the window, one hand on my service book. Someone here has to stand up for orthodox monasticism.

The train being no more than a few hours late, we arrive as night is falling. I have my first view of the Roman countryside as it goes by: ochre, yellow and blue, against an aqueduct. Washing hanging from windows, *mammas* in the streets – here I am!

It's night-time when I emerge from the Piramide station. I drag my heavy suitcase through dense traffic. Ahead is a high hill on top of which you can make out a massive and imposing building in pink brickwork.

The university of the order is perched on the summit of one of the seven sacred hills of Rome, the Aventine. I struggle up the quiet, winding street that leads to it. To right and left are dimly lit mansions. It's clearly a very smart area, an oasis of golden tranquillity amid the city's uproar – not the worst choice the monks could have made.

Suddenly I emerge onto a little baroque square designed by Piranesi: an eighteenth-century engraving. To the left, beyond an enormous gateway, an avenue of yews leads to the pedimented façade of a church. This is it.

A small courtyard, a porter's lodge. I put my case down on the marble floor. In the shadowy hallway shadows of darker black keep coming and going. And then, descending the grand staircase

behind a highly wrought banister, I see a scalp leading down to a
weaselly face and then to a black habit that moves with a sprightly
gait.

"Goot efening, Brozer. Ach, you are from France? Goot, fery
goot, velcome. I know your lofely country vell; I vas an officer in
ze Prussian army during ze var. I am ze master of ceremonies here;
ve'll see a lot of each ozer. Fazer Adalhard."

Charming welcome. A Prussian army cap would indeed have
looked good on that shaven scalp of his! He doesn't take my
suitcase, but leads the way along the dark corridors. Father
Adalhard walks sideways, just like a crab, head at forty-five
degrees – is he remembering, perhaps, the Blitzkrieg that enabled
his country to bring mine to its knees in 1940?

Come on, Brother Irenaeus – don't forget the war's over! He
steps aside for me at the entrance to my room.

"You'll be fine; you look out onto ze cloister. Ze morning serfice
is at six."

I set my case down. A desk-and-table, some shelves, a wardrobe,
a washbasin, a sprung bed. Without putting the light on, I go to
the window. The clear sky is full of stars. Drifting up from below
is a faint scent of orange blossom, oleanders and spaghetti. For
the first time I'm inhaling the scent of Rome.

2

Next morning, exhausted by the journey, I gave the service a miss.
I turned up, fresh-eyed, in the refectory.

Vast room, long and narrow, with marble floor, wood-panelled
walls and rectangular polished tables. At one end, on a little dais,
the table of the Father Abbot Primate, head of the order, who has
his residence here.

People come in, help themselves and go to sit at whatever table
they like. There's talking, of a measured, almost subdued, kind.
I'm hungry and make for the middle table: coffee, tea, cold meats,
black pudding, eggs, rolls and assorted jams. The order has 120

students here, of twenty-eight different nationalities: every taste is catered for, which suits my appetite.

Someone hands me a napkin-pouch and small card: we all write our name and country on the card and insert it onto the pouch. My identification is: "Brother Irenaeus, France".

I take a quick look at my neighbour on the right: "Spain". He's a small black fellow; he glances at my pouch:

"*Linguam gallicam ignosco. Tu quoque latine loqueris?* I don't know French. And you, do you speak Latin?"

Er... no. Anyhow, a conversation in Latin at breakfast – very bad for the digestion! I explain this to him in Spanish, very pleased with myself – and he buries his nose in his coffee cup.

On my left a burly ginger-haired lad is talking animatedly. I look at his pouch: "Brother Anselm, New England, USA".

Good, OK to use English. I force myself to pronounce each English word properly and show these barbarians what a Frenchman can do:

"Excuse me, please, er... would you be kind enough to er... give me some sugar?"

A bit halting, but very correct.

"But of course," he replies to me in perfect French, without the shadow of an accent. "Oh! but you've just arrived? Delighted to meet you. I'm Anselm. There, help yourself."

Careful, Brother Irenaeus! I am listening to him talking to his neighbours. He goes from Italian to German, then to Portuguese, with no apparent effort.

"Tell me, Brother Anselm, how many languages do you speak?"

"Oh! only eight or nine. But do you see Father Aelred over there? American. He's professor of New Testament here. *He* speaks seventeen languages, and examines the Maronites orally in Arabic. You know, it's the first four that are the hardest. After that it gets quicker."

It gets quicker, of course; that's obvious. But I know nothing of this, because four are all I speak.

I go out again into the sun-drenched cloister, an enormous rectangle, shaded by a colonnade running round each side. In the centre are pools with goldfish and fountains, flowers, orange trees, benches. And a continual movement of black gowns going, coming, calling to one another. An orgy of smiles: it's the start of the new term; the introductory mass will begin in an hour.

I'm surrounded by a whirlwind of young men, full of life and energy. Snatches of conversation fly this way and that in all the languages of Europe.

Brother Anselm has spotted me, rather bemused on my bench. He takes charge of me in a kindly way:

"For the mass, you'll stand there. We do the station in the open air, in the cloister – just follow everyone else. Afterwards you'll see the French guys; most of them have just arrived."

The station: two long black lines in the sunlight. Not so many tonsures; plenty of heads of hair. Organ music: the double column moves off and enters the church. Two thirds of the places are occupied by the monks' choir. A strong, manly chanting rises up as the Father Abbot Primate makes his entrance.

He has been elected by the congress of the order barely a month before, a slim, youthful American with an intelligent face. The French newspapers have remarked on this unexpected election to a post traditionally held by weary grandfathers. "It is the Council that has made this possible; it's all change in the Church", etcetera.

In his address the Primate speaks five languages in turn, with absolute facility:

"You are the hope of the order; you are its life. The Church is being reborn following the Council; she needs you, and the order counts on you." He ends in English: "God bless you!"

This is all going a bit fast for me: only two days ago I was on the bank of the River with its slow, measured rhythm. *Brother Irenaeus, my lad, you're going to have to change quietly into a higher gear.* On emerging from the mass, dazzled by sunlight, I come across a group speaking my language: the Frenchmen! Eight of them, from virtually every part of metropolitan France. They are easily recognized by their shaven scalps and earnest looks. Some of them are already old students on the hilltop. They give the newcomer a kindly welcome:

"Are you OK? Everything going well? We're still one short; he's only just arrived. We'll all be meeting for coffee in a moment."

I go back up to my room. At the bend in the corridor I nearly crash into a chap with fine, craggy features, close-cropped hair and lively eyes.

"Hey! Mi-ind!"

He's from home – the last Frenchman?

"Hallo. My name's Mark, I'm from B—."

B— is a big abbey in the south of France. Mark has a faintly singsong accent.

"You're called Marc, then? That makes you Marco here, eh?"

"-kus. Markus, with a K. My mother's German. Well, what do you think of it here?"

"Well… to tell you the truth, I'm a little out of my depth; it's all happening too fast."

"Nothing wrong with that. That's humility, the foundation of our life, eh?"

A sermonizer! Yet, no, there is so much masculine warmth in those eyes, the sermon is over.

"Good. See you again, Irenaeus. I'm going to get unpacked."

And Mark goes loping off, like a parachutist.

Our first meal in the great refectory. We're placed in order of monastic seniority. Beside me are a Spaniard, some Italians, a Fleming, a German. The Primate, right at the end, chants the *benedicite* with an American Midwestern accent. Everyone sits down. The trolleys arrive, pushed by brother students in spotless white aprons.

Spaghetti – in Italy one calls it *pasta*: every meal begins with a heap of fragrant pasta. On the aisles to the right and left of the Primate the reverend father professors are stuffing their mouths with trailing lengths of bright pink pasta that leave stains on the white serviettes tucked into their collars.

When the pasta is finished, the Primate rings a small bell: we can talk. From the 140 black habits rises a noise like that of a beehive – restrained, no voice standing out above the rest – while huge dishes of meat are set before us. *Come on, Irenaeus, this may not be "observant", but admit it: you're giving yourself hefty helpings. Do they eat like this every day?*

We regather in the cloister, a little heavier, heads spinning a little from talking in a mixture of languages. Each linguistic group is to meet separately for coffee. The ten Frenchmen are there, with two Belgians who do not mix with their Flemish compatriots, and a Portuguese who wants to get away from the Brazilians. We may be monks, but the squabbles of old Europe are not forgotten.

The exchanges are lively. I listen. The big subject of conversation is the follow-up to the Council, which is only just beginning. Shall we one day have a liturgy in French? Are monks going to dress as laymen? *You're crazy: it's all a pipe-dream. Besides, what's the point? Isn't our life fine as it is, timeless, inviolable?* In the hot Roman sun, after the pasta, no topic is off-limits any more. Anyhow we talk, and we dream.

Siesta time. Curtains drawn to. Sweaty in my heavy habit, I'm a recumbent effigy suffering indigestion. Someone knocks at the door. It's Mark. He comes in and sits down without ceremony:

"You know, I've done the same courses as you, but without getting to the end. 'Service to God comes first', eh?"

Always this utter conviction, which everyone but he finds hard to sustain. But his unclouded eyes, his uninhibited speech, the liveliness he exudes give all his professions of faith a tone of veracity. Is he trying to prove something to himself? Or is he really filled with that absolute certainty that is beyond my reach? I learn that his family, his mother in particular, are unquestioning believers. He has come to faith from faith.

"Well, I... I'm a converted pagan. There's nothing in our life as monks that comes naturally to me. I've chosen it because God interests me. I want to meet him, to have that experience. Unexplored territory, you understand?"

He settles back into the armchair.

"I hope, Irenaeus... I'd like us to become friends. I think I know God. We'll search for him together. I offer you my friendship. Are you willing?"

For the moment what I need most is sleep... haven't had a meal like that for years.

Friendship? Of course. There's plenty of time.

The first lectures begin the next day. The timetable is straightforward: four or five hours in the lecture theatre each morning; afternoons free, set aside for private work in one's room. We can go out into the city on Thursdays and Sunday afternoons.

At eight the lecture hall is full. It's a lecture on dogmatic theology, given by a German-Swiss professor, whose animation belies his rotundity.

All teaching is delivered in Latin: oh yes! here Latin's a living language. The German-speakers handle it with amazing facility, even constructing periods and linking subordinate clauses to main clauses in the proper order. We get our quota – obligatory in the inaugural lecture – of some subtle Swiss jokes in the language of Ovid, and the assembled students, who seem to appreciate this rare treat, burst into laughter, then bang on the desks with the flat of their hands by way of applause. Personally, I've understood nothing, but I cheer like everyone else so as not to appear too much of a dunce.

Five hours of introductory lectures in Latin: I come out with my brain pulped, and having taken very few notes. Fortunately there's pasta at midday and, as it's a professor's birthday, as much as we want of a delicious white wine from the Castelli. Perhaps the meal will help me digest what went before?

After the meal Anselm takes me by the elbow:

"We're going to have a game of basketball; it's the favourite sport of the Americans here. Will you come?"

No thank you. I just have the strength to go to my room, pull the curtains and relapse into a comatose siesta.

Those first days have left me with the memory of an unremitting struggle to listen and understand. I used to spend all my afternoons rereading my notes and trying to get them straight.

One evening, tortured by a relentless headache and unable to eat, I request permission to take a little walk outside during the dinner hour, to the foot of the hill. *Permission granted. Go and get some fresh air, Brother; it'll do you good.*

It's my first outing, and I'm wearing my great black habit. I avoid the busy road junction at Piramide and head for the Circo Massimo, the vast green area on the other side of the hill. The streets are dark and empty when I emerge onto what used to be the racecourse of ancient Rome. In front of me on the other side stand the majestic ruins of the Palatine, that humble residence of the Roman emperors. From there, without leaving their balcony, they could watch the races between the "greens" and "reds", on which huge bets had been laid.

Of the great stadium the central track survives, surrounded by dense oleanders. I am starting to descend the steps leading to the centre, inhaling with relish the perfumed air that's beginning to clear my brain, when two fellows emerge from the bushes and come in my direction, with lewd expressions:

"Hey, *padre*! You want a *bocchino*?"

My Italian is good, but I don't know the meaning of this particular word.

"I'm sorry, I don't understand. What is it?"

"Hey, *padre*! It's this, the *bocchino*, if you want – it's good."

And one of the two stretches out his finger and mimes the action.

Ah! bocchino, *that comes from* bocca, *mouth. Dammit! these fellows are suggesting… But, after all, I'm wearing a habit, I'm plainly a monk, and I'm also plainly appalled.*

"No, really, as you see, I'm a monk. No, I don't do that kind of thing."

"Ah! because earlier, *padre*, earlier… Huh! *va bene*, it's your loss, *buona sera*."

By the time I get back my brain is clear, but my heart is pounding. I tell myself that if they've made this suggestion to me when my identity is so manifest, that must mean that *sometimes* it must work with others. *Brother Irenaeus, you must take care of yourself and not stray an inch from the hill without knowing where you're going.*

Weird city, for sure.

3

Days, weeks passed. Each Thursday and each Sunday afternoon we had free. To be on the safe side, I used to join a group of seniors strolling in the city in full habit. We were aware that the number of clerics in Rome was substantial, yet very little ecclesiastical dress was visible in the streets. One day I mentioned it to Peppino, the university porter, a good family man, who had been in post for twenty years. His memoirs, had he been able to write them, would have had plenty of spice.

"Oh dear, what do you expect, *fra' Ireneo*, nothing's like it was in the old days. I can tell you this: I've known the city when it was like a big theatre, with all those priests' and seminarists' costumes. Oh yes! you could see them in every colour – whites, reds and blue. Nowadays they've all got their bums in grey; dismal it is, even in sunshine, I tell you. It's their Council has done all this, no one can make head or tail of it…"

Were we the last to wear the habit in town? Almost. One day I borrowed one of the bicycles from the basement and went into the city for a ride as night was falling, all the folds of my habit billowing out in the end-of-day traffic. Apparently my rear light was not working, though it did not matter. At one road junction a Roman, who had almost bumped into me in the darkness, wound down his window:

"So your lights have gone missing, eh, *padre*?"

Then, glancing up and down at this medieval apparition on wheels, he gave up, with a very Roman fatalism, and said:

"Of course, your light's on the inside, *mannaggia* – damn you!"

The blow struck home. Several of us Frenchmen had decided on a cycle ride on the Via Appia the next Sunday afternoon. After mass a group of us went together to the Porta Portese flea market, not far from our hill. After determined haggling each of us returned with a pair of trousers more or less matching his figure.

So it was that the revolution began. In the afternoon six French monks in their comic-opera trousers, scalps shaven and shirt sleeves rolled up, got astride six patched-up bicycles and pedalled down the route of the Imperial triumphs. We must have looked like ex-convicts on an outing, but no matter: we were bursting with life and health, our laughter travelled ahead of us, and we felt that the world was ours.

I often went out alone with Mark. One evening, returning from a long walk, we stopped at the edge of the orange grove that adjoins St Sabina's and overlooks the city from the end of the Aventine. At our feet Rome unfolded the ochre-brown of her tiled roofs, and away in the background the Vatican quarter receded into night. A few fashionable *mammas* were still walking their children on the gravel paths. It was one of those moments of great peace and serenity that the city occasionally offers to those who love her.

"Rome, Irenaeus… Do you realize, we're in Rome!"

Yes. And Rome, mother of all nations, was gently teaching me to live, without my even realizing it.

The next day I accepted Anselm's invitation, and he lent me a pair of shorts. So there I was after lunch, skimpily dressed, in front of a basketball board and a dozen Americans who had suddenly gone wild and were as completely caught up with their game as if it were a championship match. Never having trained, I definitely caused my team to lose. But it did not matter: the only thing that counted for them was the game: they launched themselves into it with yells, and it brought out the Yankee, the Texan, the Californian, the swearing, the backslapping and that laughter, that *joie de vivre*… Lions unleashed.

Then, after a shower, I came upon them in a corridor, quiet, earnest, courteous.

I learnt to understand these Americans devils, of whom so much ill was spoken in our French abbeys, those shrines of "observance". In the course of our conversations I came to realize that these "reception-room monks" were perfectly familiar with the ancient monastic tradition, much more so than I was. Several of them knew the Desert Fathers, those original founders of Christian monasticism, and were preparing theses on them. I used to ask them innocently:

"But what about the desert, the 'escape from the world'? And your universities, managed entirely by you, with their thousands of students? And your huge budgets, your endowments? And your lifestyle?"

They laughed their heads off:

"*Frenchie*, you can't understand what it is to be a pioneering country. That's how it had to be. We have a country to open up, like the eleventh-century monks in Europe. This is our way. Our "observance" is the earnestness with which we go about this *job*. We can carry the desert with us deep in our hearts, without spreading sand all round."

I also watched them living one day at a time. All the chores, all the duty rosters, were organized by them – the washing-up and other minor tasks left to the students. They were always last out of the back-kitchen after meals, when the French had long been holding forth in the cloister. And if someone or something had problems, it was usually an American who would come to lend a hand, with a Hollywood grin and nonchalant air. But they got things done.

It was then, when I watched these men the abbey had cautioned me against, these "reception-room monks" so utterly committed to whatever they were doing – it was then that I became aware, abruptly, that the error was not here but on the bank of the River. My masters, who were so sure of being sole custodians of a perfect ideal – my masters' view was wrong; or rather it did not extend beyond the bend of the River, beyond the wall of their certainties.

All at once my confidence in them was under threat. But if I called them into question on this point, why not on others? And where would this questioning stop?

I went to knock on Mark's door at the end of the corridor.

"*Avanti!*"

As a good southerner, he had been quick to adopt the melodious courtesies of the Italians. I went in and found him sunk into his armchair, bare feet in the air, wet socks on the window sill, working.

"Come in, Iré, do come in. What is it then?"

We used to talk and talk for hours on end. He had become my friend, confidant, brother. He too had lived through years of observance; he too was seeing what I saw. He realized, as I did, the artificiality of our conventions and our lifestyle, and the gulf between that existence and the simplicity of the Gospel.

But nothing dismayed him, nothing evoked his criticism. He took note, that was all.

"Iré, the Church is made up of men, and these men are like you and me: unsure, vulnerable, fallible. I have confidence in her: the Church will shift, will transform herself from within. Give us time, take time, gather in, store up and love!"

Yes, Markus, you are right. But as for me, I've thrown my life aside, I've staked everything on a single ideal; I've sacrificed my family; it's a path of blood. And if it's wrong, if I've fooled myself, if I've been fooled, there's a price of blood to pay!

Mark would laugh, and we would go for a walk. Rome, the mother-city, reconciled the extremes and soothed my soul.

But I spaced out my tonsure sessions: my hair grew, a light stubble that did not yet need combing. It was a symbol of the world I had escaped from.

And one day when the sales were on I bought a plastic mac – too short, but definitely heathen: bright blue...

4

Rome was agog. In truth, the whole Church was agog. At the Second Vatican Council, which had come to an end in this very city the previous year, 1966, mouths had opened: bishops, laymen, theologians had spoken up for a world that was changing radically. And our hilltop was like a cauldron, like a soundbox in which all these voices were resonating ever louder. Throughout the world the monastic way of life, too, needed this *aggiornamento*, this updating promised by Pope John XXIII. We were not sure what was going to change, what *could* change, in our thousand-year-old way of life. But a great gust of fresh air was about to blow through it, and we would be in the front seats, perhaps even among the leading players. Here in Rome there was complete freedom of speech and thought: we were determined, all of us, to take full advantage of it.

The new Pope, Paul VI, had turned the Church into a construction site. And that autumn of 1967 a major event was about to take place: the visit to Rome of the Patriarch Athenagoras.

Mark and I attended this historic encounter, amid the heaving populace of Rome. St Paul's-without-the-Walls was full of a jostling throng, which scarcely matched my idea of a great religious occasion. At the end of the ceremony someone beckoned to us: the Patriarch was in the sacristy and wanted to receive the monks who were present.

We made our way slowly forwards. At the back of the room, on a dais, was a small man, pallid and frail: the Pope. At his side, huge in his white beard and towering headdress, was Athenagoras. Each monk rested one knee on the ground to kiss his ring; then, with a quick and almost motherly movement, the Patriarch of Constantinople took each monk's head in both hands, bent forwards and kissed his tonsure or, failing that, the top of his head.

My turn comes; my heart's pounding. As I kneel I find myself faced with a great wall of white silk that smells of incense. Two delicate and bony hands enfold my cheeks, and a soft beard gently brushes my forehead. I see nothing, and come straight out into the street. But on my head East has just met West.

"He looked at me, he looked at me!"

Mark's exultant as he walks back with me towards the hill. He's bursting with joy, like a child. And I tell myself that I shall never be this child cradled and petted by the Church and now taking refuge within her; I tell myself that in me the child is dead, has been dead since the apartment by the Seine where he grew up too soon; and I tell myself that, if I have a place in the Church... *their* Church, it will be as a fighter, with never a respite.

136

* * *

I resumed my daily regime of study. But what attracted me from the start was not so much the theology as the city, the *Urbs*.

Rome is an ageing woman – utterly seductive, but so often seduced over the centuries that she does not bestow her favours on the first comer. I had the feeling that she had to be won, she had to be earned, and I did not know how to go about it. *Casta Meretrix*, chaste harlot: this medieval definition of the Church was certainly true of the *Mater præcipua*, the world's Mother-city.

I was speaking about this in the cloister one day to one of the professors, a Belgian; he took me by the arm:

"Brother Irenaeus, if you want to get a grip on Rome, you must have Maury and Percheron in your hand and keep it there for a long time. I have a copy: I'll lend it to you."

Maury and Percheron were two French students from the École Normale Supérieure, who had found themselves stuck in Rome during the four years of the war. They had made good use of this enforced leisure to roam systematically all over the city and had subsequently written a book that was now unobtainable. In this book were recorded, with all the discipline you would expect of the École, every monument, every least house, every least stone, arranged according to period, indexed, analysed, described in detail and placed in their correct historical context.

It was an eccentric book, unique of its kind, that one could only read on foot, while walking the streets.

I too had four years ahead of me: I took Maury and Percheron and never let it go. At least once a week, on Thursdays, and sometimes on Sunday afternoons, I set off alone or with Mark, and went through all the *Roman Itineraries*, as the book was called.

Going back and forth, and back again, we learnt what was in effect a geography of history. Each period, each stage of our civilization had left behind an imprint, a stratum, a relic in the city, its walls, its streets and its squares. To unravel this dense tangle required a patience that enthusiasm alone could supply. And, as exploration followed exploration, I became an enthusiast

137

for Rome. She talked to me like a living person, telling me, through her scars and her splendours, the long story of her past, which had made Europe a reality.

"Christian Rome" is just a figment: Rome has never believed in any god. She has endured them all; she has seen them too close at hand to believe in them; she has ceased to care about them. Rome is the most pagan of all cities, with her temples and her four hundred ancient churches. Pagan as I was myself by ancestry, I was amazed to discover this scepticism that was never cynical, always tolerant. The city taught a wise lesson – the equality of all things, and so in the end their nothingness. She alone outlasted beliefs.

If Rome is eternal, this is not because she harbours the only true religion: it is because she has been able to outlive everything, the pope and his priests included. This was the lesson that I took in through the pores of my skin, through my eyes and my lungs. It appealed to the atheist I still was, and it whetted my thirst for discovering what lay hidden behind that word that had driven me to the forest of Morvan, then to the River, and now here, onto the hilltop:

God.

5

The majority of our professors, all of them monks, were German or Swiss. The lectures were at the right level, but often short on interest, as is common in universities – professors are not expected to be geniuses, but to cover a subject fully enough to meet academic requirements. The fact that the subject in this case was theology, the science of God, made no difference: there were many professors, but few good teachers. So I was having to cope with honest grocers serving up Catholic doctrine, history or patristics in slices of equal thickness and similar flavours…

…with one exception, to whom I wish to pay homage under his true name, because I owe him much.

Notker Füglister came from a large abbey in German-speaking Switzerland. Still young, slight, and pathologically shy, he stammered a little – though this did not impair the great elegance of his Latin.

I had got used to Latin by now and understood all the lectures. During seminars I even managed to contribute in Latin; I had no style, but I made myself understood; nothing more was expected.

Notker taught the Old Testament. He had developed a method that was original and effective. Each year he would choose two or three chapters of importance in one of the four biblical traditions – prophetical, historical, wisdom and psalms. He stuck to these few pages and examined them under the microscope, word by word: it was the Bible viewed from ground level. But with each word, each expression, each key idea encountered en route, he stood back and investigated the uses and meanings of the word in the whole of biblical literature. We kept switching, of course, between Latin and Hebrew.

As a result we made very slow progress: it took him a whole year to get through a few paragraphs. It was the opposite of the French approach, which favours general concepts, broad overviews, arresting synopses. I used to feel that I was becoming bogged down in ants' work, that I was never getting any sense of perspective. Then all of a sudden at the end of a session an overall vision would come as if of its own accord, but sustained by a whole compost of meticulous observations.

"It's for you now to go on alone, each for himself," Notker would say. "I have given you the raw material, I have put it in context for you. We're dealing with the Word of God; but what God says, and even more what he is – that's not for me to teach you. It's for you to discover, and each one of you will make that discovery according to who he is, to what he aspires."

This was the only correct method, respecting as it did both our own personal freedom and the mystery of God. Because he refused to speak about God, because he remained at the door after leading us to it, Notker was a true teacher. Not only did I not miss one of his lectures, but I worked at them over and over again in the silence of my room. That first year became, thanks to him, the year of a decisive discovery.

The fact was that, monk though I was, committed by vows and confirmed in the order several years back, I still knew nothing of God. Unlike Notker, people at the abbey talked constantly of God, but the One that I struggled to make contact with during endless prayers was for me nothing more than an abstraction, a concept.

Gradually I realized that the expression *Word of God* that I heard people use of the Bible, was wrong. God has never spoken to anyone. God intervened in events at a fundamentally human and commonplace level, and his intervention passed most often unnoticed. A few men, the ones that had over the centuries written the Bible, had been able to detect God's footprints in the vicissitudes of Israel's local history. They had recounted this history – one of semen and blood – and the careful reading of it enabled God's imprint to be discerned in events.

I do not know when the light dawned on me: certainly not on a single day, nor even in that first year alone. But those hours and days spent beneath the green shade of my table lamp, while Rome hummed dully at the foot of the hill, marked a turning point. Since God was not motionless, since God was not a definition but was encountered in actions and events, the search for God must also involve movement. Therefore, the frozen immobility in which the abbey existed, clamped as it was in the bend of the River, began to appear to me as an obstacle, a hindrance, to the encounter with God.

There was no experience of God outside of events; but in the abbey we had been living a life that seemed to be wholly directed to reducing events, to minimizing their impact, to channelling them, emasculating them.

Without knowing it, I was lighting a grenade that would one day explode in my hands. And I already sensed that this was the detonator of a major clash that would set me against my community when I found it to be still the same as ever, while I had changed from within.

I frequently talked this over with Mark, who was making the same journey but did not share my fears for the future. *He* had been a son of the Church from birth, while I had had such trouble legitimizing myself. If there was a choice to make, I sensed that he would choose to trust in his Mother. I, though, would always be an adopted child.

It was you, God, that I was discovering bit by bit, with overwhelming joy, as a living being, strong yet vulnerable. Since you had allowed the features of your face to be seen by human eyes that were dim and often blind, you yourself seemed to me fragile, and therefore close to me. I was able to love you.

I did not yet know how to pray, because to talk to someone you need a measure of familiarity with him. But I knew from then on where to find you. Loneliness was no longer my only friend. Something was beginning between you and me that might be able to change everything...

...but only if my life became an event once more, and if I learnt to find you in the place where you are speaking.

The year moved on. I was engrossed in my studies on the hilltop and did not take an interest in much else. From time to time I received a letter from the abbey: inside were ten or so little notes that each monk at that end was free to slip into an envelope pinned to the noticeboard of the common room. They were most often brief messages of friendship: as nothing happened, there was nothing to say...

Sometimes there were also a few words from Father Gerard. He seemed enthusiastic about his refresher course in Paris. He was staying in a maid's room provided by friends. His letters, adorned with awful spelling mistakes, urged me to study, as here:

"Studying is very important, I now reelize. Take good advantidge of it, dear Brother, so that you can enrich us on your riturn" etc.

He was discovering the world. He had even been to the cinema, but apologized for it as a failing that he would not repeat. I smiled: his innocence, seen from here, turned him into a distinctly decent chap.

Soon it would be Easter. Ever since I had been greeted by Patriarch Athenagoras, I had had the occasional chance to meet the Pope – at the inauguration of Lent, for instance, that he celebrated each year at St Sabina's near our university. You could not live in Rome without encountering the world of the Vatican: several of my professors worked there part-time, and the echoes reached us every day.

6

Pope Paul VI was a small, frail man with a huge forehead and a very aquiline nose. Mostly he held his eyes down. But when he raised his face towards you and vouchsafed you a look – a true gift it was – you were struck by those slightly bulging eyes that were both full of sadness and profoundly gentle.

There were whispers in the corridors that in Milan, where he was cardinal at the time, he had had a quite long-standing homosexual relationship. I began to discover an immutable law of the Church in Rome: while high dignitaries of the Church are in post, one never talks of any "little adventures" they might have had.

This is the general rule: "*Una piccola avventura non fa male* – a little escapade does no harm." It is treated as a minor matter and, by common, unspoken accord, will go unremarked for as long as the prelate keeps up appearances – and, to be sure, stays within accepted standards of propriety. Once death has removed all danger of *mal'onore* – disgrace – tongues are loosened, but without malice, and even with that trace of complicity that has enabled the Roman *popolo* to cohabit for so long with the most celebritized institution in the world. As long as it is only a matter of sex or political intrigue, the paparazzi hawk the news around with no more than a knowing wink:

"*Monsignore* So-and-so? Devil of a lad! Listen, d'you know what?"

And, by being in this way closer to ordinary humanity, these gilt-encrusted princes of the Church benefit from a spontaneous affection that does no damage to their mission.

A case in point: one day I saw Cardinal N— arriving on our hilltop. He had been invited to an informal lunch with us. He was not an Italian, but had nonetheless been appointed by Paul VI to a key position in the Church.

The Romans had at first taken a dim view of this rational and high-principled foreigner, not the sort of man who would ever understand anything of their age-old wisdom. Later, though, they had found him to be a good chap. What had won the day for him was that he would go every Sunday morning after mass to kick a football around with the *ragazzi*, the kids of the district behind the Vatican.

"*Ma guardi com'è bravo, 'sto Monsignore!* – Just look what a great chap this *Monsignore* is!"

But there was one other thing. After the game, "great chap" to the end, Monsignor the Cardinal used to invite his lads of the moment to come and cool down in one of his offices. And there he took advantage of sporting familiarity to check the working of a zip fly, to pull down a pair of shorts, and let a little hand find its way into the openings of a violet-embroidered cassock.

That day we chatted with him in the cloister at coffee time, in French. The man was quite tall, approachable, eyes a-twinkle. He talked to us about the troubles of the worldwide Church that weighed him down, but we found him very direct, very relaxed.

It was in fact Sunday midday: I was unaware at the time of the sources on which he drew for his relaxation. And I used to pay little attention to the corridor gossip.

When a request came round for some monks to attend the Pope during the Easter vigil at St Peter's, I was the first to put my name forward. Strangely enough there was no rush of candidates on the hilltop, as the ceremony was extremely long and wearying. For the seniors, what is more, the pope was not a sufficient attraction. They had become Romans: they were living together with him, and the happiest households are those where people are wise enough to create some distance.

After passing along Bernini's colonnade one has to go through a security check at the entrance to the Vatican sacristy. A Swiss papal guardsman in full, gaudy-coloured uniform salutes my monk's habit by banging his great halberd on the ground; he then asks to see my invitation in an Italian smelling of Emmental. *Here you are, good fellow. Ah, it's down there. Thank you.*

The great sacristy is buzzing in every corner, like a beehive. *Monsignori* are fussing and sweating under the direction of the notorious masters of ceremonies in white pleated and embroidered albs and frowning foreheads. Here they are not just royalty: they're supreme rulers under God – or even higher.

"You are a monk-attendant. You will stand at the Pope's left, three metres away, without getting in the way of those who approach him. Never take your eyes off the masters of ceremonies, and obey their eye signals."

I take my stand in a corner. On the six great polished tables are laid out the papal vestments and insignia, embroidered with precious stones, braided with gold, stiff and heavy.

All at once the Pope is there; I didn't see him come in. I'm alerted to his presence by the buzzing of the hive, which rises an octave in pitch. He spreads out his arms and lets himself be dressed like a dummy. I cannot see his face, only his back, which soon resembles a shop window in the Rue de la Paix.

The procession slowly forms itself up – about sixty people to carry just one man's paraphernalia, encircle him, support him. For two hours he'll not flex a muscle or say a word without being accompanied by these acolytes that lead the way and guide his slightest movement.

We enter directly into the back of the basilica, where the Service of Light is to take place. Lost in the vast nave, the congregation does not look that large: they already seem restive, the silence less than total.

Finally the Pope turns towards me: two steps more and I could touch him. The liturgy unfolds, in an unending ballet of church dignitaries; they place a mitre on his head, then remove it, offer him a book, kiss his hand, advertise their presence, their existence... Trying to forget them, I watch the Pope. I only see his face when he sits up straight: intent, serious, never looking at his entourage.

Then I'm struck by something I know must be true: amid all those bear-tamers Paul VI is absent. Hands together, an expression that seems to look inwards, eyes lowered, head bowed, the Pope is at prayer – the prayer of a country priest. That man, who no longer exists for himself, whose least movement is directed by the men of power that encircle him – he's just a little priest from the Abruzzi at prayer, all alone in his mountain chapel.

At this point I too am trying to forget the choreography surrounding us. As I watch the Pope, I'm just letting myself be caught up in the prayer he's praying. But I feel a sudden, sharp nudge: a master of ceremonies, eyes flashing, is signalling to me move back. They're about to go up to the high altar; the cross-bearer is right in front of me; I'm in his way.

After his final benediction Paul VI disappears to the side. From then on St Peter's transforms itself into a reception room: there are mutual introductions, salutations, evaluations, congratulations... I leave quickly.

I return through the city on foot along the Tiber. Rome glows gently beneath the full spring moon. The city is empty and silent. Pagan Rome is sleeping her Easter sleep.

7

The academic vacation began the next day. For the first time, and thanks no doubt to the Council, students were given permission to leave Rome.

Mark and I decided to travel southwards, to Apulia. We had very little money: we made our way by hitchhiking and slept in Italian monasteries – a network of hospitable premises scattered across the land that offered monks free board and lodging.

So two large black shadows were to be seen beside the *autostrada*, raising thumbs, packs on backs – a sight so unusual in Italy (where clergy travel little) that we never waited more than five minutes before being picked up.

"*Ma, padre, come mai...* Well, well! Whatever are you doing there?"

Surprised, then delighted, our benefactors found us to be monks who were sports-loving hitch-hikers, embarking on an adventure with no precise aim but just one objective: the South.

Bari, Trani, Lecce, Brindisi... We often slept at Franciscan houses. Their hospitality was almost embarrassing, so prompt, so spontaneous, so unstinting. In one isolated little village near Noci the monastery was a simple peasant dwelling. We arrived in the evening after dark, without advance warning:

"Of course, come in, Brothers, we'll sort something out!"

A metal dish was put on the table; on it were remains of meals mixed together, vegetables, bits of meat:

"You see, we've preserved here the mendicant tradition of St Francis. This is what folk have given us this afternoon when we went on our visits. We'll share it; you'll see, it's good."

And it really was good. But the best thing was the smile of the monastery's three brothers:

"For sleeping, come this way."

The superior, youngest of the three, walked past a large cupboard, pushing the door to as he went by. At the end of the corridor:

"This is my room, excuse the mess. You'll sleep there: it's got a bed and a couch."

"But... what about you, Father?"

"Oh! I..." – he motioned towards the cupboard in the corridor, the door of which had swung open again – "I'll sleep there; that'll be fine."

Nothing would make him change his mind. As I went to sleep I was thinking that never in our "observant" abbeys would one have imagined any monk giving up his bed to a visitor in exchange for a cupboard – least of all the Father Abbot...

On the road we ate bread, cheese. We spoke little. We were at one with the stark landscape, the reserved people, the transparent sky. At twenty-eight I was discovering the East.

These were precious times that saw the firming up of a friendship for life and death. We seemed to be rediscovering a simple harmony among things: the South was stripping us bare, purifying us.

But we had to come back, return to the hill, the heavy meals, the city's electric atmosphere, the university's unceasing turbulence.

That spring of 1968 was starting well: in Rome it was already hot.

One of the Frenchmen had brought along a transistor radio and used to listen in to France Inter each morning before breakfast. He would summarize the news in a few lines on a piece of paper and pass it round from table to table – a house news-sheet that made do for newspapers, which were hard to come by on the hilltop. We called it "*France Matin*", and many of the non-French students too would take a look at it as they passed.

Then, without warning, at the beginning of May *France Matin* began to get longer: things were happening in Paris. It had started as a vast student street parade; and then it became serious. We read words like "crisis", "strike", "unrest".

Very soon the word "barricades" appeared in our news-sheet, and people scrambled for it in the refectory. First the French, then many of the others, began to congregate after matins and before breakfast in the room of the brother with the transistor.

We used to listen in to France in silence, eyes glazed, unable to believe our ears. This was much more than a crisis; it was a revolution. The reporters' microphones were stationed among the barricades; and the impression we gained, so far away on our quiet hilltop, was that the whole country was ablaze, erecting roadblocks, rejecting conventional democracy and lurching towards language unfamiliar to us: "Maoism, far left, confrontation, no holds barred..."

We held our breath. The Roman press spread the news across its headlines, but our little transistor transported us every morning straight to the Boulevard Saint-Michel, to the midst of the smouldering fires and to the side of the insurrectionist Dany the Red.

Postal communication with the abbey was interrupted. What was going on there? And what about Father Gerard, alone in Paris?

I passed Anselm in the corridor. He held me back by the arm.

"I find it splendid, Irenaeus, this capacity that France has every so often to rise up en masse!"

He raised his arm in the air, like the Statue of Liberty.

The French were in fact rather worried. None of us had the elementary idea of making a telephone call: that was not the done thing.

Suddenly the radio belched out a new item: de Gaulle had vanished. The revolutionaries were about to tip the country into the unknown, into chaos. From so far away, dependent as we were on our transistor, anything seemed possible.

Finally one morning we heard the hoarse, familiar voice stating forcefully:

"Well, I have decided: I shall not resign!"

So things calmed down, and *France Matin* returned to the refectory in nearly its usual format.

In Rome there had only been a few clashes between students and *carabinieri*, with tear gas grenades near the Piramide. But the stinging gas clouds did not rise to the top of the hill. It was now June, and time for exams.

With the return of normality the post resumed.

"My dear Brother," – it was the Father Abbot writing – "we are emerging from an ordeal that has shaken France, and the monastery has not gone unscathed. On your return you will find a change: Father Gerard has returned from Paris, after his year of study and his experience of the barricades. I have decided to appoint him Novice Master: from now on it is he who will be monitoring your progress."

The young monks always formed part of the noviciate community up to the end of their studies. But why did the Father Abbot talk of Father Gerard's "experience of the barricades"?

I understood on receiving a long letter from the man himself. When "May '68" had exploded, he had not stayed in his maid's room: he had gone down into the street and had played an enthusiastic part in the upheavals. Within a few days the man who had never left the abbey had imbibed the spirit of the barricades at full strength: total freedom, everything called into question, abolition of restraints.

He had clearly not brought all this back into his monastic life, but the shock had had its effect: his letter contained more question marks than full stops. He sent me a ringing call to hope, and if it was all a bit over the top, I was not troubled by it. Indeed, I was encouraged. I would not be bearing the weight of my questionings alone. "The man of the Second Armoured Division" had become "the man of the barricades": I could not wait to see him again.

The end-of-year examinations would bring no surprises. We were the cream of the order, and we had been working hard: there would be no failures. At the end of June, when the heat was becoming unbearable, we each left for our monasteries for the summer. The Americans were the only exception, on account of distance. They took the opportunity to go on a European tour of abbeys. Anselm promised to come for a week to the riverbank: his hearty handshake assured me of it.

8

I caught the train back north and met Uncle again at his place – my place. At last I had something to tell him about. He welcomed me warmly, but there was still, in spite of everything, that indefinable distance that squeezed my heart... Uncle had lived through May without losing composure; since the beginning of June his factories had been in production once more.

"Well then, Rome?"

I went through my anecdotes, but I seemed to be staying on the surface. How was I to tell him of friendship, of Mark, of the sun blazing down on the hills of the South? And of God, my great discovery in the Bible? Perhaps it was too soon. Maybe one day we would regain some of our old intimacy.

My mother was thrilled to find me suntanned, bursting with health. Her little one was getting on well: and I refused to see anything but her delight in that. But they were sad eyes that smiled. She had settled herself into a timelessness in which she expected nothing more from life. I could give her no transfusion of the energy that animated me: it was too late.

It was from the old bus that served our village that I caught my sight first of the River, its waters lapping lazily over the sands. Everything was green, a restrained green that matched the pale blue of the sky. No, these were not the brash colours of the South, where tones jostled harshly as if to keep their place in the sun.

And then, in the bright curve, I saw the abbey – still solid, immovable, an assertion of permanence. Everything you might think to be in motion – including the Council, and May '68 – was nothing but a mirage. Here you were marooned in another time-frame. *And if you want to clash head on with this impassive force held fast by its very nature, you'll break your teeth, my friend.*

I closed the door of my cell, as bare as it was on the first day. The only change was a glass with some wild flowers, freshly picked. That was how they welcomed the return of those who had been away. I sat at the table and fingered them gently. Were they a message of peace here? What would I find when I reopened my door?

I went out without unpacking my suitcase. At the end of the corridor I caught sight of Father Gerard. He came up to me with a smile, and there, right in the middle of the corridor – *what about the silence, Father, the silence?* – he greeted me in the traditional way and said:

"Well, do the monks still kiss in Rome?"

* * *

At the time for mass I went down to the common room to pick up my choir robe. They were all there, scalps shaven, greeting me with a smile, a nod of the head. Then we were in the passageway for the station, like fish in an aquarium, beneath the filtered light of the modern stained glass. And I knelt before the Father Abbot to receive his blessing: Brother Irenaeus was back, that was that.

I took my old place in the refectory, while the intoned reading flowed on like clear water; I found the apple again in the hollow bowl, the pot of vegetables, the fish that smelt a bit too strong. So nothing had changed here. And yet, in the looks, in the sign language used for silent communication, there was, it seemed, a rather mournful weariness. But, then, I had not been getting up at 2.25 a.m., had I? I had seen places; I had eaten meat. In order to become one of their kind again, I needed to experience anew how long the days could be.

Father Nicolas had been appointed manager of the workshop that occupied the whole basement. At siesta time I went to see him. As I descended the stairs, a faint smell, delicate but acrid, assailed my nose. Nicolas was sitting behind his desk, a malicious glint in his eyes. Planted between his lips, discreet yet provocative, a foaming pipe gave off the smoke of a Swiss tobacco:

"Yes! What can I say, Irenaeus? The bad old habits are back! The Father Abbot has given me permission to take up a pipe again in the workshop."

This was a revolution to match that of the barricades!

"Well, you know, people were very frightened in May. Everyone was bracing themselves; they were expecting the commissars of the great Revolutionary Republic to turn up. It's the first time I've seen it since I've been here. How shall I put it? They haven't had William Tell here; they don't realize it all ends up every time with an apple."

We chatted on, like old friends. He had not needed the events of May to recover his freedom of spirit; he had never lost it.

151

"And you know who was most frightened? It was Father Du Bellay de Saint-Pons. He kept his eye on the abbey's investment portfolio, and the more the share price plunged, the more his face lengthened. He sits opposite me in the refectory: he quite lost his appetite, I can tell you; he didn't touch his pot of vegetables till after the demonstration in the Étoile, when the stock market pulled itself together. Strange, isn't it, when we've placed our lives into the Lord's hands?"

Nicolas was stuffing his pipe, with a twinkle in his eye.

"We need ready money; you can't just live on your tonsure. I'd like to develop the workshop. Of course, it'll be necessary to play the commercial traveller a bit in order to analyse the markets and capture them. But the Father Abbot has got the message; he agrees."

The next day is very hot. In Rome there used to be a supply of cold water in the corner of the cloister, for everyone's use. Here I have a water tap in my cell, but I cannot touch it without permission: that's the rule.

So, at eleven in the morning this lad, who's studying for his third university degree, goes along to knock on the Father Master's door at the end of the corridor. He goes in, kneels down, asks: "Father, can I please drink a glass of water?" "Of course you can, Brother" (kindly smile). He gets up, says thank you, rushes to the other end of the corridor and finally turns on the tap that he lives with twenty-four hours a day.

9

Two days later Father Gerard took up his duties as Father Master. There was a short meeting in the novices' room. We all stood – could our deliverance from the benches mean other deliverances? The summer began under the star-sign of new blood.

After several weeks, a first revolution: there was talk of abolishing the night service. The community, and particularly the youngsters who kept it going, had had enough. The Father Abbot proposed an uninterrupted night, then getting up early in the morning.

There was no escaping it. Yet everyone clung onto this section of wall as if they felt that, once it fell, others would fall too. These men with baggy eyes and frayed nerves were refusing to give up the thing that was wearing them out, because it was something they had always known.

There were epic discussions in chapter, then they resigned themselves to what meant death for their souls.

I observed all this with anxiety. If there was so much resistance, if it took so many struggles to modify one doomed item of observance, what about the rest?

As I saw it, it was a whole system of thought, tradition and custom that stood in the way. Without really knowing how to move forwards, I reckoned that it would not be enough to alter this item or that: there was need to inject a new spirit that would work from within. Not that I wanted to do away with monastic life, rather to give it back its freshness, its exemplary and prophetic value, so that within the Church – and why not in the world at large? – it could become once more an ebullient source of refreshment and evangelical renewal.

I spent long hours in Father Gerard's office telling him all this, though I was still unclear about it. We were no longer on our knees before him from then on, but sitting on a stool, a relief to my kneecaps.

He listened, and as always he agreed with his interlocutor. I felt myself understood, even if I had little idea where I was going. But he was with me, and I took one more step forwards:

"In the end our way of life, our way of prayer, depends entirely on the idea of God that we form for ourselves. It's this that has to change: God is perhaps more than the one we believe him to be!"

And I told him of my discovery, in all its freshness, of the Living God.

This elderly monk, who was so reticent about his God but certainly not ignorant of him, listened to the young convert exposing his dreams. The enthusiasm was sincere; the discovery a real one: it must be encouraged, vague though it still was.

"Yes, Brother, everything will fall into place bit by bit, like the notes of a symphony!"

As he said the word "symphony", he lifted his hands, and, when I left him, I felt that it was to a background of grand harmonies. This man, who knew so well how to win people over, calmed my anxieties: I had no more fears for the future; I was on the right path, and I could rely on him.

That summer, then, I entrusted myself to him, rather as one might entrust a newborn life.

True to his promise, Anselm's with me in the garden beyond the cloister. With his air of earnest and elegant patrician, and with his experience – he'll be starting the fourth year of his degree course – I need him to help me make myself understood by Father Gerard.

But Anselm first wants to hear the story of the barricades and questions the Father Master at length – not only on May '68, but on its philosophic and theological implications. Has Father Gerard not done a year at the Catholic Institute? Hasn't he been through a refresher course? I need him to reply to Anselm's precise and deliberate questions.

We're sitting on a bench. Father Gerard's talking, tossing words about. Faced with Anselm, who has read and reflected so much, surely he'll be clear and explain himself?

"In the last analysis" – grand wave of the hand – "what would be needed is a rethinking of the whole of theology in the light of Hayjel."

Hayjel? I realize that Father Gerard's speaking of Hegel, the mentor of Marx and Heidegger; I realize that he has never read anything of Hegel's, that he's repeating commonplaces he has heard at his lectures, but doesn't know... no, he doesn't know what he's talking about.

I glance anxiously at Anselm, who is pondering, then smiles:

"You know, Hegel's only a small bit of the picture; and rethinking our faith as disciples of Hegel... I don't know if that would do any good. I think rather that we need to return to the Bible, and to what's best in our tradition, provided it's properly understood and assimilated..."

But is he wasting his breath? In a flash I realize something that I try very quickly to forget: has Father Gerard really understood the fundamentals? Is he really going to be the man of renewal that I, along with the youngsters of the order, am hoping for?

I needed too much to believe this was so. But somewhere a vague doubt lodged within me. Hayjel...

Father Gerard asked me to give the novices a series of lectures on the Bible during the summer. I took my place at the teacher's lectern, an unusual occurrence that only my status as a "Roman" made possible. I tried to pass on Notker's system of arriving at an understanding of the nature of God's Word: something living that people experienced in life, that summoned them to life. Father Gerard was delighted:

"Excellent! You're giving us the basis for true renewal. Carry on."

At the end of the summer the Father Abbot summoned me:

"Brother, we're going one day, for sure, to have to tackle a major task: the rewriting of our liturgy – the heart of our life, the cement that holds the community together. You're returning to Rome: the mission I'm giving you is to lay the foundations for this undertaking. You've still three years ahead of you: put yourself to work."

Message received: David face to face with Goliath.

The leaves were turning to ochre on the bank of the River, which basked in the gentle autumn light. One fine day I set off again to catch the *Palatino*.

10

Before returning to the hilltop I needed to take my bearings; I needed a brief time of solitude, to come once more face to face with myself, face to face with God.

Near Assisi, on the far side of Mount Subasio which overlooks the town, there was a mountain hermitage belonging to a small community of Franciscans. I asked if I could spend a week there before the start of the university year. *Of course: the hermitage is empty. Come along.*

The track left the village and climbed far up the slopes. The landscape was mountainous, bare and stony, beneath a sun that scoured the contours. Umbria, elusive and understated, was giving me a welcome.

On an escarpment a shepherd's hut seems almost one with the mountainside. It's built of dry stones with a grey slate roof. The door creaks, opening onto a room with earthen floor. There's a bed, a table and a little air circulating through the uneven stones of the wall. At the back is another, smaller room: a mat on the floor, and on the wall a crucifix, icon and candle. The oratory.

In one corner are pasta, rice and some tins of food. The nearest house is eight kilometres away by mule track. Down below stands a clear, slow-running spring.

In my hand I hold a Bible, that's all. Around me a sky of dazzling clarity, and the mountains. And God, perhaps. I have a week before going back down.

I've folded my body so as to break it, so that it would lose itself gradually on the oratory matting. If time proves long, there'll be nothing but the sky, the rock and the light revolving slowly in the intense blueness.

God.

I want to listen for that soft voice so long awaited, to let it rise up. *I know that you do not talk in human language. I shall await you. For too long you have let yourself be yearned for. I shall await you, because I love you already without knowing you.*

In the doorway a grey and russet bird has come to look. It tilts its head, hops around and flies off in a flurry. Maybe it's one of those that St Francis instructed, long ago, on the other slope of Mount Subasio?

* * *

The shadows are slowly revolving. Yesterday I heard the bells of a flock, but didn't see it. In front of my shelter there's a thicket of junipers. When I go out in the morning, at a daybreak hard as granite, it gives off a strong scent that heralds the light. My beard's growing thickly. I've interred myself in my stone hut that's of a piece with the mountain. Around it the stars of the sky unfurl themselves like a reassuring scarf.

God.

God, I shan't tell in this book what happened, what there is now between you and me. I don't want to talk about it.

What I know, now that the years have left their mark on our story like a patina of time (but what is time?) – what I know is that you have drained me of all the strength I had for love.

God, I believe I really loved you. Maybe I had never experienced that emotion, but with you I have learnt what love is. You are the God that cannot be grasped, the unknown God, the God that is not satisfied with a little but demands the whole.

Here I am as you left me, unable henceforth to love. You have killed love in me. You have taken everything.

The next day will be the last. There's no more pasta, but the water is cool at the spring. I intend to cross the mountain and go to Assisi on the far side to find St Francis there. My eyes have widened; the sky has cleansed me; my limbs are supple.

Gripping a strong staff, I set off with the last star of night, leaving the hermitage open. On the mountain the scrub scratches my bare legs. All of a sudden, over the crest, there, in full sunlight, are bell-towers and roofs clustered in the valley: Assisi!

There are tourist coaches in the basilica square. I push open the church's double door and notice a paunchy Franciscan sitting at a little table counting notes and coins.

He looks up at me briefly, and with an imperious gesture, finger outstretched, he points me to the door:

"Out!"

157

"What? But... I'm a pilgrim; I've come from the mountain; I've been walking a long time to get here..."

"Yes, but here it's not the mountain; here it's a church. You can't come in wearing shorts: you can see very well what's written there: 'Decent attire'. Go on, out!"

Thanks, Brother. And it's St Francis's tomb right here! As he carries on counting his small change, I go out again into the square. *You've saved me time, Brother; at one stroke you've plunged me back into humanity and the Church. Thanks, Brother!*

11

Rome. Steaming pasta on our plates, cheap white wine from the Castelli, crisp grapes in bunches. Friends, smiles, hugs in every language. Mark, Anselm, life bursting everywhere...

"He's a great guy, your Father Master. Of course..."

Anselm's too nice, too tactful. It's his last year in Rome; plans are already in place for his future in America. He has brought back a flute, and I sometimes hear him playing in the empty lecture theatre of an afternoon. "Reception-room monk, uncouth..." *He* is an accomplished gentleman.

The usual round of lectures has resumed. I have to choose the subject of my thesis: it will be St Irenaeus, my patron – the first of the Church Fathers, author of monumental writings from the end of the second century. I'll be studying his theory of the summing up of all things in Christ. The text that has come down to us is in Latin, the original being partly in Greek, partly in Armenian. Shall I need to learn ancient Armenian? Why not? It's similar to Hebrew, it's not so difficult. When you've passed the threshold of the first four languages, you get on faster.

One day news reaches us that some Italian Sisters are asking for help in building a convent for themselves in the suburbs. I go along with Mark one Sunday. It's a work site for youngsters. In the sandwich break we chat with a group of students from the city, Calabrians all of them. An architect, a medic, an engineer: they have state scholarships, and live in a Catholic hostel, as you'd expect. We make friends. They've never seen monks in shirt sleeves, wielding a pickaxe.

"Here the clergy live off the backs of the people. Their only blisters they get from sprinkling holy water. You're different. We'll come and see you on your hilltop."

Amedeo and Piero sit in the refectory in front of a dish of pasta. They're a bit ill at ease, but after a good laugh the ice begins to melt. Of course they're all Catholics – how could it be otherwise in Italy? But at least one of them is also a paid-up member of the Communist Party; in Italy people go to church, party card in pocket. And why not?

A friendship is coming into being. These Calabrians are more Greek than Roman. They talk to me about the South where they belong, the *magna Græcia* that has never forgotten the East.

"In Italy the West stops at Rome. Naples is the first eastern capital: we've nothing in common with the Milanese, those barbarian invaders. It's due to them that the Mafia came into being. And it was their oppression that caused the Mafia to survive."

The Church has sheltered everything beneath its cloak. But they invite me to visit them, in that poor and noble country. And they make me want to explore their East, which is so close, only a few hours away by train.

That was for the next Christmas holidays. In the meantime I neglected a little the streets of Rome and went into the city's museums in search of Greek art.

I was amazed. The Romans had invented nothing; the Romans were barbarians – a nation of soldiers, engineers and colonists. The art that had outlived the centuries – the art here was Etruscan or Greek. Even the arch, which enabled them to build their basilicas – the Romans had not even fathered that; they had stolen it from the Etruscans and had simply developed the technology.

Sculpture too was copied from Greece, from Praxiteles and Phidias. In all Rome's museums there are just copies, scores of copies. Only the subjects – the faces with their raw realism – are Roman. The beauty and the grace are Greek.

I fell in love with those sensual figures. Above all, I took a liking to Greek ceramics, depicting as they did with a faultless and precise elegance the everyday life of a people that loved the body, that loved their youth, their flesh.

The Capitoline museums, the Villa Giulia, the museums of Naples, Taranto, Brindisi... Everywhere the rooms were chock-full of scenes of everyday life, of lithe, athletic bodies with almond-shaped eyes and profiles that were at once masculine and languid.

Through seeing all this, through deciphering the inscriptions – KALOS MYSCOS, Myscos is beautiful, Myscos is lovely – I became aware of the obvious: love here was the love of boys, of lads in the first flower of youth. The females I saw were in the women's quarters, spinning or looking after children. Woman was the genetrix, the wife and mother, or else the stylized goddess, creature of myth. But the object of admiration, of passion, was the boy, the young man.

I was discovering Greek sensuality.

Absolutely nothing had prepared me for this. But there was, after all, no harm in developing an enthusiasm for classical antiquities; that was part of the reason for being in Rome. My eyes were taking in the serene eroticism, unembarrassed, uninhibited, of a civilization that I was coming unreservedly to admire: it was after all the mother of us all.

At Christmas and at Easter I returned to the South. Naples was an obligatory staging point. I was rediscovering the city of my labours as a student biologist; but this time it was as a tourist that I came, nose to the wind. I saw now what I had never seen: Naples was a Greek city, the city of Petronius's Satyricon. There everything was possible. The Neapolitans used to say with a laugh that in Naples it was no more surprising to see a priest walking the pavements than a prostitute preaching in church.

I stayed at the Franciscan monastery of Santa Chiara, an

attractive and picturesque building. Wearing blue jeans and a tee-shirt – things were changing quickly – and with a key to the monastery in my pocket, I made visits to the museum and to the Castello Angioino, the castle of the Angevins, overlooking the port.

There in Naples I rediscovered the characters from my Greek ceramics, alive and well – a population of *ragazzi*, with alert eye and quick rejoinder – you could recognize them immediately by their cheeky look and hand constantly lodged above the flies. A proposition? I do not know, since I had no wish to respond. I was simply noting, involuntarily. And my sexuality, like a baby in its mother's womb, gave a few kicks, quickly repressed.

I was unwise: I should have shunned those streets flooded with sunshine and shouts. But what harm was there in having a walk around for a few hours, for a few days, before returning to my books and the discipline of my studies?

I witnessed scenes that took me aback. As I spoke perfect Italian, I mixed easily with this populace for whom pleasure seemed the only god – an innocent, spontaneous pleasure, without regrets, like that of the Greece of their ancestors that was till so close.

It's late afternoon. At an angle of the castle, on a terrace in the lengthening shadows, a prostitute is leaning back, legs apart. Pressed against her, trousers half open, a man is at work in silence. Several people are passing by: nothing untoward, everything as usual. When she has finished and pocketed her fee, she comes up to me. At her side is a *ragazzo*, a streetwise kid, perhaps her brother – or her son?

"And you, big fellow, do you want a go too?"

"Er... no thank you, really."

"Well then," she motions towards the kid, "what about him, do you fancy him?"

"Go away! Good night, *arrivederci*."

I went back up onto the terrace that looked out over the castle moat. A good-natured crowd was taking a walk – *mammas*, soldiers in uniform, engaged couples. Below, in the empty moat, a car drove up at top speed and drew up by two girls in short dresses. Night was falling, but the castle was floodlit. Passers-by, chatting calmly, stop to watch. The two girls get into the car, one on the right and one on the left. A pause, while the crowd waits. The right-hand car window opens; a girl's head leans out and spits. Then the left-hand window.

"*Bravo, bravo!*"

The crowd cheers in delight. And the car drives off again.

Never would the young middle-class lad, schooled by the fathers, disciple of St Thomas Aquinas, monk par excellence – never would he have imagined such a scene. But the dirty-minded student of earlier times was not dead, and found it funny. And in any case that city had a sort of magic: it whispered to me at every street corner:

"Come off it! *You* may not realize, but this is life. There's nothing happening here that isn't absolutely normal!"

After that it was the harsh mountains of Calabria, and my friends' families in their little village houses. A biblical welcome: everything was at my disposal, the house, the car, my friends' friends.

"How's our son getting on? Is he studying, at least? Rome's dangerous: there are savages there, people from the North…"

And they spent the whole morning making me the *pasta casalinga*, fresh pasta made the traditional way.

On my return to the hilltop it felt to me as though those ten days of holiday had lasted a year. I resumed my seat under the green lampshade without regrets…

…but not without memories.

The academic year is coming to an end. Anselm has put on a recital for us in the great lecture theatre. While Debussy's melody rises and falls as though hanging in mid-air, I watch that distinguished face, bent over its flute. *Adieu, Anselm, ciao, goodbye. I shall never see you again. A long clasp of your hand: there are tears in my eyes.*

12

I was happy to rejoin my brothers on the riverbank. They were endearing, those extremists of God, who pushed to its furthest limit the logic of having made a gift of themselves. I became acutely aware of all that our life contained of anachronism, and even of falsehood. But, as individuals, they were not responsible for that. And after all they were my family; I had done everything to ensure that I had no other. You can be hurt by your family, but you do not disown them. It was for me to bring them, if I could, the fresh air that they would surely not reject. It was a delicate process, demanding infinite patience: *they* had not been out of the monastery; *they* had been faithful day after day to the "observance" that must lead them to God. I had no right to scorn that, or even to ignore it. Change would come, as Father Gerard had assured me; and I had put my confidence in him, once and for all.

At the start of summer there was a little event that showed that anything was possible.

In the refectory the reading was always performed *recto tono*. With voice pitched high, the reader strung out his text on a smooth thread, separating each syllable, like children chanting their tables. We were used to it. The reading was as flavourless as the food.

For a week at the start of that July a group of army officers were attending a study retreat at the abbey under the direction of a Jesuit father. With their epaulettes neatly lined up in the refectory, they were slipping into the rhythm of our ways.

Someone had chosen for them an entertaining book *The Longest Day*, which told the story of the Allied landings in 1944. It gave a little holiday feel to the start of our summer.

One day, then, midway through the retreat, the reader reached the scene where the troops first set foot on the Normandy beaches:

"And as the ma-rines leapt on-to the sand, the Ger-man sub-mach-ine guns be-gan to spit out with a hell-ish din: ta-ca-ta-ca-ta-ca-tac."

There was a blank moment at the guests' table: the epaulettes quaked, and then there was an outburst of laughter, heroic, uninhibited, soldier-like. Our guests were creasing themselves:

"Ta-ca-ta-ca-tac!"

They wiped their eyes with their white napkins:

"Ta-ca-ta..."

Never did the refectory react to a reading. The very purpose of the *recto tono* was to avoid any possibility of comment from the listeners. But this had been too much – the expressionless falsetto voice pronouncing from on high:

"Ta-ca-ta-ca-tac!"

The Father Abbot was obliged to use his little bell.

The next day the reading was resumed, but in a natural voice. As no one had learnt to give public readings in a normal way, I was given the job of tactfully taking over from the reader. And the book was changed, to make a start on *Everyday Life in the Ports of Brittany in the Seventeenth Century* – indeed, a much less perilous subject.

Father Gerard joined us in the novices' room.

"Brothers, you may have heard mention of Taizé. Next week all the novices are invited to go and spend three days there. We will leave on Monday."

Taizé, on its hill in Burgundy, was a Protestant monastery. Inconceivably – something that must have made Luther turn in his grave – a Lutheran pastor, Brother Roger Schultz, had back in 1947 begun to live a life there that was inspired by the Rule of the monks. Others had joined him. Unencumbered by any outside pressure or tradition they had reinvented monastic life: people talked about it a lot, and all eyes were fixed on this new and refreshing experiment.

It was the first time that the novices had made such a journey in an organized group. Father Gerard, who sensed that everything must move forwards, but that nothing was changing, had decided to strike out boldly – to get us to make tentative contact with a different embodiment of monasticism, to enter his Catholic monks into the Protestants' school. Without a doubt, the Council had opened doors! We were overcome with the excitement of things forbidden, things dangerous.

On the set day, then, we squeezed into the workshop van, and the novices crossed the frontier of the River.

Three amazing days. Along with my brothers I was discovering a place where one could talk without breaking the silence – a real silence that enveloped you from your arrival in the village, a silence that left space for God without crushing human beings. They were manly folk, these Protestant brothers, living in trousers, and only putting on their white habits to go to church.

There my dream became a reality – a liturgy that was gripping and moving; services that were quite short, few each day, but extremely compressed: a few psalms only, a few readings, and some Lutheran hymns; everything in French. So one could actually pray in French? So I could talk to God in my own tongue, and his Word could reach us through our everyday language, in our everyday lives?

Finally, during the services there were long stretches of silence. It was no longer a matter of gabbling off psalms at top speed, of filling up every vacuum: the Word was mounted in a setting of silence that displayed all its worth, all its lustre.

At that time Brother Roger had not yet become an international celebrity, and spiritual tourists were few. We lived among the Taizé Brothers, our black hoods mingling with their white vestments in the bright church that was becoming a place of revelation.

I returned full of enthusiasm. So it was possible. My brothers had witnessed it as I had: the seed would sprout within them; we had only to let it happen. Father Gerard's gamble had paid off: my confidence was well placed. Unhesitatingly I left matters in his hands. The future was ours.

Back in the abbey our liturgies seemed to me even more ponderous, even more deficient: but patience! I kept hearing Mark say:

"Wait, Iré, give us time, take time... and love!"

I waited.

13

It was the beginning of my third year in Rome. So I was now a "senior", getting by in all the languages. Because of my past history I had been entrusted with the post of Nursing Brother for the university – a delicate job that demanded tact and a gentle touch.

There was always someone under treatment: my room doubled as a surgery, and every day I saw colleagues lining up for injections. Abbots passing through Rome, priests, students: they all came to present their posteriors to the unpitying needle.

So it was that one day I saw a Swiss student come in. I had already noticed his reticence, reclusiveness almost. He handed me a prescription without a word:

"Penicillin. 3,000,000 units a day, intra-muscular."

Clear enough. I looked up at him, and he burst into sobs. Distraught, racked with choking fits, the poor lad told me his story.

He had been very young when he entered his snow-girt abbey. Never had anyone talked to him about sex there. (*I know, I know*…) Since his arrival in Rome he had lived as a martyr:

"It becomes all hard, you understand, and I don't know how to deal with this thing that burns me between the legs… I've talked about it to my confessor here, and all he's said to me is: 'Sublimate, Brother, sublimate!' But what can I do with 'it'?"

The inevitable had happened. Alas for him, he had come across an infected girl. He had not got much pleasure from her, but had contracted syphilis, which for him was a stamp of shame, the end of his world.

I dried his tears. No, he was not damned; no, his days were not over. He had encountered life, that was all, and had become a man. Of course, I would keep it a complete secret; nobody would know anything. I was holding his life in my hands.

For ten days I administered massive doses of antibiotics to him, for which he showed low tolerance. To his moral anguish was added real physical pain, of which I must be the only witness. Our injection appointments were also therapy sessions: I soothed him, helped him to see his future, assured him that God condemned him no more than I did.

He recovered and resumed his academic work. The following year he returned to his abbey in Switzerland. At Christmas I received a box of chocolates, without a message. Afterwards I learnt that he had become Father Master, a well-merited appointment. I, I alone, knew that he was sure to be a better novice master than others. His painful adventure evoked respect, not blame.

But I was myself having to struggle with my own sexuality. So long held in check, forgotten, mastered, it was sprouting in the Roman sunshine like a vigorous tree. Women, all too clearly, were condemned objects. What was left, then? During my forays with Mark, we had seen little in the streets of Rome but matrons. Like the whole of southern Italy, Rome was a city of mothers, and of men. Young girls were presumably kept cloistered at home, and only made an appearance once they had lost their figures through a life of housework and pregnancy.

There remained the characters from my Greek ceramics, those young lads who populated the city with their sensuality. Of course, I had no dreams of anything, but over time images left their mark on me.

I wanted to get my mind clear about all this, and after dinner one day I broached the subject in the cloister with the professor of moral theology. He worked very much under the eye of the Vatican, and his teaching represented in some degree the official line. He replied to me with a smile:

"For us, when a misdemeanour takes place with a woman, it's extremely serious. The act of love is only acceptable within marriage, as you know, and as a conduit that channels our weakness, our con-cu-pis-cence, to the Creator. With boys" – he began to laugh – "it's less serious: there's no risk of producing a child!"

No doubt this was only a quip, an after-dinner proposition that would obviously not have formed part of his teaching in the lecture theatre. But nonetheless, the words had been spoken: *una piccola avventura*...

I continued to reflect and went bravely on with my struggle for chastity. Men did not interest me, and women were forbidden. I was better off, for sure, immersing myself in the works of St Irenaeus.

14

By now my Calabrian friends were well acquainted with the route to our hilltop: in return they used to invite me to their students' hostel. Armed with the necessary permissions, I would often go there of an evening and come back late at night.

They were all Catholics, but as anti-clerical as they were believers – a typically Italian combination. Up to that point they had been content to shun churches and the practice of religion. But as I got to know them I discovered a phenomenon that the aftermath of the Council was making possible: "base communities".

All over the city these groups were coming into being; they were the consequence both of established Catholicism's inability at the time to transform itself and of the Italians' profound and deeply rooted faith.

Because the Church, both in outward manifestation and in essence, seemed to them unhelpful to their faith – indeed frequently it repelled them – they began to create small underground cell-churches in parallel.

"We hate the clergy; the Church is so antediluvian it's lost our respect; but we believe in God and we want to live out our faith. The Church, after all, is us too, isn't it?"

For these groups to be able to celebrate mass, they needed a priest. And here was the new phenomenon: from this time on it was possible to find in the city, notably among the non-Italian clergy, priests who were willing to risk their reputation with these marginalized people – meet with them, and sometimes celebrate clandestine masses with forms of service that were uncustomary and unauthorized.

Amedeo and Piero belonged to one of these base communities

called *Ora sesta*. This group of about thirty people had been brought together by word of mouth and used to meet every week in a shabby room in old Rome near the Campo de' Fiori. After talking to me about it they invited me along: the only condition was that I come in lay dress. I readily obtained permission: these communities were as yet unknown on the hilltop.

We sat round a large table, beneath a light bulb hanging from a ceiling from which the paint was flaking. Men, women, all participated on an equal footing – for there were several young women there accompanying their husbands. The priest went unrecognized among us, dressed as the rest.

The meeting began with a "sharing of life", on the pattern of Catholic Action. Each person would mention what had struck them most during their week. All of them were active on the political left. I particularly noticed a judge from the Rome bench, Giampiero, a stern man with an impassioned way of expressing himself. Then a Bible was placed on the table, and a passage was read.

Everyone contributed their comments. At a prearranged moment a hunk of bread appeared on the table, with a bottle of Chianti. The priest, who had kept himself to himself till then, pronounced the words of consecration. Large lumps of bread were passed round; then a glass of wine: it was the communion. No chalice, no ornaments: just a kitchen plate, a Duralex glass.

Another short time of prayer, and then abruptly someone brought in some steaming pizzas purchased from the *trattoria* on the corner.

It was always very late when we split up. Everyone went home with the feeling of having done something forbidden as much as something new, but also of having lived through something important.

Ora sesta brought me a completely new experience that counterbalanced a life that was now dedicated to study. I learnt there things unknown to me: the protest of May '68 carried to the heart of the Christian faith, the struggles of the trade unions, the injustice (to which Giampiero testified) of a system of justice set up to serve the establishment alone.

169

I spoke very little, having little to say. But they had quickly accepted me as one of themselves, and they used to chaff me in a friendly way:

"Well, Irenaeus, are you a protester, yes or no? And those monasteries of yours, when are they going to become, through and through, patterns of life according to the Gospel?"

I could not even make poor knowledge of Italian an excuse for staying dumb. *If you only knew, brothers, the battle that still needs to be fought in our monasteries! It may seem footling to you, distant and muffled; but it's my battle, and my life is at stake there, just as yours is in your workplace...*

Little by little these base communities spread; and one fine day one of them gained recognition from a parish in Rome. After that they used to meet in the parish church, and I went there sometimes.

The church of Sant'Egidio was full. But the altar beyond was ringed with a band of laymen, some of them young and bearded, who were taking the place of the priest. The priest himself came out of the sacristy for the short periods when his presence was indispensable – to consecrate the bread and give the blessing. But the microphone was held by the laity, in the form of a parish council.

And held it truly was! I discovered something that dismayed me: from the time they gained the microphone and the power to speak, from the time they took the priest's place, the laity showed themselves more clerical than the clerics, and they wielded over the congregation a power more absolute even than that of the clergy.

Was this just the laity turning the tables, as was inevitable after so many centuries of silence? Or could it also be the corrupting effect of power, of spiritual and religious power?

So there was no escaping clericalism, which was now the clericalism of the laity – clericalism unending, with a continuity that I was just beginning to discover:

"There is only one truth, and that is ours. If you do not share it totally, there are only two possibilities: either you're a bit stupid, and we'll enlighten you, for your own good; or else you reject our line of thought, and you become our enemy: then we'll crush you, for your own good."

Many of these progressive laypeople had been through the ranks of the Communist Party, or were there still, and I observed that Marxist totalitarianism translated perfectly into clerical totalitarianism. In truth, it was the same language, the same methods, the same outcome: an obedient proletariat under the spiritual and psychological control of their masters.

Alarmed by what I was learning here, I talked it over at length with Giampiero: he was older than me; he had more experience and used to show real insight:

"Irenaeus, this is something as old as the world. The Church is the bride of Christ, the channel by which human beings experience the presence of God. That's the theology. But in the way it behaves, as you rightly see, the Church acts like a sect, just like a sect conforming to worldly standards, and it's recognized as such. As for communism, I believed in it, as we all did here. But in reality it's also a sect that seeks power for itself and control of the human spirit – and not only the spirit of society, but also the spirit of individuals. As long as there continue to be free men, these two sects will find their growth constrained. Don't be surprised at anything. These laymen that you see taking power, they're replaying the scenario they've already lived through, be it in the party or in the Church."

I responded with a laugh, as though he were a cynical old Roman. But deep within I felt that he was right...

...except that I was an official member of one of the two sects; and I must continue to live within the Church.

That evening I returned from *Ora sesta* late at night, by bicycle. The city was completely deserted. I knew that I would be unable to sleep, so I rode along the Tiber and crossed the Ponte Sant'Angelo. In front of me St Peter's threw wide open the arms of Bernini's colonnade.

I made a circuit of the vast round square that is known to the whole world. It was empty and silent. Then, up on the third floor to the right, I saw a lit window, just one: the Pope's office. The Pope was working at that hour of the night. We were alone, it seemed, he and I, watching over the city. Think again! The Church was not just a sect, but something more. I rode off to bed, under the protection of Paul VI.

15

It was summer again, and my last return to the abbey for a "Roman holiday". My brothers knew that next time it would be for good and that from then on they would have to live with me…

In truth I did not sense any anxiety among them: they were too caught up in the changes that, in small increments, were already impinging on our life on the riverbank.

Changes? Oh! quite imperceptible things, negligible against the pace set by the world outside; but, for these contemplatives rooted in the cloister, they were taking on the significance of affairs of state.

In a life reduced to basics, like a country landscape unchanged for generations – something more than familiar that conditions your very being from the outside – the smallest tree one cuts down, the smallest hedge one removes, require a new equilibrium to be found. We were like old country folk that see their earth shifting, their clay being reshaped. People of the soil are slow, they do not like change.

In the first place, the practice of silence was no longer what it had always been – a sort of cellular membrane isolating us from one another, making us into hermits as we lived together. From then on we used to speak to each other – in a deliberate fashion, for sure, and without breaking the spell, but freely enough. Human relationships came to be expressed, and so too preferences, likes and dislikes.

Then, the French language made a shy appearance in our services. The Latin liturgy, that great impersonal edifice, found itself under-mined, endangered. This was the big change.

The Father Abbot had seen correctly: the liturgy was the crucible of our common life, the public and official expression of our faith. I had learnt in Rome the old proverb that can be translated: "Tell me how you pray, and I shall tell you who you are." To disturb that was to disturb, in the depths of the subconscious, what caused us to live such a distinctive life together. All the fears, all the worries felt in the face of renewal, inevitable as that was, crystallized around this very point.

But no one at the abbey had any experience, any expertise, in the subject. It was out of the question to adopt the liturgy used in the parishes, which was regarded with scorn. No, there was need of something that would be "monastic", in harmony with our tradition – something that would be "us". So everything would have to be composed afresh – texts, music, even rituals.

It was like poking a stick into an ants' nest: huge agitation. The Father Abbot calmed his people down with a refrain that became routine:

"When Brother Irenaeus returns from Rome…"

When he returns from that remote and somewhat mythical place, there'll be someone who'll know perhaps a little better what course to take, what directions to give. When Brother Irenaeus returns…

I had no idea that such a weight of confused hopes, fears and resentments was being piled onto my head – and that one day this weight might well crush me. The weather was fine, and I was delighted to see my colleagues ready for life.

Father Nicolas had given the workshop a new impetus. The first result was the acquisition by the community of a powerful Citroën car, since future building jobs had to be investigated and orders won. Nicolas spent a great deal of time on the road, devouring distance with an utter disregard for all precaution. In two or three days he accomplished insane itineraries, sleeping little, cooking huge pieces of meat on a stove – permissible in view of his distance from the monastery. Father Du Bellay de Saint-Pons watched the cheques come in and decided it was all fine.

I often used to go and find Nicolas in his workshop, pipe

constantly alight. He was happy, overflowing with life and projects. Talk of liturgy left him unmoved:

"All that I ask is to be allowed to pray in church. If what you fellows are cooking up for us, Irenaeus, is as good as what we have, or better, that's fine by me."

So it was with a heart at peace, full of hope for the future, that for the last time I set off again for Rome.

16

Like an old mistress, a little worn out, a little tired, the city offered me no more surprises: but I came back to her with feelings of affection. On the hilltop I was now part of the furniture, and Vatican rumours reached us without causing me any more dismay.

Mark had not returned; he had been detained by the needs of his abbey. He used to write to me, but I missed his warm friendship. So the academic year seemed heavy-going, a little dismal even.

I continued to attend *Ora sesta*, and I was putting the last touches to my thesis. The final examination – for a degree at the level of a good university – would be in June. I have the memory of long winter hours spent beneath the green lamp at my desk. To be ready: I had to be ready, so as not to disappoint the abbey's expectations on my return.

The Father Abbot wrote to me more frequently than usual. He was a very reserved man, very hard on himself, but he poured out his feelings more easily on paper and at a distance.

I am weary. This adjustment of our life to the renewal desired by the Council is now beyond my strength. A younger man should run the next lap. I do not feel myself capable of dealing with the conflicts and tensions that arise with every step forwards.

I saw it coming: towards the end of February he gave me notice of his intention to resign during the summer:

I have given my best, my life, to this community. I want to leave my post in peace and later withdraw to a hermitage somewhere.

In the meantime I had to keep the secret: an election would be taking place; the community would choose his successor, a new Father Abbot.

But this piece of news was almost outshone by another: my mother was to come at Easter and spend the holiday with me in Italy. For this woman whose life had ended when her one love had betrayed her, when her son in his turn... for her, this was an immense joy – to leave her humdrum life, rejoin her big boy now he had some free time, almost as much free time as on Tamatave beach, the little king!

Uncle had of course given financial support for the journey. I felt the web of love and well-being weaving itself anew around me – the web that I had severed so brutally in order to go and live an incomprehensible life that my family were quite unable to share.

Florence, Rome, Naples: I showed her my museums, my South and its sunlight. Brotherly and gentle, the city gave her a warm welcome.

"Then soon I'll be at the abbey again, won't I, closer to you, eh?..."

She answered me feebly:

"Closer? I don't know..."

I was being self-centred, as so many men are with women, allowing their occupations to become preoccupations. Perhaps on that last day before her return, at the end of this parenthesis in her life – perhaps there by my side in the streets of Rome, she lived through a second separation. Mothers are sensitive to things, and a mother she was.

The degree exams did not bother me: they were not the first. By the end of June I had my degree, and an honourable mention into the bargain.

I had two days to straddle my bicycle, to make love with my city, to miss none of the sun's caresses on its pediments, its grey stones, its great ochre walls, its warm motherly body; two days to absorb its serene delights, to listen to its ancient wisdom; two days for a last pasta with Amedeo and Piero, a last unauthorized mass with *Ora sesta* and a last deep and gloomy conversation with Giampiero.

It was the porter Peppino who came with me to the door that led out onto Piranesi's elegant square.

"*Ecco, fra' Ireneo*: I… I was born here, and I'll die here. You go and show them over there a little of what the Romans are capable of!"

It was well after midnight when the train stopped at Modane for the frontier formalities. Leaning out of the window, eyes wide open, I was still awake. And when the train pulled slowly out, gathering speed for the race to the north, I was resting against the glass, my mind a blank.

Part Four

Explosion

1

"On the Gospel I swear it!"

We're about to undertake the election of a new father abbot. The monks, in great black habits, have gathered in the half-light of the chapter house. The wooden throne at the end is empty; to its right stands the Father Provincial, who has come to preside over the election. On the table in the centre lies the Bible: each monk in turn moves towards it, places a hand on the book and vows solemnly to write on his voting paper the name of the one he judges, in good conscience and before God, to be worthy of election.

During the preceding days the abbey had been in turmoil. In a stable community of men who spend their whole lives together, there are no electoral campaigns, no declared candidates. In the course of meetings, first in small groups then more widely, the Provincial had got us to talk informally. What should he be like, the man we wanted to have at our head?

There were only two men that might match this identikit portrait of our ideal: Father Joseph, candidate of those with clenched jaws and concrete certainties, and the attractive and enigmatic Father Gerard. Very soon the preference of the monks swung towards the latter. But there still had to be a vote.

"On the Gospel I swear it!"

The last brother has given his oath. Pieces of paper and pencils are handed round. Silently each monk quickly writes a name on his paper and folds it in four; then he goes to drop it in the ballot box on the central table in front of the Provincial, who stands there motionless.

The Provincial takes hold of the box, opens it and tips it upside down on the table: a little heap of white squares falls out that

179

then have to be counted. There are forty or so papers; it'll soon be done.

Then he unfolds the papers one by one, reads aloud the name pencilled there, and places them in little piles.

I watch my brothers as they sit in a rectangle along the walls. Their faces are entirely expressionless. Yet it's their lives, for many long years to come, that are at stake here. Not a muscle twitches, not a breath quickens.

"Father Gerard... Father Gerard... Father Gerard..."

Very quickly one pile wins out over the other: by an overwhelming majority Father Gerard has just been elected father abbot – plinth, pillar and master of the abbey.

His eyes have not blinked; he remains undismayed. What is going on behind that unruffled brow?

The act of allegiance follows immediately, whereby the monks recognize the elected candidate as their new abbot. Father Gerard goes to take his seat in the patch of light, on the abbot's little throne. Beginning with the most senior, each monk kneels in front of him, silently places his hands together and presents them to him. The Father Abbot then enfolds them in his own hands, that meet over the hands offered, and holds them thus for a moment without moving.

This action comes from the ceremony of "dubbing" in the age of chivalry. The vassal would close his hands together within those of his suzerain to signify that henceforth he belonged totally to the other, along with his lands and his extended family; and that the suzerain had power of life and death over him.

I'm kneeling before the throne. I join my hands and feel two warm hands enfold my own, clasp them tight. Father Gerard's head bows forwards and almost touches mine. Along with my hands I'm entrusting him with my future and my life.

On my return from Rome I had talked at length with the Father Abbot. Without his telling me outright, I had come to understand the inner reason for his resignation. This man of intelligence, this old fighter, had been weighing up the nature and extent of the changes that were required of the monasteries and the whole Church, if she wished to become alive and attractive once more. It was not just that he no longer felt he had the strength to carry forwards this process: more profoundly, more confusedly, he realized that it would not happen, or only very partially; he realized that the immense hopes engendered by the Council would not be fulfilled, that the dead weight of the system and of things generally would prevail over life and its vigour.

He did not want to witness all that at close hand; he did not want to be an actor in this scenario. Perhaps he foresaw that all these convulsions, everything that was in prospect, would be wearing and pointless. In his old days he would have greeted a rejuvenation of the Gospel with joy: but he did not believe, he no longer believed, it would happen.

So he asked for peace, he asked to withdraw from the abbey so as to live for a few years in freedom, as he understood freedom – freedom to be human and uncomplicated before his God, stripped of the symbols of power that were now for him so many barriers.

He would go alone, then, to a little parish in Lozère where he would also be priest. Silence, poverty, utter self-giving – he would find them there without having to create them, without fear of boasting of them or of attracting the admiration of some audience or other.

"Be on your guard, Brother Irenaeus! You grasp things quickly, you want to travel fast. But the Church doesn't move like that, and the Society to which we belong doesn't like to change our brand image. As you'll discover, though everything might be possible everything is not achievable. I think that Father Gerard will be elected abbot: good luck, God preserve you!"

With my hands still enclosed in his own, Father Gerard has raised his head. Our gazes meet. I can read nothing behind those creased eyes, that faint smile. *Will you be a father to me? Shall we receive from you the life that I am waiting for?* My unvoiced question meets with no response.

Slowly his hands part. I get up and go back to my place in the

181

shadow. Next week will be the abbot's benediction, a ceremony with full pomp, at which the bishop will preside.

Father Gerard was the candidate of renewal. He signalled it in an original way: the abbot's benediction was to take place in the morning; and in the afternoon, for the monks' families, the abbey would be open house: enclosure would be lifted for a few hours. Everyone would be able to show his dear ones what this regime of life was that stayed forever hidden from the world.

I used to write to Uncle very regularly. This time he replied to me that he would be free: he would not come to the morning's "religious nonsense", but he would be there in the afternoon.

After six years Uncle was going to make the journey to the riverbank to see me! – to recognize in some sort the choice I had made, draw a line through the past, accept me for what I was, for what I had wanted to be!

Uncle here! Floods of joy coursed through my veins. Yes! All this would lead to something, there were no two ways about it: life would triumph!

He's there in the middle of the garden, in his grey suit, with a strained smile. There are lots of people; I grab him by the arm:

"Come along! We're going to walk round inside."

His wife follows him: she understands that this brief time is for the two of us, that she should keep to the background, not obtrude. We walk the length of the cold, stark corridors. Uncle doesn't unclench his jaws. I bring him into my cell.

"Well then, is this where you live? Is this where you write to me from?"

He loosens up, sits down on the bed – and makes a grimace: *the devil it's hard!*

"Do you sleep well on this?"

Now he's at his ease, opening doors, rummaging in corners, going down to the workshop, giving a connoisseur's appreciation of Father Nicolas's tobacco. The ice has melted; he asks a thousand questions, takes an interest in everything.

It doesn't matter what you say and what I reply: you simply want to make me understand, to make me feel, that you love me, that nothing has changed between us. Yes of course, I've chosen this extraordinary whatsit of a life, but if I'm happy, that's what's important. "Are you happy, Michel? Tell me, are you happy?"

Yes, Uncle, I am happy, wild with joy to see you here, to know that your wound has healed over. I have been so wretched, you know, to have hurt you of all people! But you're here, and you're smiling, and I'm smiling at you. The abbey – you couldn't care less about it, I realize. What counts is that we're together once more.

That evening I was soaring with the summer swallows over the village roofs towards the River bend, in the rays of the setting sun. Was this it – happiness?

2

And there was evening, and there was morning...* Father Gerard is seated at the Father Abbot's desk. We're discussing what my activities at the abbey will be: study time, holiday time, are over. Now I have to put my hand to the dough.

"The liturgy, of course. You know that there's everything still to do, and that we've been waiting for you. Then, welcoming outside visitors, and the abbey journal."

Like all monasteries we used to produce a periodical each quarter. From a simple news-sheet it had gradually become an attractively presented magazine. We reckoned on nearly two thousand subscribers, the important thing being of course the income that they contributed each year. These were the friends of the abbey, women to the fore. It was a matter of maintaining contact, of providing a shop window for the monastery. It contained the inevitable "little message from the Father Abbot", a few virtually unreadable articles on doctrine, a diary of daily life (the three months took up one page) and appeals for financial support.

* * *

Welcoming outsiders was a rapidly developing field. In the great upheaval that was shaking the Church, monasteries were becoming fashionable. Many people – believers or not – came on tours, to look around. It was not the ancient and traditional activity of monastic hospitality. Visitors came for the day: they took a little sniff of liturgy, gave themselves a few cheap mystic thrills, then gaped at how these funny monk-people managed to live.

Television had got involved in it. They sometimes screened documentaries, always based on the same clichés: the university graduate sweeping corridors, the pretty young girl who had taken the veil and who was so, so happy! The picture that the small screen gave of the abbeys was an idealized one, the one the public demanded.

Progressively schools and parishes had discovered us: whole classes and old folks' guilds in organized groups treated themselves to "a day with the monks". As they were not admitted inside, we had to devise new ways of entertaining them: a visit to the church, an interview in the garden – "What time do you get up, Father?" – and a tour round one of the reception rooms that had been converted into a permanent exhibition. At the end of the visit the welcoming monk held out a basket: contributions were not inconsiderable, and Father Du Bellay de Saint-Pons eagerly gathered the baskets up at the end of the day.

I was to be much occupied with these fringe activities at the abbey. They were distasteful to the pure and hard-line monks, but they certainly matched my need for human contact.

Then there was the fearsome and delicate responsibility for revision of the liturgy. Everyone, without telling me as much, was looking to me for this. The Vatican kept sending us directives that were thoroughly Roman – that is, equivocal: yes, abbeys must adapt themselves to the new era, but at the same time they must preserve all their traditions.

Father Gerard had set up a committee, with me as coordinator and leader. Four brothers were to work with me in preparing drafts for submission to the community. The task was to take our liturgy apart, bit by bit, like a piece of precision engineering; to select, retool and reassemble the bits; and to be sure that the whole machine was fully coherent and homogeneous. Each word, each text, each change that I proposed was discussed in committee.

I thought I would be able to look to my colleagues for support and share the burden with them. As months, then years, passed, I realized that they were there, rather, to keep an eye on me, to curb my initiatives, to avert the excesses that were feared of me. To be sure, they were never given any instruction of this nature. But they were representing a community that desired above all not to have its routines shaken up, and they knew this.

This committee, which met weekly, was formed, then, of a locomotive pulling four trucks whose brakes were jammed.

My enthusiasm was such that it took me time to notice this. I found it hard to conceive that someone could at the same moment be entrusted with a mission and not want to fulfil it.

If there were disagreements, they were for Father Gerard to resolve. I went to see him frequently, and he assured me of his support:

"Brother, you are touching there the most sensitive nerve in our body. But I have confidence in you; carry on!"

What is at stake here, God, if it's not the way your Word can get through to this group of men? If we hear you as something strange, if nothing can pass between you and us other than what's artificial and conventional, can you truly be for us the living God that I've discovered?

I don't conceive of you as other than fascinating, off-putting, original. You're not for me the God of the banal or the repetitious; I want to be alive, and to be confronted by you every morning...

The truth was that I regarded myself more as missionary than as agent. But were the old, established monks prepared to listen to the tune of a johnny-come-lately, a pagan convert?

Trench warfare was about to begin: every inch of territory

would be fiercely disputed. The monotonous years that were to come, each long day indistinguishable from the next, would be full of these arcane and silent battles. I was thirty-two by then.

I loved these brothers, nonetheless; and I was fully aware that I had no exclusive claim to the truth… But, since we were seeking the same God, why this constant hanging back, this underlying inertia? Was it in fact the same God? Or was there perhaps, elsewhere, something that I had not yet glimpsed?

I tackled head-on the thorniest problem, that of the psalms. The heart of the liturgy was made up of the chanting of the 150 psalms. The Latin text that we used went back to the fourth century, and the music – the Gregorian chant – to the eleventh. It was this that had to be changed.

There already existed in our country a French-language version of the psalms that was widespread in the parishes. It certainly was not perfect, but it was at least in use everywhere, to tunes that were simple and popular.

It was exactly this that the abbey could not stomach. The Gregorian chant was not to be replaced by something commonplace and therefore vulgar: we must have a special liturgy that brought out the difference between us and the people.

So contact was made with a musicologist, a professor in a conservatoire. Certainly, this project interested him; yes, he would compose for us tunes that were completely modern and that would be uniquely ours to chant.

Honour was preserved.

For more than a year we spent whole days at work teaching ourselves this music, then singing it. Our tousled-haired Wagner of the abbeys got us to swallow dissonances, syncopations, strange modern rhythms. I had, it is true, envisaged something friendlier, something less esoteric, more like what I had witnessed at Taizé. But it was difficult and strange, and therefore monastic:

the community accepted it, embraced it. No cause for complaint there.

One fine day our fat Latin books, which had lulled generations of monks in the comforting monotony of a dead language, were replaced in the chancel by little psalters in French. The whole of the last part of the office was still to be sung to Gregorian chant, first to appease those who clung to the past, but also because there was nothing yet available to replace it in our language.

With knitted brows, eyes riveted to the music, my brothers yielded to the inevitable: for the first time beneath the medieval vault, the inspired words rang out in French.

3

It was a Sunday afternoon. A few weeks earlier Rome, having encouraged the "necessary liturgical renewal", had issued a little rhapsody about "the intrinsic worth of the immortal Gregorian chant".

I had just finished taking a group of tourists round the church and was walking towards the door to the enclosed section of the monastery. A small, spare young man, in plus-fours and crew cut, springs out from behind a pillar.

"Father! Can I ask you a question?"

The eyes behind the glasses are anxious; the voice is affected, stressing the sibilants.

"Please go ahead."

"I'm about to attend your office of vespers with my children. Tell me, Father, the psalms are of course sung here to Gregorian chant, aren't they, in Latin?"

He has come all the way here to attend the service with his two children, who are staring at me.

"No, sir, the psalmody is now in French, but all the remainder of the office…"

He cuts me short, stiffens his legs, and rises on his toes, buttocks drawn in:

"What! In French? After the instructions from the Holy Father the Pope, you've the audacity, you've the audacity?..."

I mumble something and withdraw to the enclosed quarters, the value of which I appreciate on this occasion. His barking follows after me: you've the audassity, you've the audassity?

Outside the monastery, too, a change is making itself felt. For a small minority of the population we're an ideal, a secure repository of eternal values. I'm accustomed to think of myself as working simply to improve the quality of our worship. But in the current climate in France, some people are making a political issue out of what we have done and aim to do. Are we going to witness a commando unit of beefy fundamentalists striking up Latin psalms to drown out our singing, as they have done in Paris?

"Grown-ups do behave in a quite extraordinary way!"

"God, you are my God; I have sought you since daybreak..."*
Slowly I am letting the phrase of the Psalm seep into me. There are not many of us in the chapel at this morning hour. I often come here at the end of the night's great silence. I leave my body on the ground and make myself ready for you.

At the start of our relationship I used to talk to you a lot. Now, more and more, I stay quiet before you. Are you not aware of what I am about to say, even before it comes to my lips? I keep silence in your presence. It is not that I really know you: but that is how I love to be. Do with this moment whatever seems good to you.

I am learning to pray.

There were veritable palace revolutions. One example: services are led by a monk who to some extent plays the part of leader of the orchestra. He starts the service off, intervenes at various points on the way, and brings it to a conclusion. He is called the "celebrant".

Over the centuries his role had been whittled down to the point where his voice was hardly heard any more. The liturgy lost out in liveliness and three-dimensionality, while the father abbot, by a natural shift towards authority, gradually took over the role, affording him, as it did, a lasting enhancement of status – a classic transformation sanctioned by history throughout the Church.

I had studied the matter at length at the historical level, and I proposed that in the liturgy the father abbot should give ground to the celebrant, who would once again play his role as leader of the service. As there was a change of celebrant every week, our liturgical life would gain in variety, each monk stamping it in turn with his own personality.

In principle there was no room for debate: the case was compelling and unanswerable.

In practice, however, the father abbot would have to give up the central place that he had been used to occupying in all the services; he would have to re-enter the ranks – *primus inter pares*, "first among equals", for sure, but on a level with the rest of the brothers.

Father Gerard saw no problem with this: he understood that this small change would lead to each celebrant taking over the service for a week; he did not rely on things like this for any consciousness he might have of his primacy as abbot.

It was the community, in fact, that could not stomach it, and the members of the committee in particular. It was an assault on the image of hierarchy that they had apparently formed for themselves. My proposal had a whiff of egalitarianism about it; they could not help suspecting me of socialism. Then, too, the fifteen or so celebrants that followed each other in this position saw themselves suddenly invested with a responsibility that thrust them forwards, in public: this was something that they really did not like.

Their reluctance was such – you would have thought the whole world order was in peril – that I had to stage a *coup d'état*. The church furnishings needed to be rearranged, the father abbot's throne moved. With Father Gerard's agreement, Nicolas and I carried out this little task at night, while everyone was asleep.

At morning service the next day, boo! With the furniture moved around, the men just had to follow along.

Three months on, everyone felt fine about it; no one would have wanted to put the clock back. But, underneath, I was resented for my forceful tactics.

And this infighting – hard to imagine in any other context – was slowly wearing me out.

It certainly was.

Fortunately, God, you are there. I am trying hard to keep my eyes on you. But how far shall I be able to carry on?

There were a few months of respite. Then, with the approach of spring, it was decided to have a go at Holy Week and Easter.

For this crucial season of the church year, we had inherited a liturgy distended by the passing centuries. So it was with the earthquake that according to the Gospel would have accompanied Christ's death: when this passage was read during the office of *Tenebræ*, everyone used to go down on all fours in the stalls and imitate the rumbling of an earthquake by banging their hands and feet on the floor. It was a droll and baroque diversion, and it had in any case been abolished by the Council, but it shows how far unnecessary accretions had gone in the end to smother those liturgies that were already lengthy and complex creations.

Here too I had an unchallengeable case. Father Gerard asked me to give a series of talks to the community to set out the whys and wherefores and explain the purpose of what we were proposing to do – restore the value of those symbols that were important and unforced, adapt the readings, and rediscover for the Passion story what lay behind the liturgical antics of the high Middle Ages.

During my talks most of the brothers heard me out with patience and did not react. But there were a few who were acquainted with history or liturgy and who kept seeking substantiation for the least of my statements: I had to back these up with irrefutable evidence that they could check. This work had, of course, already been carried out in committee, where I used to have to present myself in front of a small board of examiners before the general examination.

One needed to have strong nerves. Fortunately Father Gerard seemed to be behind me, giving green lights. We moved forwards, slowly.

Easter that year was late, and the weather magnificent. For a month now everyone had been rehearsing the rituals, the words (some of which I had had to rewrite) and the chants.

The monks' smiles testified that we had had a good Holy Week. Congregations, too, had attended in ever greater numbers: the word was getting around fast that the abbey was making efforts, that the liturgy there was becoming livelier, while still beautiful.

For the Easter vigil, which lasted almost four hours and concluded the week, there were about two hundred people present, something never seen before. The lighting of the candles began at the back of the church, proceeded up to the altar, then travelled back down again among the congregation. We went on to the blessing of the baptismal water, which would later be sprinkled among us... It was a serene ballet, a sharing in the mystery, with the cosmic elements recovering their original significance as spiritual aids.

I had organized two great bowls of mulled wine at the church door for when all was finished, in the middle of the night. A few nominated monks began serving it to the chilled and grateful congregation. Then some of the others shyly joined the crowd who had thrilled and prayed with us – a brief time of great brotherly concord. On the Easter Day walk comments flowed freely: people were tired, but pleased.

And then the following year it all had to begin again – meetings, exhortations... People couldn't quite remember any more, they had not really understood, they had forgotten.

Like a patient Penelope, I started to weave my tapestry all over again.

4

My mother used to come once a year to spend a few days at the abbey. At the beginning of that summer she found me tired and tense.

"No, Mother, really: everything's fine, no problems!"

I was unable to admit to her what I was reluctant to admit to myself: the task was a heavy one, and the struggle was wearying me. But I was acting under orders; I had placed my confidence in Father Gerard. He was not letting me down; he was backing my efforts; he was providing me with the wherewithal. I explained it to my mother, passing over the details.

But she was a mother. Without telling me she asked to see the Father Abbot – the one that had authority over this son of hers, this son who was relying on him.

So this woman, whose wounds had made her so reserved – where had she found the courage for this initiative?

It was only very much later – "afterwards" – that she let me in on the secret of this interview. I can still hear her words, and I do not question them:

"We had a very candid discussion; he didn't beat about the bush. He spoke of you with affection, but he concluded sadly: 'I didn't think your son would return from Rome. I don't believe that he will stay.'"

Woman, you obtained this admission, and you hid it in your mother's heart. How did you regard me from then on, once you knew? With what foreboding did you watch my path? Was there still, then, somewhere within you, some part susceptible to pain?

Suspecting nothing, I carried on: Penelope – or Don Quixote? Or perhaps just Voltaire's Candide, insisting that his mentor Pangloss was incapable of misleading him: *all is well in the best of all worlds.*

Strangely, God, these sources of distress do not touch me in that secret depth where I meet you. Am I running away from the reality of my everyday life? I do not believe so.

I believe rather that you are the sole reality. That may be why our relationship seems so little affected by what is going on outside.

Is "relationship" the right word, though? I am silent for a lot of the time with you. You talk seldom – or, rather, you talk in a strange manner: you come to confirm, in a kind of way, the words that are familiar to me from the Bible – by an inner certainty, as if you were addressing them to me, yes to me, that very day.

Silent God. I love to listen for your word.

All monasteries in France were faced with the same problem of adjustment – of transforming their liturgy and so their innermost life.

At the starting point patterns of living were identical everywhere – with subtle variations, often important, between Benedictines and Cistercians. Our traditions were not the same; our historic paths had not marched in parallel; but as far as liturgy was concerned, we were very close to one another.

Under Church law each monastery enjoyed great autonomy. With renewal under way, therefore, there was a danger of significant differences developing between sister houses. What was needed was not a central authority – abbeys recognized no authority beyond that of far-off Rome – but an opportunity to link our efforts, and maybe coordinate them.

And there was also a need to circulate information: expertise was scarce, and some monasteries were very isolated, with no knowledge of what to do or how.

A national meeting of father abbots took up the issue. It was decided that there should be a "liturgy secretary", who would put himself at the disposal of the French province of the order. He would inform each member of everyone's work-programme and achievements; he would facilitate progress, slow as it had been, not by the exercise of authority, but by providing material for discussion, case studies and expertise.

The Provincial summoned me: was I prepared to accept this job and to carry it out on everyone's behalf?

I asked whether Father Gerard was in full agreement: yes, it was he that had put my name forward.

It was only after the event that I realized that from the abbey's point of view, and perhaps also the Provincial's, the exercise had a double purpose: certainly to resolve a general problem and secure the availability of expertise; but also, yes, to give me an outlet, to offer an opening for my activities that would divert it somewhat from the self-contained world of the abbey.

As you had a locomotive, you added trucks to it, and you put it on the national rail network, where it could let off steam without champing away too much in its local station.

So I began to travel a bit around the country, from one abbey to another, bringing together information, organizing meetings, giving talks.

It was an opportunity for me to take the pulse of the order, to gain an overview of French monasteries. I realized that tensions were not my abbey's monopoly: everywhere newness gave birth in pain, with brakes being applied sharply, whether by communities or by authority. And I observed that the houses that survived this difficult transition best were the simplest ones, the ones that were poorest in human resources: rural abbeys in remote locations, Cistercian houses lost in the depths of forests, little-known monasteries without any brand image to protect.

The small ones, the lowly ones, despite lack of means, adopted the French language without protest and selected uncomplicated tunes that they often sang with enthusiasm. Very well, it was no longer in the great tradition of Gregorian chant; they were moving, in a small way, from the splendours of Versailles to the unpretentiousness of Fontainebleau, but the new liturgy gave them nourishment, and concord was granted them as a bonus, as though in reward for their humility.

With the great monasteries, the popular and famous ones, it was all more complicated. Here knights clashed with swords unsheathed; blood was shed. In what was said, of course, good form was always observed between brother coreligionists. But although these contests were not disclosed to anyone, not even to the provincial secretary, I became aware of them.

The rules of silence had been eased everywhere, and during the course of my discussions and walks, I was able to observe the relationships that were becoming apparent between monks.

Something began to strike me, something quite tenuous, marginal and hard to define.

I had already had plenty of experience of working relationships between men. Confrontations took place face to face, things were out in the open. People disagreed, they said so, and once the matter had been settled there was no further talk of it.

Similarly I had experienced friendship, and even affection, between men. Such feelings were forthright and wholehearted, unafraid to manifest themselves in word or gesture. My friends placed a hand on my shoulder, we kissed on special occasions, gave a close hug or a slap on the back, looked each other in the eye and shared smiles.

But among monks it was different – and hard to define. Often – not always, to be sure – I noticed a sort of affectation, exaggeration or ostentation in relationships. People did not touch, they brushed by each other; they came close, while all the time keeping their distance. Gestures, looks, gait sometimes, had in them something slightly feminine. Was it the gown that these men wore? I do not know.

In the abbey, where I was well acquainted with the little world of fondnesses and antipathies, I used to witness those mottled exchanges, those stings wreathed in smiles, those disguised declarations appealing for the sympathy and affection of someone you went in awe of.

And I kept repeating to myself the question that never found an answer: where had the sexuality of these monks got to? How did my brothers experience and manage their sexual urges, beyond the official pronouncements – "Sublimate, Brother, sublimate!" – or rather in their absence?

Then I remembered in my heart a phrase my mother had tossed out a few days before my departure for the abbey, so very long ago.

5

"And anyway, for a start, all monks are queers!"

The poor woman had been at the end of her tether, her arguments exhausted: the only remaining objection she had been able to muster against me had been this stock imputation, like a final barrage to deflect me from my purpose.

No, the monks among whom I lived were not practising homosexuals: the popular tittle-tattle was totally without justification.

On the other hand, yes – now it is glaringly obvious to me – yes, monks are very often homosexuals in their minds.

Will I have the skill now to find the precise words for describing a reality that is so delicate that I only became aware of it long afterwards and that it was impossible to speak of?

I had met Mark again in his remote abbey. Here was a friend to whom I could say anything. But whenever I timidly broached this subject with him, he closed up like an oyster – the topic was taboo, impossible.

Our sexuality had not vanished when we became novices. But it is in our heads that everything goes on – emotions, desires, pleasures. Our heads might be shaven, then covered again in a hood, but that changed nothing: no "destructuring", no restructuring, could neutralize that potent alchemy that is the alchemy of life itself.

We were a select group, and we knew it: one indecent action would have caused us to lose our identity, the image we had of ourselves. Permeated as we were with our moral superiority, indoctrinated by our recognized authors, we were also surrounded with admiring looks, and these protected us. To stoop to homosexual practices was clearly unvocational, if not unnatural.

And yet in our communities there prevailed an ambivalent atmosphere.

On entering an abbey monks become orphans. Moreover, I often noticed that a monk's physical father, whom he had left behind in the world, played an offstage role in his new life. It was the mothers they talked of when they talked of themselves, the mothers who had suffered most from their son's departure, the mothers who came often to visit them in the interview room.

But abbeys contain one omnipresent father, the father abbot. He possesses an absolute authority that is physical, moral, spiritual and emotional. That is how he is constituted under the Rule, in the image of the Roman *paterfamilias*.

Convention insists that the father abbot addresses each monk as "my child" – even if the child, white-haired and deeply lined, might have been the youthful father abbot's grandfather. A French abbot in transit once said to me in Rome, where the balmy evening air invited confidences:

"What do you expect, dear Brother – a man enters our abbeys as a child, he lives there as a child and he dies there as a child..."

Relations with a father abbot are complicated. Once a monk has joined his own hands within those of the abbot, he has yielded himself to the abbot body and soul. What the Rule says is very true: an abbot's fatherhood is simply the image, the incarnation, of divine fatherhood. So the abbot, almighty father that he is, fades away before God, the only Father. Then the monk finds himself again with an offstage father – a father present for all the restrictive purposes related to fatherhood, but absent for the crucial purpose, which is the transmission of life, the gift of life.

I was well aware of what Uncle had given me in becoming my father: not only his own life, but a life of my own as well. I was aware of his solicitude in following my progress, of his joy – so much greater than my own – at my successes, and of the mysterious bonds that linked us together. The conflict that had divided us was that of one flesh being torn apart.

No abbot, whatever his fatherly intentions, could have come near what I had gained in Uncle.

A father off-stage, but almighty; a father we were obliged to love, but were not always in love with; a father in charge of our lives, but also, and above all, committed to secure our observance; a generous father, devoted to his children, but only to a certain point: for he too has to live his own life alone before God, God in whose eyes he has to recognize himself as a child. A father-child; an orphaned father of orphaned children.

Consequently the monk-children develop a kind of inverted relationship among themselves: duty-bound as they all are to love each other, but unable to love everyone, they often choose to love some more than others, but with a spiritualized love. Those couples that come together in the course of work or study – we called them a "team".

I knew one such team, who lived for years in what one can only call a perfect love.

Father Anscar came from old Flemish middle-class stock. Tall, fine-featured, distinguished-looking, he had a nervous instability that bordered on the pathological. A hypersensitive man, he spent half his life unearthing and then publishing a medieval manuscript that had been discovered in the abbey library, a Benedictine work with a potential world readership of barely a hundred specialists.

His jerky movements, his fretful outbursts against a recalcitrant typewriter, the cries he would utter alone in his cell as he pored over his famous manuscript, his twitchiness and abruptness – none of it surprised us any longer, but it had certainly isolated him from the rest of the community.

Alongside him was a brother, third or fourth of a prolific family that enjoyed a lifelong discount card for public transport. All muscle, head shaped like a breeze block, he was a manual worker who liked to think himself incapable of study: in fact, he was certainly no more stupid than others.

With him everything was meticulously arranged, prepared and coordinated – ponderously, to be sure, but with never a comma missing. He had been appointed master of ceremonies – that is, organizer of our services. Each night he pinned up the next day's schedule with electronic precision, but I reckon that even a computer had more sense of humour than he did.

Once the revolution had made it possible for the *lectio divina* to take place in small groups, these two monks began meeting every morning to read the Gospel together. They were an astonishing couple, the tall hypersensitive intellectual and the young tough who looked like a cement mixer, taking turns to sit in each other's cell and exchange thoughts on a page of St John or St Mark.

They complemented each other, I suppose, and these two less-than-happy men ended up by becoming inseparable from one another, to the point where on all the walks – the aim of which was to shuffle the cards – they were to be seen side by side – sometimes in a group, sometimes on their own – as though through magnetic attraction or in order to seek refuge together from the rest. When one nodded his head, the other would smile, and the older one usually voiced the joint view of the two.

As a pair they were perfectly chaste, perfectly innocent, and so perfectly accepted – admired, almost, as examples. Were they not the living ideal of that brotherhood formed around the Gospel that alone could have brought together two such dissimilar beings?

Yes; but if ever one was attacked, the other flew to his defence; and if one had a success, the other was the first to congratulate him on it. It was the Greek heroes Achilles and Patroclus, without declarations of love, but not without armour.

The formation of such couples, motivated as it was by the noblest of sentiments, was common. I do not believe I ever myself took part in such a special, private relationship that excluded any other. My friendships with Mark and Nicolas did not lock us into a lonely twosome, but remained open and unpossessive.

Only the passage of years enables me to understand what there was of ambiguity in the stilted language we used within our group, in the acute consciousness we had of being a self-selected minority with a duty to defend itself. Anyway, once we had taken the decision to enter, all other choices and struggles that form a man over a lifetime were spared us. From then on most of my colleagues were incapable of taking a decision without prior reference to the one that held them in the hollow of his hand.

All the ingredients had therefore come together for it to be possible to speak of latent homosexuality – all of them, that is, except the act, or even its stimulus.

6

Autumn had come. In the course of the academic year the welcome programme for outside visitors attracted more and more young people's groups. This time it was chaplaincy groups led by their priest who were asking to spend two or three days at the abbey. We quickly arranged accommodation for them in the village school, where they slept on the floor. Rather than just a tour of the place, they wanted a real retreat, including in particular an introduction to prayer.

These older adolescents, mixed boys and girls, came voluntarily and were keen for anything. I took charge of them and assumed the role of leader for their short retreat.

One does not give talks to youngsters; one helps them to gain hands-on experience. They needed therefore to be not just spectators but active participants in our liturgy.

To start with, I requested that we bring them in beside us into the monks' stalls. There was considerable resistance: the monks saw their private domain invaded, desecrated, by blue jeans and long hair. On each occasion I had to get my way by dint of persuasion and discussion with the brothers.

Early on I saw that this was not enough. The very contents of the service needed to take into account this unaccustomed presence of the non-initiated. It might be necessary to change one of the set readings, choose one song rather than another and adapt the language – to ease their path into our world and its mysteries.

These youngsters were thoroughly well motivated, ready for any experience. Once they had got over the initial strangeness, they were quickly able to enter into the liturgy and receive its message. I met them afterwards in the school-turned-chapel for short periods of directed silent prayer. I sat in on their discussions; I heard and saw what was happening within them – the discovery, in wonderment, of a God of whom they had till then been ignorant, or nearly so.

When I went back to the community I found it impossible to convey all this to my brothers, to get them to realize that important things were happening there. The God whose life we were leading, who was the sole reason for our presence beside the River – could we keep him for ourselves alone?

Could we not share the bread that nourished us with those hungering for it who came knocking at our door?

Two attitudes were coming into conflict. On the one side were the brothers of the abbey, wanting at all costs to safeguard the choices they had made. Escape from the world, a desert existence – that was the aim they had set themselves, the path they had taken; they had willed it, and it was needful for them. It was their right, after all, and I understood that.

On the other side were the ever-more-insistent expectations of a world that was losing its values, that was suffocating spiritually, and that was discovering in the abbeys a special place, a protected place, which could provide an experience unobtainable elsewhere that would illuminate lives with an enduring light.

When you have met God once, even fleetingly and incompletely, you never forget it. These young people that were like a wave breaking against our walls – they might later become convinced atheists. But I was familiar with atheism: I had come from there, and I knew that there was no unbeliever that did not have hidden within them somewhere a secret place where God could one day find a tentative foothold.

It was my own experience that I was reliving with those youngsters, lacking God as they were, yet hungry for him. Besides, was I so sure of having found him myself? Was I not too, like them, searching for a God who was yet to be discovered?

Whenever I came back among my brothers, whenever I witnessed the serene assurance with which they seemed to enjoy a God that was familiar, comfortable, conditioned in a way to their own environment, I used to wonder if we really belonged to the same world. Sometimes I felt more at ease with those unsure and eager youngsters whom I would meet for a fresh plunge into worship.

I was the eternal trainee; my brother monks, on the other hand, behaved like landlords. I wanted the abbey, I begged the abbey, to change its stance towards the outside world.

And the abbey, standing as it did by the water that had flowed at its foot for centuries, was not ready for that opening. Who was I, after all, to ask the bed of the River to change its path? It was for me to fit myself within this mould – there was no other.

God, I have to speak to you today; you must hear me.

What is happening? Are you just an illusion? – you, who have slowly made me accustomed to your presence; you, who used to be enough for my happiness... But am I mistaken? My brothers, the brothers whose life and destiny I share – they can't all be wrong and I alone right.

But then, who are you, if you're not life in full flood? And as for me, what value does my life have, if it's not a constant walking in your footsteps?

What sort of life is a stationary life, God?

Year by year, step by step, festival after festival, our liturgy was taking a little more account of others – of others that were just passing through, it is true, while we stayed put. Our life was there; it had its roots there, its *raison d'être* there. For whose sake should we alter it – for those folk who came, and went?

This was the unspoken message that my brothers were sending me, through all the obstacles they were putting in the way of my initiatives.

I went to see Father Gerard.

He listened to me, seeming to understand.

"We must respect the sensitivities of this or that brother. But, if you like, I'm ready to meet with your groups at the school and talk to them."

Was this not a gesture of goodwill, a way of sharing my concern, of being by my side?

He really did come to talk to the young people. They listened to him in awe: you don't meet a father abbot every day. But he sat facing them, whereas during our prayer initiation sessions I placed myself among them, looking with them towards the icon of the transfigured Christ. The demeanour was not the same; nor perhaps was the result.

Father Nicolas watched my manoeuvres in silence. He was taken outside more and more by the building jobs he was securing for the workshop. He travelled a great deal, was often away. While manufacturing took place in the monastery basement, he used these days to go out and supervise installations, then sometimes lend a hand himself. In the end he put on blue overalls, which he never left off, and became a builder.

How did he live during those long absences? Did he at least celebrate mass? The seniors used to wonder.

There was one building job in the Vosges more difficult than usual. He was allocated a young novice to go with him and give his back some relief. On their return we would find out a little more.

The account of the journey took up several walks. Father Nicolas still drove like a madman. Once they had reached the building site, he put on his blue overalls and joined in fully with the workmen, spitting gently on his hands before grasping the handle of his tool.

This time the workers were Arabs from Morocco. The novice had witnessed a strange scene. One of the Moroccan workmen, who scarcely spoke French and was working without a permit, was doing some earth moving with a shovel, while Nicolas was up a ladder finishing off a fitment. Suddenly the shovel handle broke in two with a snap. The Moroccan was speechless with panic: *What's going to happen now? What will I get for this?* The foreman, fortunately, was looking the other way.

Nicolas had seen it all and had understood the mini-drama. With an agility improbable for that huge frame, he had climbed swiftly down his ladder, had grabbed his own shovel – an abbey one, strong and new – had gone up to the Moroccan, put his shovel down in front of him, gathered up the bits of the other one and climbed back up his ladder.

All this had taken a few seconds. It was the monk who had broken his shovel – no problem: those folk are well off; they will buy him another.

The Moroccan had taken a long look at this untypical Christian holy man, who was whistling to himself now at the top of his ladder. Then he had gone back to his work, new shovel in hand, the holy man's shovel.

"What about mass? Does he say mass?"

Yes, certainly, in the village churches. But that building job was in the back of beyond. So one morning, when the mist was rising from the valley, Nicolas had set up an improvised altar on the bonnet of his Citroën, and there in his boiler suit he had celebrated mass with all reverence. They were alone, the two of them, in the mountains, among all those Muslims. It was really great, the novice kept saying.

The story of the mass on the bonnet did the rounds of the monastery, and Nicolas was summoned to see the Father Abbot:

"Father, when working away from here you're still a priest, and you must celebrate mass with solemnity; at least, at least with priestly accoutrements."

Nicolas was an obedient monk. Six months later he found himself stranded in the Ardennes by a heavy snowfall. That morning, as an icy dawn broke, he set chalice, paten and candle out on his car bonnet. Still wearing his blue overalls he put a small travelling stole round his neck – and had Christ come there between his calloused hands.

The requirements of solemnity were met.

7

Time flowed slowly by on the riverbank, but the outlook was growing darker. Within the Church there were numerous signs that the momentum created by the Council was slackening.

This was not yet the "clamp-down" that was to take place several years later under the Polish pope, John Paul II. But Paul VI was getting old, and his staff were gaining the upper hand. It was these men – whose names were never mentioned and whose faces even were unknown to the public – that were securing the long-term future of the Catholic Church. Was the ship veering off a bit to the left or the right? They could wait. Time was on their side: fashions, those momentary gusts of wind, would pass. The Church had seen it all before; the Church was eternal. They were the Church.

The Council, which had been a forerunner of the revolution of May '68, would be controlled, channelled. It would be reduced to a momentary spasm, just another twitch, while the huge body would resume the aspect it had always had: there would be more speeches, more encyclicals. Right to its furthest extremities the Church was guarantor of a system that could not be called into question.

At the abbey the room for manoeuvre was becoming tighter and tighter. I began therefore to give more of my time and energy to the journal: as the proverb says, "The one who can no longer act writes a book."

From one quarter to the next, from one year to the next, I had endeavoured to give the journal more substance, and then to widen its appeal. Several issues had been devoted to famous writers and painters. Studies of their work provided the context for discussion pieces illuminating this area where art and literature stand at the frontier of faith.

The circulation grew: we now had nearly four thousand paying subscribers. The journal was moving beyond the narrow circle of the abbey's uncritical friends.

In this area at least I was free, because there were no practical consequences. I decided to produce a special issue about the life of monks: testimonies from my brothers, a full account of our life, the issues it raised and its prophetic value, written in a language that was no longer wooden but comprehensible to anyone, speaking straight to the heart.

The issue was well received, with a print run of six thousand; copies were offered for sale in some Paris bookshops.

In the abbey it was greeted with silence. The only comment was a remark from the redoubtable Father Joseph during one of the walks:

"That issue of yours is a two-dimensional portrayal of our life.

You've taken all the mystery out of it, which is what makes it what it is."

The situation was clear: I was deliberately placing myself outside that unspoken consensus to which a monk must stay inwardly loyal – if he wanted to remain within the invisible circumference of the circle defining the group's true membership…

…if he did not want, simply, to be forced out – made to force himself out.

A new spring was on its way, the fourth since the start of our liturgical reform. At the big festivals our church saw ever larger crowds – a direct result of the awful chaos into which, as seen from our bell tower, the parochial liturgy was sinking – trite words, music borrowed from the world of popular song, meaningless symbols. The fundamentalist movement was born from this rubble and came to beat on our walls, and along with them a mass of good folk who had simply lost their bearings and were seeking to rediscover the roots of their faith.

Safe in our enclosure we were not in direct touch with these tensions that racked the French Church – I perhaps even less than others. It seemed to me that politics should not interfere directly with the way we expressed our faith.

I was so naive.

The result at Easter was a church that was packed: several hundred people overflowing into the side-aisles, standing behind pillars. To check the situation, I spent part of the mass in the nave: people could see nothing, could hear nothing.

There would be the same crowds for Pentecost. I reconvened my committee. Something had to be done to adapt ourselves to these conditions. I proposed bringing the altar forwards in the direction of the congregation and placing it on a platform. Then at least the crowds would see and hear.

I was met by a wall of silence. It was too much; Brother Irenaeus was asking too much. A platform, and what next? Our liturgy was primarily for ourselves, and for God. If people came, they should take what they found. We were not monks for the sake of the public, we were monks for God's sake alone. Let our desert teem with crowds, but they must accept its emptiness.

I went to find Father Gerard.

"Listen, Brother, this practical issue of a platform is not one for me. It's not my place to intervene over details that are within the competence of the committee. Sort it out among yourselves, and do it for the best."

A detail... Yes, the platform was only a detail, but it indicated the stance we intended to adopt towards the surrounding world.

The night before Pentecost, with the help of a few novices, I carried a heavy piece of wooden flooring to the entrance of the chancel, and with difficulty we placed the altar on it. It was, once again, an attempt at a *coup d'état*: this time too the men would follow the furniture.

It was brilliantly sunny that festal morning, and the crowds were beginning to gather well before the hour for mass. I spent a fair time in the chapel, endeavouring to quieten myself before taking my welcoming position in the nave.

The bells were pealing cheerfully. When I entered the church, the platform had disappeared and the altar was back in its usual place. The people, as usual, would see and hear nothing.

The abbey, to its relief, had just had a narrow escape.

On leaving mass I took one of the scraps of paper that the monks use to communicate without breaching silence:

Dear Father,

I think that it is best that I cease henceforth to have anything to do with the liturgy and the welcome of outside visitors to the abbey. The most important part of the work that you had entrusted to me has been achieved; and the committee has no further need of me. With your leave, I offer you my withdrawal from that task.

I slipped the note into Father Gerard's pigeonhole and awaited a response. I had put my confidence in him; he understood me so well; would he not support me over this too?

A reply never came. Maybe my withdrawal arrived at the right moment: Father Gerard would not have to take sides.

So it was a platform that extinguished my enthusiasm and brought my dreams to nought.

For sure, I was beginning to become a nuisance. The platform was only the symbol of something much more serious: I had a vision of our life, and of its relationship with the outside world, that the community did not share. Nothing amiss with that. But I suddenly found myself beyond the boundary, intangible and indistinct as it was, that defined the abbey. I needed to withdraw, to submit. My withdrawal was a done deed. But my submission…?

It was obvious that I should give up my national role too: less need was felt for it now. A short message from the Provincial informed me of this: how could it be otherwise?

"It's a pity that you've given up, Brother Irenaeus. There was a breath of fresh air in our abbey, and I'm not sure if it'll continue…"

Father Nicolas was calmly filling his pipe. The workshop around us was quiet. Nicolas was just back from a trip and was off on another at the end of the week: more and more he was using the car as his cell. This bison from Vaud said nothing; he was too shrewd and too discreet. But I got the impression that his work and his incessant travels had become for him a kind of escape.

"You see, with us, when things don't go as we wish, we need to go back to our cell, to our books. And wait. Maybe the weather'll brighten up?"

There was less sparkle in his eyes than usual. He wanted to encourage me: he was worried about me and sent long puffs of grey smoke up to the ceiling.

For the very first time I went out of the back door without permission and walked by the tracks over the fields as far as the River. Behind the forest screen on the far bank, shadows were gently spreading: it would soon be evening. The water at my feet was dark blue. The tourists had gone home: a deep peace was slowly settling over the valley. The River as it flowed smoothly along seemed incapable of sound. I made my way back: no sound came from the abbey either, towering calmly there in the distance. It was I that was ill at ease; it was I that wanted to be talking, doing. I had entered the abbey to find life, and life meant forging ahead.

From now on I would have to learn to live a static life.

Violence. After all that time I was encountering the full force of violence, in the way violence manifested itself among us.

It had seemed to me in the early days that violence had been removed from our way of life; or at least it had been channelled to the very edge. The Greeks, our forebears – had they not discovered *apatheia*, the curbing of the passions, which stemmed at its source the very propensity for violence?

Everything was done to instil among us this "apathy", this absence of discord. And in this life of ours without friction or conflict, it was in a secondary form that violence manifested itself – in the struggle for ideas.

No one had sought to supplant me: humility ruled out such fantasies. It was on behalf of the group and its convictions that I had to move over, or be overcome. Violence was unleashed invisibly, in a cause to which no one gave their name.

It is now my belief that this is also the way in which repressed sexual impulses manifested themselves among us – in conflicts over dogma, in battles for ideas. The monks of today were assuredly more chaste than those of the Middle Ages; but, like their predecessors, they were ready quietly to bludgeon the one, or ones, who in an indefinable manner were no longer their own.

It's over. The enthusiasm, God, in which you were one with ongoing life – that enthusiasm is shattered now. And you yourself, these days, when I come to present myself before you at dawn – you seem absent too, God.

And yet you're still the same. You haven't changed because I've ceased to hope. Am I now going to have to wear myself out with your absence?

Could you be an imaginary God, like water that runs away?

*Or rather is it I that am now unable to hold you in the hollow
of my hand, to drink you?*

*God, I may be able to live without expecting anything of the
morrow. But how can I live without you?*

Father Nicolas was right. Salvation was in my cell, among books.
One thing was certain, the contract that I had signed when I
entered the abbey was not a contract made with men. Through
these men, my brothers, I had entered into a commitment with
God. That I would never put in question. If needs be I would have
myself put to death on the spot; but I would not break my vows, I
would not give up the monastic life.

I suggested to Father Gerard that I prepare a series of lectures
for the following year. It would at the same time be a piece of
research that I had wanted to do for a long time, on Christianity's
Jewish roots.

"Yes, Brother, that's an excellent subject; it's an area that's been
little explored. We'll certainly benefit by it. Carry on!"

Father Gerard – didn't he always support my initiatives with his
smile?

So I went on a tour of the library and returned to my cell with
a stack of books.

That is the day, or maybe a similar day during those months,
during that year… That is the day that I died.

Nothing had come to a standstill. But somewhere within me I
had died. Brother Irenaeus went on coming and going and smiling.
I did things, I talked of the future, but I was dead.

I had come into being on the ocean shore, in my Razanne's arms.
I had endured, unscathed, the folly of adults who behaved like
children. I had stayed alive through the restructuring of the new
man.

And then one day, stupidly, there I was, dead, done to death by
a platform.

And life went on.

8

I made a bold start on my studies. The point of departure was clear: Jesus of Nazareth was after all a Jew. This obvious fact had quite simply been erased from contemporary teaching: the Jesus mentioned in books and sermons was from no country. Was he perhaps a Greek or a Roman? In any case, Jesus had been commandeered by the West, in its service.

If Jesus was a Jew, he had lived as a Jew, he had spoken as a Jew, he had thought as a Jew. I needed first to immerse myself in the age of Christ – its feeling for things, its local colour, its way of life. Once I was better acquainted with the customs and practices of that Jewish world in which Christ had been steeped, I would be able to reread the Gospels with new eyes.

So I opened the first book of the Jerusalem Talmud, the *Berakhot* tractate, and I spent several months scouring it, pencil in hand. One section of this book went back to the third century: that was close enough to give one an idea. It was necessary of course to pick out the old part from the more recent material: by using a rigorously critical approach I had a mine of information available to me.

After that I investigated all the available documents of what is called "inter-testamental literature": written between the first century BC and the first century AD, these documents have not been incorporated in the Bible. But this was precisely the period in which Jesus lived, and these texts reflected the conditions of life, the religious climate and the contemporary atmosphere from which he had drawn breath. Gradually Jesus became no longer a meteorite that had dropped from heaven, but a man who had lived at a specific time in a specific place. Like every one of us, he belonged to the culture with which he was imbued.

I was on my way to discovering the man who had assimilated his native soil and had then one day set himself apart from it to launch his message. The novelty and originality of this message – the Gospel – I would come to appreciate better; and at the same time it would regain its tonality, its original Jewishness.

* * *

211

I did not have all the documents available on the spot: I needed to go to Paris, to the Fathers of Notre-Dame-de-Sion. There I found several men who had had the same idea long before me and were applying the same method, though as experienced professionals. They knew their way around the Talmud, that jungle of case law. Though they were Catholic priests, they also bore some resemblance to rabbinical scholars: there was a whiff of the *yeshiva*, the Jewish school, about their workplace.

That is presumably why their activities, and the results of their research, were so little known to the public. There are taboos one does not challenge.

The Jewishness of Christianity at its outset – that period that had always been the basic reference point for all Christian churches – that Jewishness gave off a smell of sulphur. For centuries the Inquisition had burnt Jews, or Christians suspected of sympathy with Judaism.

Jesus, the God of Christians, could not have been a Jew. Or if he was, it was by a historical mishap that should be hurriedly obliterated in order to use his words as the foundation of a theology that was wholesome – and Western.

The Fathers of Notre-Dame-de-Sion were therefore very circumspect. But they lent me all the documents then available. I had to content myself with provisional texts, but that was fine for my purpose.

Slowly, pages of notes piled up on my table – as the daylight waxed and waned on the banks of the River.

"Brother Irenaeus, telephone, from Paris."

The meal has just finished. I'm on washing-up for the week. Standing by a basin of steaming water, with suds to the elbow, I'm scouring piles of plates. The guest quarters are full: it's summer, and there are thirty guests in the refectory at midday.

"Would you mind taking my place? I'm on my way, thank you."

Wipe hands; go to the telephone on the kitchen wall, nearby. So who can be ringing me from Paris?

"Hallo?"

"Michel, it's me, it's Mother."

There's a crackle on the line. I recognize my mother's voice, but I can't make out her tone. She seems to me faint, hesitant.

"Hallo, Mother! Yes, I can hear you: what is it?"

My mother had never rung me at the abbey: there were few telephones; the rule about silence was strict, and she heeded it.

"Michel, my big boy, it's awful... Michel, your uncle had a car accident. He was killed at once, he's dead. I've been asked to let you know. Hallo? Michel, hallo?... Can you hear me?"

I had taken the telephone from my ear. Around me everything was reeling. The kitchen, the washing-up basins were going round and round.

"Hallo? Michel, my child, answer me! Hallo?... Say something!... Michel?"

Slowly I hung the receiver up on the wall. I must have gone outside like a robot, because I came to in the garden, near the cherry trees, at the entrance from the abbey fields.

At last, at last I was able to cry – a man's heavy sobs, choking me; the sobs of a child, a lost child; the sobs of the little king when he used to graze his foot on Tamatave beach, and Razanne, motherly and anxious, would enfold him in her gentleness – take him in her arms and make a fuss of him:

"Zere, m' li'le king; zere, it's nozing; zere, your Razanne's here m' darling; zere, zere..."

Razanne, where are you? My uncle's dead, Uncle's dead! Uncle, who had come all the way here on a journey of love, to promise me that his affection was always with me... Uncle, who loved without ever showing it, whose hardness concealed a tender heart – Uncle is dead!

I walked over the fields that stretched flat into the distance. It was the season of the lettuce harvest: labourers, hunched over the ground, were cutting the green balls and stacking them in heaps. I glimpsed them in a fog, through the tears that ran down to my chin.

Uncle, my uncle!

I must have gone as far as the River, but I did not see it. Then

213

I came to again in the abbey garden. Over there a black shadow was coming towards me, book in hand: the Father Prior, taking his walk before the afternoon rest.

"Brother Irenaeus... but... what's up with you?"

I was facing him, deathly pale, my eyes brimming.

"What's the matter, Brother? What's going on?"

"Nothing, Father, nothing. Let me alone. Nothing."

He could not have understood. He did not know who Razanne was, and that it was her, only her that I needed. He did not know who Uncle was, and that a part of me had just died, had just been torn from me.

There was no one here that could have understood. *Let me alone, it's nothing, it'll pass. Nothing has happened to me. Let me alone.*

Loneliness, my closest friend,
loneliness, my fellow traveller,
here you are again beside me,
you will never let me go.
You stand by me, no one else does,
loneliness, my closest friend...

I took up my books and my work again. The lectures were beginning in a few weeks; I must be ready.

In the chancel during services I clutched my missal absently. Both heaven and earth were empty.

Loneliness, my closest friend...

9

My lectures commenced at the end of October. They were intended for the whole community, but were scheduled for an hour on Sunday afternoons: people were free not to attend.

About two thirds of the monks were present in the great hall, its windows open to the valley and to the River down below. I began at the furthest remove, by describing the land of Israel to them, that land that was, for the Jews, proof of God's election. It was more than their possession: it was the pledge that God had chosen them, that God was with them. It was a land with the attributes of divinity, with a mythical status; for its sake each Jew was ready to give his blood, his soul.

They listened, with attention or indifference. There had been, there would be, so many talks in their lifetimes! I gave the best of myself. It was my way, the only way I had left now, of loving them – of being one of them.

Week by week, the panorama unfolded. The village, the synagogue – Jesus' own parish – the markets, the festivals, the Jewish liturgy of the time: a scenario was taking shape that conjured up a Jew's everyday life – that daily life from which God is never absent, where every event is prefaced by a blessing that sets it into the context of a wider, all-embracing future.

I expounded these blessings to them one by one, in the original Hebrew. I do not believe any of my brothers knew Hebrew: but I endeavoured to have them savour the sonorities of that language of peasants and priests, a language at once crude and immeasurably rich, with extraordinarily complex resonances. Like the land, the language of Israel was a gift of God, a promise and a pledge of his presence.

They listened, sometimes in rather smaller numbers, but apparently with interest. Winter had arrived: I had not forgotten my wound, but I dwelt on it less.

It's you, God, that are always the subject; it's of you, after all, that I talk day in day out.

And yet you seem to me more and more absent. I used not to imagine any relationship with you but love, impassioned love. Is this now the tepid indifference of old couples who have lived together too long? I could not endure that, with you.

I had set out on a path of adventure and exploration: and here I am now, a teacher. Is dust from the blackboard going slowly to smother my irrepressible God?

215

As weeks of study went by, to be followed by other weeks – a future without incident and maybe, maybe, without hope – something began to break out inside me that I had almost forgotten: sexual desire.

It was an overpowering, overwhelming desire that I no longer knew how to control. Did I, in any case, have the wish to control it? Chastity is only possible if it is driven by a life that outpaces it, just as a frenzied *farandole* ends up by getting the most stubborn, the most stiff-jointed and the crippled to join in the dance.

But nothing, in reality, was driving me any longer. My craving – powerful, domineering, derisive – was gaining the upper hand. It was becoming an unruly animal, wayward, uncontrollable. Wild.

Sometimes I resorted once again to the lonely pleasure of my boyhood. That residuary sexual activity is only as potent as the fantasies that accompany it – the fantasies that it arouses and that give it a semblance of life. And the fantasies that were assailing me I could only draw from my own memories.

Women were so far off! But, like a diabolical round-dance, the characters from my Greek ceramics kept coming to unfold their mocking beauty in my loneliness, which they began to populate. Then after them came, in dim outline, the *ragazzi* of Rome and Naples, brazen, scoffing, hand at the ready, eyes cheeky and enticing.

I did not believe that I had really looked at them, still less that their image had imprinted itself on me to that degree. They mingled with the *Kalos Myscoses* of the museums of the South, of the *Magna Græcia* that I had so much admired, and they awoke in me something unknown till then that alarmed me: a desire that I cannot name, a desire whose nature and form – vague, ill-defined, but importunate – I did not recognize.

I did not like the direction things were taking at all. I rejected these fantasies, warding off their every onslaught, but a feeling of danger, ungovernable as the craving itself, seized me by the throat.

I buried myself in my studies, like an ostrich in its hole in the sand.

* * *

We were just completing a long voyage: at the end of it one could begin to discern the face of Jesus, his feelings as a believing Jew, his innermost thoughts, even, indwelt as they were by a pervasive liturgy – just as the first green patches were starting to be discernible in the valley as it emerged from winter. I was now ready to embark on the key phase of the course, the rereading of some passages from the Gospels in the light of all this.

I had informed the community of my intentions at the end of one of the lectures: what would follow was research, in an area little explored. If we were to engage with it, it would require an active approach on their part. It would not be enough just to listen: they would have to take part in this research themselves. There would be exchanges of view, to discuss theories and to assess the material that I was sharing with them.

For me too this would be an experiment – to ascertain their state of mind each Sunday. Did they support my methodology; or were they just onlookers, filling up the vacuum of an empty afternoon?

I suggested that they gave me their opinion before embarking on this process: those who wanted it to go ahead need only drop a note into my pigeonhole. If everyone was in agreement, we would proceed: it would surely be exciting.

I waited. During the week there was one note, then two, at the back of the pigeonhole.

Excitement was not in the abbey's prospectus.

The position was clear. By a brief note pinned up in the common room, I announced that the lecture would not take place the next Sunday – nor on the Sundays following.

So I was totally isolated within the community – with no activity to undertake, physical or intellectual. There was the magazine to keep going, and the welcoming: but, please, no rocking the boat! Get up in the morning, go to bed at night. Be friendly, smiling, colourless, odourless, flavourless. Search for a rootless God that I no longer knew how to reach.

217

Become in fact part of the River, in its sluggish course. The water came from who-knows-where upstream, maybe from the mountains, maybe from the forests. It departed downstream, watering other valleys and flowing out, presumably, into the wide ocean that stretched to the Caribbean.

But, as for us, we were there on a few hundred metres of sandy riverbank where the River seemed unchanging. Its tomorrow would be the same as its yesterday; the only subtle change was in the light, the fleeting light that illumined eternity.

10

"Brother Irenaeus, please come and see me at the end of the morning."

It's a note from Father Gerard in his small, neat hand. What does he want me for?

"Brother, as you know, they're getting ready for an international congress of abbots in Rome in a few months. Nobody these days can speak Latin fluently, and the organizers are looking for simultaneous interpreters. Do you feel competent to take on this task, and are you willing to go?"

Was I competent? For sure. Was I willing? Of course – to see my city, to be on the move. *Agreed. Reckon me in.*

"Dear Mark,
Thanks for your letter. So you've been appointed master of novices: you're one of those people that inspire confidence. Not so with me. Mark, I don't know what's happening... I don't want to talk to you about it; not now.

I've been summoned to the Rome Congress as an interpreter: I'll give you an account of it.

God bless you, Mark. *Ciao.*"

It was a Roman September. The city, battered into a stupor by the summer sun, was recovering a bit of freshness and life.

The hill had not changed; but the huge building was now full of father abbots, who had gathered from all over the world.

I took my seat in a narrow cubicle like a telephone booth. Wearing headphones I began to translate, translate... Speeches were uninteresting, expositions laboured: nothing ever happens on conference platforms. It is in the corridors, during chance encounters, or ones that have been adeptly prearranged, that the real discussions take place, that the conclusions are worked out.

As I translated, rivulets of sweat trickled slowly down my calves. The heat was oppressive, as oppressive as the tedium.

We used to have free time between two and four – a holy interval when even God takes a siesta, since Rome's churches close. I would put on my jeans and immerse myself once more in the city.

Never had I found it so beautiful, indolent and voluptuous. At that time of day there were few people in the streets: the odd tourists, and *ragazzi* on holiday. When I saw one of them, I kept my distance, walking by in the sun, something never done in Rome.

I was instinctively taking care of myself: *Kalos Myscos...*

That particular day my meanderings took me to the foot of the hill. Traffic was moving slowly: Rome, crushed by the heat, was catching its breath.

I went in the direction of the temples – among the oldest in the city – that rise in the middle of a garden of oleanders stretching along the left bank of the Tiber. Behind the temple, circular and exquisite, of the Vestal Virgins stands a rectangular edifice that used to be called the "Temple of Manly Fortune". Each of the columns of its peristyle – erect, muscular and capped with an acorn of Corinthian leaves – reminded the informed visitor what its dedication had been.

Having nothing to do, I looked around the temple. It was approached by several steps, and at the top I caught sight of a typical woman tourist sitting in the shade of the columns: shorts, sunburnt thighs, tired appearance. Then I heard a high-pitched laugh: a kid was prancing around her chirping, "*Moneta, moneta!*"

I took a step forwards and discovered the reason: in her slumped position, the exhausted tourist was showing her two ample breasts.

The child was circling her: he had his hand to his flies and was massaging them frantically.

At the foot of the steps a bigger boy is watching the scene. I can only see his golden hair.

He notices me and comes up to me with a smile:

"She's a smasher, eh, sir! You like her?"

"Not particularly. And you?"

Blond as a Slav, he has a rather large nose and almond-shaped eyes.

"Oh me, I'm too small; I'm fifteen, but my family call me *piccolo*. You want to see the theatre?"

At the end of the street the Teatro di Marcello is offering the cool shade of its ancient colonnades.

"Yes, why not?"

"Can I come with you? You give me a *moneta*, and I'll show you round."

"Listen, I haven't any money, and in any case I already know..."

But the kid is trotting along beside me.

"What's your name?"

"Kikko. Say, sir, do you want to see my *cazzo*?"

I talk Italian well, but that word doesn't have a place in my vocabulary, I've not heard it on the hill.

"*Cazzo*? What's that?"

He stops and turns towards me, beside himself with excitement.

"It's this, sir, it's this!"

And there in the open street he undoes his trousers.

I almost die.

"You're crazy. Put it back. Off with you!"

We're passing beneath the Roman arches of the theatre. Kikko is talking non-stop at my side, but I'm barely listening. The place is completely deserted. Everywhere among the ruins scrawny cats are going, coming, vanishing.

The shade is cool; I've rested my elbow on the shaft of a column.

By now Kikko has come right up to me: his face is at the same level as mine. I've turned to stone and don't move. He's placed his lips gently onto mine. His lips part. I return his kiss.

One moment, one century later, Kikko has vanished; I'm alone.

I've escaped. *Get away, get away! Regain my hilltop, my earphones, the tedious speeches, my own self: Brother Irenaeus, graduate monk, serving the order. Serving God.*

What terrifies me is what I've felt: pleasure, smothered for so long; my body, reawakening. But to what end? And how far would it go? "Death begins at the very point where pleasure begins"... Anything is possible, so where might I be carried by this mighty wave I cannot control?

I was shattered and in a state of shock. What had they done with me, those people I had entrusted my life to? All that conflict, that fighting inch by inch of the way, the persistence in that adventure in spite of my family, in spite of myself? Was this the outcome? "You will arrive"...

"Una piccola avventura non fa male": yes, that's what they say. But I'm not interested in this "little" adventure. A life has greater weight, greater value.

At once I took a bicycle and rode along the Tiber all the way to St Peter's. The church had just opened, and there were few people in the huge nave. I looked for a confessional. *"Italiano"*: a Franciscan was reading his prayer book within the shadow of the box.

I fell on my knees at his feet. The confessionals in the Vatican have no grille: his face was almost touching mine. *Unclean, Father, my face is unclean, don't come near!*

I told him everything, the theatre, its shadows, Kikko...

He heard me out, then smiled:

"It's nothing, Brother; nothing has happened. You will say a *Pater noster* over the Apostle's tomb. Go in all peace."

So everything was coming to an end on a tombstone.

No, I did not go "in all peace". It was true, nothing much had happened. But I was in danger. One kiss could be the ruin of a life.

221

MICHEL BENOÎT

I was unwilling, unable, to stand by as my own life crumbled away. Something had to be done.

I had offered up my life, given it up, entrusted it, to those men, my brothers, and to their system: "You will arrive"…

I had ended up not just at an impasse, but in a situation of dire peril – peril that I alone was in a position to appreciate, and to avert.

Since there was no alternative, I would resume my life, in order to safeguard it.

That evening, from my window on the hilltop, I caught sight of the friezes of the Theatre of Marcellus, just projecting above the ochre roofs in the setting sun. Rome was slipping into its nocturnal silence.

Michel, your life is yours and no one else's; once again you must take a decision.

Loneliness, my closest friend…

11

"I know maybe what you should do."

It's a Jesuit friend; we're sitting in a bar near the Palais du Luxembourg. The "Jes", he knows a mass of people; he's a one-man encyclopedia. And he likes me a lot; he wants to help me.

"Iré, do you know Father Denis?"

"The Tioumliline chap?"

"Yes. You know him?"

To be sure, I know him. Everybody knows him. I've never actually seen him, but he's been much talked about. He's a monk, a Frenchman, who founded a Catholic monastery after the war in Morocco, in a remote village in the Atlas. There had been headlines in the newspapers, books, fantastic publicity: "Christian monastery on Islamic territory", "The cross raised: challenge to Muslims", "Summer conferences at Tioumliline: record attendance this year", "Christianity and Islam: a new understanding"…

Etcetera. Tioumliline had lived under the spotlights; then suddenly had vanished. There was no more mention of it. The celebrity-founder, Father Denis – what had become of him?

But my Jesuit friend had met him.

"You ought to go and see him. He's quite old; he lives in the Paris area now, with people who are mentally handicapped."

Mentally handicapped? What does that mean? Lunatics?

"Listen: go and see. Believe me, it's extraordinary, but it's true. Go along."

All right, I'll go. Father Denis is a recommendation. But even so, mentally handicapped...

I had returned to the abbey after the Congress – with the thanks of the Father Abbot Primate:

"No, no: you're an excellent interpreter; you've done a fine job!"

A fine job...

I had taken a nasty throw from Kikko. That short, fleeting encounter in the shadows of the *teatro di Marcello* had left me stunned. I was now picking myself up very gingerly, feeling my ribs.

Una piccola avventura... Not something I wanted.

To see my male identity gradually gnawed away, to become perhaps one day womanlike, a bit this and a bit that, in Gregorian packaging: no thank you. To bring fantasies back to life that were instantly repellent, and yet find pleasure in them: no thank you. To exist no more, yet flirt with a sensuality that did exist, and fool the spectators: no, thank you!

I would not be fooling myself – nor God either, supposedly at least.

Cyrano, flaunt your plumes again! I went to see Father Gerard, smiling and friendly as always.

"Yes, I understand, Brother. (*He doesn't understand, he can't understand.*) Go and have a meeting with Father Denis. And if God wants you there, he'll know how to make it clear."

What God wants, I don't know. But I do know what I want: to stay on my feet.

* * *

A house on the main street of the village, on the edge of a wood. A high wall, entrance gates open, gravelled drive. Behind, a garden. To the right, against the wall, what must be a garage.

The house has the well-to-do look of Île-de-France residences: two storeys, and an attic with dormers half-open.

"Then it's you, Brother Irenaeus? Come in, if you don't mind our squalor. It's not the abbey here!"

The tone of voice is light, bantering. Father Denis wears his monk's habit with elegance. He has a mane of white hair; thick, bushy eyebrows, also white; and beneath them eyes that are lively, alert, penetrating, intense.

He's someone, this man.

"Come along. This way: this is our common room, our lounge, our chapter house – call it what you will."

The room is lined with books. In the angle of two walls are benches of dark wood, placed very low, spread with bright-coloured cushions.

"All this is Tioumliline furniture. Those benches of Atlas cedar were designed by Maître —, the famous architect. Their dimensions are based on the golden section."

Father Denis is very relaxed; he has sat down and crosses his legs, a worldly posture forbidden to monks. But he's apparently one to maintain a very loose attitude to "observance".

"Well then?"

Well, what? I've not much to say; I've come to listen. A silence falls.

Then the door opens abruptly: a young man comes in waving his arms, walking jerkily but fast. It's hard to guess his age. He comes towards us, but his eyes are straying to right and left, without resting on anyone.

"Well, Ricou, what's the matter?"

"Fa-a-ather, it's no good with the plates, they keep brea-a-aking; I can't ma-a-anage."

"Come along, Ricou, go and find Luisa and sort it out with her. You can see very well that I'm busy."

Eric, known as Ricou, is son of a big family of French industrialists; he's mentally handicapped. He goes off again with his uneven gait, talking to himself.

"There, you see: these are my brothers now. Tioumliline was the adventure of a lifetime. When we had to leave – politics – I didn't want to go back to my abbey straightaway, just like that. I still had some potential, some things to achieve. You understand?"

I understand – all too well in fact. While he's speaking, I slowly fall under his spell, that masterly ease of manner that must have disarmed the French settlers, the Moroccan peasants, the king of Morocco himself. Father Denis is straightforward, but regal. And he knows it.

"The life we led over there was too intense, too stimulating. I'll certainly return to my abbey, one day... But I wanted one more adventure in life, something in line with my capacities and with what I'd become, a tired old man. Then I found this house, and these disabled chaps who'd always dreamt of being monks. The only thing was, none of our abbeys would have it. Do you understand?"

I understood – completely. I could hardly see Ricou, with his absent look and dangling arms, capering along beside Father Du Bellay de Saint-Pons.

"These disabled folk aren't mad, you know; quite the contrary! They have a feel for things, for reality, that society's attitude to them cannot suppress. They're very close to the Gospel, very. Here we've adapted monastic life to their capabilities. That's what I've brought to them. They've brought me all the rest: to be genuine every moment, to shun all that's abstract, to make do with little, to live simply. It's a rough school, but I'm learning. The most handicapped aren't the people you think they are. In God's eyes I'm more handicapped than them."

We talked for a long time, till the shadows began encroaching on the garden.

"Tell your father abbot that, if he's willing to let you come here and help us, and live with us, you'll be welcome."

I'm moving the car forwards over the gravel. Suddenly there's a drumming on the car window: it's Ricou.

"Are you going then, Brother? You'll come back and see me? Say you will."

This time the eyes in that disfigured face are staring straight at me. He's grinning all over, jumping from one leg to the other, clutching at my arm.

"Yes, Ricou, I'll come back to see you; it's a promise. But now move away, I have to leave."

"What? Speak louder, I can't hear very well."

The face that was creased with a thousand smiles suddenly turns serious:

"I'm n-nandicapped; but that doesn't matter, you know: there are things – you don't hear them properly with your ears, you hear them here…"

And he bangs his fist on his chest.

Ricou, you don't realize that someone else said that before you, a poet-airman. You haven't read St-X; you can hardly read at all. But evidently you don't need to read.

As the car speeds off in the direction of the abbey, I repeat Ricou's phrase: "You don't hear properly with your ears!"

Yes, there's something there, in that house in the village. Whether God wants me there, I don't know. But I can picture myself there, perhaps.

For sure.

I had a talk with Father Gerard. I told him what I had seen, what attracted me: a desperate experiment, as desperate perhaps as my dreams.

I did not tell him that I was wanting most of all to save myself from something desperately dangerous – the danger of a slow but relentless disintegration.

He heard me out sympathetically, as always.

"Yes. You might well go and give Father Denis a helping hand – at least for a while, for a year or two. The abbey will send you. Talk to the community about it this evening, at the chapter meeting."

I'm amazed at so ready an agreement – no objection, no reluctance. What lies hidden behind Father Gerard's smile? Is

it support? Or rather – also – relief at the prospect of having a problem for the abbey sorted out?

The chapter meeting listens to my brief account of what has happened and to my plan. There's no reaction. Evidently no one wants to discourage me; no one seems to be opposed to my departure, or to be sorry about it.

I wonder in the end if I am not doing the abbey, as well as Father Denis, a service in going off to serve the handicapped.

But this is not the time for regretful musings: tomorrow Father Nicolas will be taking me over in the van. I pile my papers and notes – the most precious things I have – into cardboard boxes, along with some clothes: a monk's packing is soon done.

It's grey on the highway leading to the house in the village. Father Nicolas drives in silence, pipe in mouth. Suddenly I realize that I've not even been to see the River. Not to worry: the abbey is only an hour's drive from the village; I'll be back.

Father Nicolas's pipe has gone out. He's grave, solemn, with a bitter crease in his lips that I don't recognize.

As we draw near the village and can make out in miniature the house at the edge of the wood, he slows down and finally speaks:

"What the hell are you going to do there, Brother Irenaeus? What's a chap like you going to do there? What's the reason?"

And then, after an interval, while we turn the last corner:

"Do you want me to tell you what I think? You won't come back to the abbey – ever again. You're not going on secondment, you're leaving. And I'm driving the vehicle you're leaving the abbey in. For me it's…"

The sentence is left hanging; we're arriving. I turn to look at him. A tear seems to me to be hanging, too, from his eyelid, which quivers. *Father Nicolas smokes too much: it's the pipe.*

But the pipe has gone out.

227

Part Five

The trapdoor

1

"The ways of the Spirit are ins... insc... ins..."

"Inscrutable!"

We're at table. Everyone's there, in a rectangle: Ricou, Raymond, Jean-Pierre, Max, Father André, Luisa... a gallery of Daumier-style portraits.

Father Denis has decided that at the start of each meal at the village house we'll have a short reading, since as we dine there'll be talking, as in a family. Marcel has been given the book and is having difficulty deciphering it, while the soup steams in his plate.

"Inscrutable! It's a rather complicated word; it means that you can't see anything there. A bit like you, eh, Father André?"

Father Denis, regal as ever, is sitting enthroned in the midst of this extraordinary court.

"OK then. Marcel, that's enough, leave the book; we'll come back to it tomorrow. Hey! Father André, mind! You're spilling salt on the tablecloth."

Father André is an elderly monk from Tioumliline who has followed his prior here, rather than go and bury himself in his abbey's infirmary on his return from Morocco. It is not that he can't see at all; he sees right in front of him through an angle of ten degrees. Father André loves spicy dishes: he adds salt and pepper to every serving, but he regularly misjudges, and his shaking hand sprinkles the tablecloth, the bread or his neighbour's plate.

"Father André, that brings ba-a-ad luck!"

Father André gives Ricou no reply. He never replies, speaks very little and always ends up smiling, as if to say: "Well yes, what do you expect? I'm the way I am. You'll see when you get there!" He lost a leg in the war, in 1918, and the rhythmical tap-tap of his wooden leg marks his rare comings and goings.

231

There are smiles and laughter aplenty in the house. Apparently that's normal among the handicapped: their development has been arrested somewhere along the line, and they have the ready and infectious jollity of children. Father Denis maintains this atmosphere with mischievous irony: it seems to be accepted that nothing will be taken seriously, least of all the various residents' eccentricities.

"Father André, don't forget, please, that it's me that washes the linen!"

Luisa, for her part, wears an almost permanent smile. When momentarily she turns serious or solemn, her round face takes on a look of gentle, almost resigned, suffering.

This community was a complete medley of misfits, who had found themselves there partly by chance and partly by favour of Father Denis.

And, yes, there was one woman, Luisa. Originally from Portugal, she had lived in France for ever. When still very young she had got herself a child, whose father had vanished into thin air. She had brought her son up single-handed, and he was now twenty and working. Luisa was the house mother.

"We're a religious community of lay-folk, but we're also a home for the disabled; in a home there has to be a mother, a mum. Luisa, I consecrate you mum of the house. Would you please go and fetch the next course? Marcel, move yourself, go and help Luisa. Go on!"

Luisa looked after the cooking, organized the housework and made sure everywhere was clean. Father Denis used to call her "our Mother Abbess", which made her laugh. Her room was next to mine. Luisa, then, was my mother, a mother only slightly older than me: I never imagined that she could be anything else.

She had viewed my arrival with relief: Father Denis overawed her somewhat, and she found herself having to run this unusual house on her own. But Luisa was conscientious, she worked from morn till night, and the premises were well kept.

Each day at the start of the morning Father Denis had instituted "the meeting". Luisa brought in coffee, rather stronger than the breakfast coffee, and we had a three-way discussion as we stirred our drinks.

"Well now, Brother Irenaeus, call this our inner chapter, if you like. This is where the spirit of the house is being built up. It's more effective than the abbey chapter, believe me!"

Always this hint of ridicule, of irony. Father Denis is mindful of the lessons of May '68: everything here will be reinvented from scratch, because nothing's the same as elsewhere. The meeting is also the time when he talks to us, at length.

"Don't forget that we're *all* handicapped here. It's only a matter of degree, if that. Some handicaps are more obvious than others. Ricou is visibly handicapped; that's why society has sidelined him. But you, Brother Irenaeus, you're handicapped somewhere too. The only thing is, it shows less, or maybe your handicaps are recognized and shared by society at large. Our brothers will help you find them, and accept them – and accept yourself!"

Luisa's been with them a long time, and she smiles: she's already accepted being what she is. But will *I* be able to accept? Where's this new venture going to take me?

Downwards. I have to go deeper down into myself, lower still. I'm no longer anything in this place. Qualifications, learning, experience – none of that exists for them. For them, I've only just that moment come into being. The Church doesn't recognize them: it's an "experimental" house, tolerated by the order because no one can refuse Father Denis anything. Officially I've been seconded to them by the abbey – even though I know at the bottom of my heart that this has been the abbey's neat solution to the problem I've been setting them.

Seconded? or banished among the disabled? *Don't ask questions, my lad. After all, it's you that wanted it. Move forwards. Move forwards today, and tomorrow you'll see.*

"There, it's the gree-een vegetables; I need to wa-a-ater them, and then get rid of the wee-eeds."

Ricou, in working clothes, walks along the kitchen garden paths, talking at the top of his voice. Or else, he talks to the vegetables. His job is to look after that patch of ground, and that's his way of gardening. If I don't interrupt, he'll spend the whole morning talking to his plants, explaining to them what he'll need to do to coax them into growing as they should. That's his handicap: he approaches real life through the spoken word. But if things don't fall in with what he says, he becomes completely distraught, and there's a crisis.

Father Denis has put me in charge of work:

"If you like, my lad" – he speaks to me familiarly now – "you're Cellarer. As there's barely three of us, we've a whole heap of titles to share out. Work with the chaps: that'll be the best way to become one of us."

So I've taken up the spade again and spend long hours turning over the soft earth of Île-de France – along with Ricou, who capers around beside me talking to the spade.

"Max, we're going to read the story of the Good Samaritan. You know the Good Samaritan? Sa-ma-ri-tan!"

"'es, 'es, Sm-errri-t'; Max knows, Max knows't well, ver' well!"

Max is a deaf mute from birth. He lip-reads, and he's learnt several sounds by placing his hand against the speaker's vocal chords. On top of that he has a mental disability, which doesn't stop him being quite sharp at picking up plenty of things. Max smiles all the time, amid constant gesturing. He has a prominent stomach, a prominent behind, and smokes Virginia tobacco. His upper-middle-class family from the North has brought him up perfectly. He'd upset a flower vase by jumping aside to let Luisa go through a door ahead of him:

"Aft' you, Ma'am, p'eese; aft' you!"

Max has a love of life: he savours our table plonk as though it were a fine Bordeaux, rolls his cigarettes like a connoisseur and bursts into peals of laughter whenever Father Denis smiles.

Max is my comfort and joy. Each morning I read a passage from the Gospels with him and explain it to him.

Explain the Gospel to someone who's deaf, Father Notker: you didn't teach me that in Rome!

But Max understands; and his jowls quiver with laughter every time:

"Max 'derstood, Max 'derstood, nice, nice B'other 'Renee's!"

I do indeed explain the Gospel to him in my own words, enunciating carefully so that he can lip-read. But he doesn't so much understand the Gospel as live it. He turns into each of the characters in turn: the Samaritan is him; and the injured man huddled by the roadside, that's him too!

Max has long been at home in the Gospel, a land that I have only entered with my head. In truth, I begin to wonder which of us is actually explaining the text to the other. Father Denis is right: I know nothing – or rather, what I know is nothing compared with the knowledge that Max has.

2

A large shed at the corner of the garden has been converted into a chapel. Everything inside is beautiful: exposed stonework, furnishings from Tioumliline, icons.

Three times a day, and once more before bedtime, we gather there for regular worship. Father Denis has quite simply taken over the form of service used by parish priests: a few psalms, a few short readings.

But, such as it is, it's still a feat for the mentally handicapped. Yes, they sing, stand up and genuflect at nearly the right time, and listen to a reading by one of the "abled". The contrast with what I have lived through is absolute. Our byzantine discussions over liturgical details seem ridiculous here in the face of this strange fact: people with no education, with nothing to recommend them, disabled people, are engaging in the most esoteric activity there could be, the regular celebration of a Catholic liturgy!

My brain's undergone a complete clean-out. Everything I've

struggled so long to achieve, the wellspring of so many confrontations – here, all that has become pointless. How could we – we the "normal" – have torn each other apart to such an extent on something that, here, seems straightforward and natural?

Of course they sing out of tune; of course they don't understand everything. But when I watch them each day in chapel – Ricou of the thousand smiles, Max with his gesticulations, Father André and his wooden leg, Luisa sad and cheerful – I wonder whether those doughty warriors I've been tilting at are not just windmills.

Adapt – I need to adapt myself to this slightly mad, out-of-the-ordinary existence. I need to enter into the traditions of this house, make them my own. I'm here, in theory, for one year: but might I find here, perhaps, something to live for, something to fight for, something to build?

The morning meeting takes place in Father Denis's study. It's here he spends the best part of the day, seated at his table, receiving various callers.

The shelves of the bookcase facing him are covered with photographs, many of them yellowed: Father Denis arriving in Morocco, building Tioumliline, kissing the king's foot and hand, greeting government officials... and then success, French and Islamic intelligentsia at his side, international conferences... Father Denis always at the centre.

The foundation of Tioumliline had been planned and supported by the French government; they had seen in it a key element in the establishment of colonial power in Morocco. Was Father Denis aware that he had been playing the game of financial interests and of French government policy at the time? That question was never broached between us. Maybe he was sincerely convinced that he had acted for God alone. So deeply compromised is the Church with the right-wing forces that underpin it in return, that people are no longer able to pass sound judgement on their actions.

Anyhow the politics had changed. Independence had not only become a fact, but an attitude. Departure became necessary – evidence that Tioumliline had never been an independent venture, that the holy-water sprinkler followed the sword and shared its fortunes. The lovely estate became royal property, and the young Hassan II undertook to maintain it. But the monks had got their return ticket.

Nothing was left of it all but those photos, with Father Denis mounting guard over them like a sentry at a memorial.

"It's my graveyard, my mortuary chapel!"

He had returned to France by a roundabout route and had encountered the charismatic movement that was coming to birth on the debris of the May '68 barricades.

The "base communities" that I had got to know in Rome with *Ora sesta* took a special form in France, called Charismatic Renewal. The theory was simple: believers had discovered that the Holy Spirit existed and that they could tap into the Spirit directly. This filling with the Spirit was received during worship meetings of a very special kind. It was mediated by "pastors", who gathered around them a drove of charismatics with hands a-tremble and eyes enlarged through experiencing the Spirit.

Communities were formed, then very quickly expanded and developed into an organization. At the outset they were regarded with mistrust by the authorities, who saw their flocks escaping them. These communities were a motley assemblage of people disillusioned with the Council, anarchists of every hue, idealists, neurotics and the generous-hearted – all sincere in their approach, all on the Spirit's wavelength. The movement had what was in effect a distinctly right-wing orientation and was often tinged with an innocent and naive fundamentalism.

The bishops had realized that this was something they could not ignore: when the Church is unable to control things, it has always had a remarkable talent for adjusting to them, infiltrating them and taking them over.

So the charismatic movement had ended up by being officially recognized, like the "base communities" in Italy. There were charismatic bishops, charismatic priests and charismatic members of religious orders.

237

The charismatic movement played mainly on the sensitive string – the emotionalism, the exaggeration – of feelings displayed in public, and on the need for reassurance. Several theologians had hurriedly constructed a doctrine showing that the charismatics had invented nothing and were in the mainstream of Catholic tradition. The "baptism of the Spirit" experienced during ecstatic worship-meetings led to the creation of a cadre of initiates.

The genius of the Church had been to capture this movement in time, in order to control it. The excessive clericalism of the laity, which was burgeoning in France as in Italy, was considered a lesser evil: priests were a vanishing species, and lay-folk were effectively taking on their dominant position and their authority. If they adopted the priests' quirks and their appetite for spiritual power, that would change nothing for the flock, passing as they were from one tyranny to another.

It was on this islet, about to become a continent, that I was setting foot, without being too much aware of it. Father Denis had received the baptism of the Spirit. We were in frequent touch with charismatic groups, which considered us to be among their number. To care for the handicapped was well regarded, the thing to do. A few tens of kilometres from the house a community called "The Road" – the road to Emmaus – was growing fast. They used to come to us; and we often used to go to them.

Why shouldn't I too take a few steps along this road, after all? I've nothing to lose. My path at the abbey is reaching a dead-end, shut in on every side. Go for the open road: at the other end, maybe, is life?

"Alleluia! Brother Irenaeus, hallo, alleluia!"

A load of girls in long skirts, with childlike faces devoid of make-up and hair drawn back or in plaits, is getting out of "The Road" minivan.

"Brother Irenaeus, how are you?"

"Fine, thanks, I'm fine."

"Aaamen, amen! And old Father André?"

"Oh! his aching joints still, you know, his wooden leg…"

"Grief!... Oh, Ricou, you well? Alleluia!"

The sect has a vocabulary of its own, expressing the predominant human feelings in three words:

"Alleluia" – it's going well, it's all fine, that's brilliant;

"Amen" – oh good, that's all right, OK;

"Grief" – what a shame, oh so sorry.

With that one can get around, it's all there is to know. Further shades of meaning are expressed with the eyes, hands and face. It's a good idea, communicating with three words; it avoids fuss. There's the good, the bad and the middling. Life's a lot simpler that way.

3

The setting sun has just disappeared from my room. It's a great time of peace in the house, after the labours of the afternoon. I've spent almost all the time with Raymond, in the shed behind the chapel. Raymond carves wooden crosses from boards of sippo wood, passing them to Marcel, who's supposed to rub them down by hand: they're to be sold as first communion crosses. But Marcel has an amazing gift – the gift for doing nothing. And if I'm not present, those two will soon murder each other.

Life has settled down, in a strange, unreal way: Ricou, Max and the others, Father André, his wooden leg, Luisa, King Denis... a tranquil house, a sleepy village. *Michel, are you going to sink into a gentle slumber as well?* The months pass, winter comes, a very mild winter that year.

Is this what's come over you, the sleep of hibernation?

There's a noise of tyres crunching on the gravel. I crane my head: it is the abbey's Citroën. A large, heavy body is lowering itself to the ground; a car door slams.

"Father Nicolas, what a joy!"

"Irenaeus, I was passing not far from here. I said to myself: 'I'll go and see him.'"

239

"Excellent idea; come in, it's cold."

Nicolas greets Father Denis, and meets Luisa and some of the disabled. I've the feeling that he's avoiding my gaze, and I find his joviality a bit forced.

"Good then, I'll leave you: you must have things to talk about."

Father Denis, head held high, leaves the room.

Nicolas fills his pipe, then lights it painstakingly. Silence falls. I cannot say what, but something... yes, something seems different about him. Is he perhaps a little thinner? The bison from Vaud seems shrunken, less vigorous.

"Well then, Irenaeus," he has lifted his eyes behind the cloud of smoke, "what's new? How's it going?"

"Listen, Father Nicolas, it's going fine. But there's something that surprises me: I've had practically no news from the abbey. You're the first to come here in six or seven months. Almost no letters, nothing. Complete silence. What do you make of it? What does it mean?"

"Oh..." – wave of the hand, he's relighting his pipe: is he going to reply? – "you know... nothing; it's just that you're not there any more. People start by getting used to your absence, then they realize that they can get by without you, then they get by fine, and in the end they even forget you were there... It's a bit like that, I suppose."

"But, Nicolas, it's my community, I've surrendered my life to it, I've surrendered my life to them! We've lived together; it has shaped me, and I even think that I've shaped it a bit too. Isn't that so? I've kept my place there, after all!"

"Absolutely, Irenaeus, absolutely..."

Father Nicolas seems to me like an animal going to earth in a burrow: he doesn't want to reply; this conversation is infinitely painful for him.

"Absolutely... listen..."

He finally raises his head and looks me in the eye:

"I could be wrong, but I have the impression that you've given all you could, and that anything that might follow would be too much, more than people could take..."

"How do you mean, 'more than people could take'? But Father, I've given myself for life, I've been accepted for life. You can't cut a life into slices: 'this bit's good, that bit I'll throw out'!"

"But that's how it is!"

He thrusts himself forwards, face strained, pipe held away. He shouts almost:

"That's how it is, Irenaeus, that's how it is. They've taken the best of you, all the good you were able to give, and that was tremendous. You've helped us move from the old world to the new one, you've done a marvellous job; it's brought fresh life. And then, now..."

He slumps back into his armchair:

"Now, they're getting along without you, and they're quite happy. They've taken the best, and then, when it might be getting awkward, it's good riddance, or virtually."

He relights his pipe. It certainly keeps going out often enough. I cannot believe what Nicolas is saying. He's weary, you can see it in his face; something has got him down. But he repeats, hidden now behind his smoke:

"They've taken the best..."

There's a long silence. Then Nicolas shakes himself and gets up.

"Well then, I must go."

"What about Father Gerard?"

"He's fine. He never speaks of you – though it's him who ought to give the chapter news, if he has any. But you say, he doesn't write..."

"I'm about to write to him; it's for me to do it; I've been remiss. It's really strange here, you know!"

"Indeed it is! Wait a bit; leave it to him."

We're moving towards the car. Then, as if to change the subject:

"So tell me, Irenaeus, what do you people live on here?"

"What remains of the old friends of Tioumliline. So there's no financial problem, we're comfortable, in fact."

"Comfortable..."

He looks at the house, merging as it is into the dark night, into the silent village.

"Comfortable... Goodbye then, Iré, I'll be back."

I can't pray any more. Those long periods reserved for God, when I used to expose myself to his radiation, when I used to abandon myself to his presence – I still spend those periods in the chapel, but they're empty. The stones in front of me are bare, they loom above me oppressively. It's all over. That special dialogue – wordless, internal, living, life-giving – has been cut short, snapped like a fine thread stretched to breaking point.

Why, why has this happened?

But then... was it God I used to encounter? Or was it a facile echo?

During these times of prayer I feel like one of the stones in the wall opposite.

The waters of the River must still be flowing placidly down below. It's slow, of course, seems motionless sometimes; but even so it moves forwards, onward, at the foot of the abbey walls.

A kind of lassitude is coming over me: I've struggled too hard up to now. A rest here would be nice, maybe.

4

"Alleluia, Brother Irenaeus, welcome!"

Two girls are waiting for me when the bus arrives: I'm coming to spend the weekend with the charismatics. It'll make a bit of a change from the mentally handicapped – at least, I have to hope so. In their Île-de-France hamlet they've bought up four or five houses, their "homes", plus what's known here as the "château": an eighteenth-century manor house deep inside a park, which serves as headquarters, chapel and workshops. The charismatics don't seem short of money...

"You're staying at the château. It's easier, and pretty. Is that all right?"

"Absolutely, no problem."

"Amen! Give us your bag. We're coming with you."

The hamlet was dying, with no more than a few pensioners left. The arrival of the community has given it new life. Girls and young lads move up and down the single street, going from one "home" to another. Dress style is post-hippy, mixed with Hindu – long skirts of madras cotton, Nehru shirts for the lads; there's colour and exuberance in this fairy-tale scenario.

"Irenaeus, you know our pastor?"

He's a round man, with quick eyes and thick beard. He seizes hold of me, pulls me to him, wraps me in his arms and sticks his beard into my neck: this is the brotherly hug, the kiss of welcome. There's plenty of kissing in the community – brotherly and sisterly, of course. I gasp for air.

"Brother, be welcome. If you'll excuse me, the sisters of this home are waiting for me. We'll see each other at mass, and at the meal. He's staying at the château?"

"Yes, he's been put in the new wing."

"Aaamen, see you soon, Irenaeus, alleluia!"

So there I am, enveloped in the Holy Spirit, like an English sweet in its cellophane wrapper. All I have to do now is let it happen.

Mass: they're all there, men, women and children (there are several couples in the community).

The chapel occupies a beautiful room on the château's ground floor. From the windows you can see the lawn sloping gently down towards the main road.

Everyone's seated on the ground; the floor is covered with thick rugs. At the far end, behind a fine table decked out as an altar, is the elderly Dominican, the community's chaplain, in priestly vestments. He lives here, and it's here he'll end his long years.

A fellow in a white cassock-like gandoura, his long hair knotted with an elastic band, does the reading. Kids are larking about around his feet and right up to the altar: these are the community's children, and they rule the roost here. From time to time a mum gets up onto one knee, reaches out an arm and retrieves a youngster: it all happens very quietly.

"Aaamen!"

The reading has just finished; the congregation closes their eyes and raises their hands to their face for a short interlude of free prayer in the Spirit.

You have to be initiated to understand: in time everyone'll express in words or sounds what they feel. A gentle humming arises – moans, and unintelligible words – that merge into a pleasantish kind of harmony. There's no intermediate relay: we're in live contact with the Holy Spirit.

After mass I call on the old Dominican. It's actually for that purpose that I've come – to meet him.

He has one quite extraordinary quality: though he's been stone deaf for years, his answers to questions people put to him – which he doesn't hear – are always full of meaning for those who come to consult him.

So he has become an oracle, the community's Delphic priestess. When one goes to see "the Father", it's the Holy Spirit speaking directly through his mouth.

I find him sitting in his armchair, wearing a Dominican habit of grubby white. The study is dim, barely lit at all. Come what may, I've decided to have a go and to open my heart to him.

It's true: he can hardly hear and keeps fiddling with his hearing aid. Nonetheless, I feel that he's totally focussed on my presence. Behind thick round lenses his protruding eyes remain fastened on me.

I explain about leaving the abbey and about the house in the village. I don't talk to him of the virtual ostracism that I'm becoming conscious of. But this extraordinary man senses his interlocutors more than he hears them.

"Very well, Brother, very well" – the voice is faint and quavers a little. "Wait till the twelve months is up; let your superior take the initiative to get in touch and tell you the abbey's intentions for you. Come and see us often. I'll pray for you."

That's all. The oracle has spoken.

He's confirming Father Nicolas's advice.

* * *

Time passes gently, drop by drop, like a liqueur being distilled. The seasons seem to me less distinct here than on the bank of the River. Or might it be I that am less receptive to nature? Anyhow spring is already well advanced. Soon it'll be summer, and my life continues to run on, or rather run out, without my being able to hold it back.

None of those moments will I be able to live again; and what have I done with them?

There's one thing at least I can be grateful for: now that peace of mind has returned, my sexual feelings have abated. *Myscos* seems to have left the scene.

As no message has come, and summer has arrived, I pick up my pen.

Dear Father Gerard,

It is a year now that I have been here. I have found a place in this house. But it seems to me that I belong in the abbey. What should I do now? Can you give me your view?

The summer ends almost without my noticing: I'm waiting. The garden produces a full crop; Luisa periodically launches jam-making campaigns; the acid smell of stewed plums wafts around the house.

Eventually Father Gerard's reply arrives. At the abbey the telephone is only used in direst emergencies; serious matters are dealt with by letter.

His is short and clear.

You may return to the abbey, if you want – but on one condition, that you comply with observance in its entirety, that you accept our way of life as it is from now on, without wishing to have it changed.

"If you want" – in other words, I am not wanted. Nothing can debar me from going back, nothing short of a grave misdemeanour certified by Rome: Church law is explicit.

Father Gerard must have been aware of this. And he knows me. So he's setting conditions for my return of a kind that he has good reason to believe I'll not accept. Return to the abbey with an outlook no further than the River, with observance as the sole motive for living, surrounded – it must be certain – by general mistrust? No, that's a death I can no longer choose of my own free will.

And Father Gerard is aware of all that.

There was a day, long ago now, when I had placed my hands between his: they're now closing in and crushing me like a nut.

There's no choice: at the abbey I'm at risk; here I can live and be of use.

I've gone to speak to Father Denis: he listens to me gravely. He gives his agreement: "Stay, you are at home here."

Father Nicolas has returned as he promised. It's a damp November, and night has fallen. His car's there in the courtyard when I come down to dinner.

"Father Nicolas! You'll eat with us?"

"No, I have to be at the abbey this evening. I've been absent a lot this month, been driving a lot. Let's go and sit down for a moment."

I find him a bit bent, and definitely thinner. His features are drawn.

"Well then, have you had a reply from Father Gerard? The fact is, I haven't seen him for weeks."

I hand him the letter without a word. He reads it slowly, and his face darkens:

"There's no mistake, Irenaeus. They know you, and I know you. You're not a man to inflict a slow death on yourself. To put things as he has, it's to get rid of you without taking responsibility for it."

"Yes. That's just how I took it. I'm staying here."

"Here?"

He gives me a surprised look.

"But... for what kind of life?"

I reply to him gently:

"You know, Father Nicolas, I've stopped asking myself that question for several years now."

A silence. He mutters:

"I see..."

We part in the garden. Nicolas turns to me, his hand on the car door:

"Irenaeus, it's lucky you're not there. One can sense reaction coming from every side – from Rome, from the Provincial, from Father Gerard, who swims with the current. There was a time, just after the Council, when anything seemed possible. Now..."

He takes his seat ponderously:

"Now, we're returning to the past, while dressing it up otherwise. You wouldn't tolerate that."

And how does *he* tolerate it? Isn't it his own life he is reappraising, by way of the rebuff I have received?

"See you soon, Irenaeus!"

I watch the lights of his car moving away down the road. I pause there a moment motionless, while Father Nicolas disappears into the night.

5

It's a long winter this year. Every morning since Christmas, in the room in the attic, I've been giving an introduction to the Bible to those who are up to it – to some of the handicapped, and Luisa.

What a journey I've travelled since the high-powered teaching I gave at the abbey, so many... centuries ago! But these talks, which I prepare with care, mean as much to me as the others did. The passing on of knowledge doesn't draw its value from the level of the participants – be they teacher or pupils – but from the exchange that takes place, from the electric charge that passes to and fro.

Very basic it may all be, but the knowledge is not my property: it has been given me to dispose of for the benefit of others. Handicapped or not, no matter! Pass it on...

It's good in the attic, with the raw light of March flooding in. My own head is almost touching the studiously bent heads of my pupils: we're reading a passage from Genesis. With these beings that society regards as unfit I'm using, with some adaptation, the most up-to-date methods of exegesis.

A door opens: Father Denis comes to the bottom of the narrow staircase:

"Irenaeus, phone call for you, from the abbey. Come and take it in my study."

I rush down the stairs. What could be going on? The telephone, only in cases of emergency…

"Hallo?"

"Brother Irenaeus? It's Father Du Bellay."

"Yes, Father. What's going on?"

"Brother, Father Nicolas had an accident the day before yesterday, at daybreak. He was discovered in the crypt, dead. The burial's taking place this afternoon; the family are expected. Father Gerard realized that we'd almost forgotten to let you know."

"This afternoon? OK. I'll jump into the car and be there."

Father Du Bellay de Saint-Pons's voice was clear, businesslike, neutral. If the man's feeling any emotion, he's hiding it admirably.

Father Nicolas! My God, I had my suspicions, I ought to have known it, expected it. The strange feeling that I had at the time of his last visit here – what happened later? And what happened two days ago, that icy dawn by the River? And the crypt – why the crypt? What was he about to do there?

I'm pushing Father Denis's 2CV to the limit. *My, these cars are feeble, feeble! Get a move on, old lady, get a move on!* The minor roads flash by at high speed without my seeing them. I'm wholly elsewhere, in the medieval crypt barely touched by the first milky glimmer of that dawn two days ago. What happened at that precise moment?

Nicolas!

"We'd almost forgotten you": don't they heed anything then, even death, even friendship?

But what do they know of friendship anyhow? The friendship that bound us together, Nicolas and me, was a friendship of human beings. It had not been restructured by observance. The hand twisting your guts, the parched mouth, these human emotions – do they only feel them at the level of dumb animals?

Nicolas, Nicolas! Gone for ever, that pipe of yours, that twinkling eye, that warm heart – the heart that persuaded you to make one more detour, after all that driving you'd done, to come and say hallo to your friend... But why, Nicolas, why?

Suddenly the car emerges onto the bank of the River – that broad bend so familiar, yet always new. And there's the abbey bell tower looking out over the valley. Is it one year, or two, or more, since I've been here?

At the back of the church, towards the crypt, black shadows are moving quickly to and fro: I'm immediately aware of the uncustomary bustle that marks special occasions. Then all of a sudden I notice that I've forgotten to put on a habit: I am in lay clothes, and my trousers seem out of place among the rustling robes that are hastening downstairs.

I've pushed the door open. The crypt is dimly lit. In the centre, in front of the altar, is an open coffin. Nicolas, in formal habit and priest's stole, fills the narrow box. His countenance is at peace, as always with the dead. But there's a deep, tumescent cut across the forehead. What happened?

On benches along the walls sit black shadows, motionless. I sit down too: no one seems to have seen me. My lay attire rather sets me apart. What's taking place here concerns no one but the shadows – the true monks.

I've been here a long time without moving, by the box from which Nicolas's profile barely projects. Every now and then, in absolute silence, shadows stir, withdraw, advance. A few come up to touch my shoulder, without a word. *Mass is about to start; it's not the right moment; the family must have arrived from Switzerland.*

All of a sudden the crypt comes alive with light; the priests are entering in procession, while the bell begins its melancholy tolling over the valley. I awake to the fact that I'm in the front row, an anachronistic impediment to the service. I go to sit at the back, in the gloom, with the sparse lay congregation.

As the service proceeds, I realize that I've become a stranger to these men, to this world. Yet I've spent almost twenty years here, the best years of a life. *Michel, not the time for self-pity!* The mass is ending; the coffin, closed now, is lifted onto the shoulders of four monks. It's to be buried in our cemetery, by the apse of the church.

Nicolas, what happened?

It is only later that I learnt what they were willing to tell me, and guessed the rest.

For months Nicolas had been leading a disordered, crazy existence. He had dashed from worksite to worksite, devouring thousands of kilometres, sleeping in the car, returning seldom. The workshop's development was used to justify this escape onto the roads: did the abbey's finances not depend on it?

Then several weeks back Nicolas had complained of a sharp pain shooting across his chest. As often happens, he did not think it important. Father Gerard had insisted that he take medical advice.

During one visit – fleeting as always – Father Gerard had asked him the result of the medical check.

"Oh, the doctor! Yes, well… He said that it's my back. For years, you know, my back…"

No one had questioned this statement.

The procession is making its orderly way through the bare, cold church towards the exit. Black shadows, priests in violet, the coffin, Father Gerard, the congregation… "*Requiem æternam dona eis…*"*
I am somewhere at the back. I've not felt able to place myself among the monks: trousers and hair give substance to my alienation.

Nicolas…

Then, very early that morning, around five o'clock, a young brother unable to sleep had seen the lights suddenly switched on in the church. He had, nonetheless, not got out of bed (*mustn't put a foot wrong*), but had noted the strange time.

On arriving for the first service of the morning the brothers had found the church lit up and the crypt open. Dressed in a black cape over his pyjamas, Nicolas was lying at the bottom. He had felt faint, collapsed and cracked his head against a bench. He was dead.

The procession has come outside and is skirting the church by a pathway through the cemetery. An icy wind is blowing out the candles, buffeting the robes and chasubles, and ruffling the pages of the great service books. I've not looked at the sky since morning: it's grey, with clouds billowing up fast towards the River.

There at the angle of the church I see a heap of bright chestnut-coloured earth and, beyond, a gaping hole around which the community are lining up. The absolutions are about to begin.

I was able, later, to reconstruct the course of events. Nicolas had never been to see a doctor; enquiries throughout the district confirmed this. Nicolas was aware that he had contracted an illness that was unforgiving if ignored: heart disease.

That pain, stretching from one shoulder to the other, he had recognized. It was a coronary, a heart attack, which could be fatal. He had done nothing, said nothing. This attack was his heart refusing to pump blood to a body that was overweight; it was his heart facing demands for the impossible month after month – he had watched it coming, this attack, coolly and calmly, as he stuffed yet one more pipe.

And then one morning he had realized the moment had come. Clumsily – for time was pressing – he had grabbed a cape in the disorder of his bare cell and descended the stairs clutching the banister, making no sound.

He wanted to see once more the church he loved so much, to go on to the crypt where he had prayed his life through... *Turn on the lights... Stagger if you must, but move to the back. Quick – the pain's unbearable; the dizziness... Go down the stairs.*

251

The crypt – there it is.

In a universe where death is not the property of individuals and can only come from God alone at a moment of his choosing... Father Nicolas had, in effect, turned the general rule to his advantage one last time: he had killed himself.

The coffin slowly sinks into the grave. They make a show of busyness: it looks better that way – not to give way to sentiment. Father Gerard, standing by the tomb in his pontifical robes, seems to merge with the earth. His puckered eyes are expressionless. He's very pale, that's all, and his hand keeps folding back mechanically the pages the wind is turning.

I've come away immediately without approaching him. *He's with the family; it's not the moment.*

Tomorrow maybe?

One of our number has just died, of an absolutely unforeseeable heart attack. Yes, tomorrow, if you want. Not now.

Father Nicolas, I shall declare who you were – you were a living being. I shall declare that you died from being unable to live on – in that lonely state of mystery where one day death comes to take each one of us, alone face to face with ourselves, alone face to face with God.

I know myself that you chose to die quickly, through being too much alive. I shall declare that, without realizing it, without intending it, they killed you – the very ones that always talk of new life, yet do not know it. I shall declare that you took the risk of living, and that is what you died of in that dark crypt one winter's dawn.

The next day the abbey received a letter, which some time later I was able to read:

Superior monk, Sir,

I am Ahmed; I'm a Moroccan; I can't write; it's my friend who's writing for me.

Here at the worksite people have said Father Nicolas is dead. It's as God wills.

Superior, I want to tell you, Sir: one day Father Nicolas saved my job. He gave his shovel because my shovel it had broken.

I want to tell you, Father Nicolas's shovel is still there at my place. Now I have proper papers; I live in a low-rent flat. The shovel is in my bedroom against the wall, beside my prayer mat. Father Nicolas – I can't forget him.

Yours sincerely.

6

Months, seasons, pass. Like a boxer taking more punches than he can give, I'm still on my feet, but that's all. I have very few letters from the abbey. Father Gerard – has he not always supported me? – lets sleeping dogs lie. Over there by the River life is running on without me. Perhaps it's better thus: I don't have to witness the "clamp-down" that must be taking place little by little – insidiously, inexorably.

I need to limit my own prospects to those of the house in the village. But what are those prospects?

The friends of Tioumliline, who supply us with funds, have asked me to prepare a draft deed, to turn our little fellowship into a charitable trust. Father Denis is leaving this work to me, as he does increasingly with the day-to-day routine.

But at the same time I now and then feel him to be tense and reserved. This house is his final achievement, the child of his old age. Next, as he well knows, it'll be the abbey infirmary, till the end.

Logically, he should be training me up, making me more and more his partner, then his successor. No one else is going to join us. Human beings are living here in a kind of contentment, or at least in equilibrium. He'll leave the stage before them. Max, Ricou, Luisa and the others, shouldn't they be assured of their

MICHEL BENOÎT

future in this community created for them, but also created by
them?

Is Father Denis ready, though, to yield control? Will the king
accept a crown prince?

And me, am I prepared to don this robe that's been specifically
tailored for him?

"Brother Irenaeus, I know Father Denis well. He won't agree, he's
incapable of agreeing."

Luisa's sitting on the edge of my bed, in my room. I've come
more and more to appreciate this woman's dedication, so clear-
sighted, so unconditional. We're friends, and used to opening our
hearts to each other.

"Even if he were willing, he couldn't have a successor. He's made
like that: he's an initiator, but he has to be in complete control."

"But in due course, Luisa – in a few years, when he's unable to
carry on?"

"He'll close the house. I'll go somewhere else, so will the disabled
ones. He'll look after each of us; he won't leave us in the lurch. But
for someone else to take his place – never. Out of the question."

"You know what that means for me?"

"You're still young, Irenaeus. You've got the abbey to fall back
on. You'll go back there. That's where you belong."

"You really think so? Can you see me living for observance and
nothing else, counting the passing days?"

Luisa falls silent. What an understanding woman…

"No" – she looks me straight in the eye – "no, I can't see you
doing that. And you mustn't. For you it would be tantamount to
suicide. I know you now."

I have recently learnt the circumstances of Father Nicolas's
death. The suicide that he has, in a way, committed is something
I have no wish for, no stomach for. I owe it to him, and I owe it to
my family – and to myself – to go on living.

"Go and talk it over with the chaplain to 'The Road'. He's fond
of us; he's known the Church inside out for a long time. Listen to
him."

Luisa's right. More and more frequently I go to spend a day or two with the charismatics.

"And why not enter this place and become a member of our community?"

The old Dominican is lying back in his armchair. I've told him the whole story, breaking down once or twice. What has he heard? I don't know. But he's understood; he's trying to help me.

Enter this place? Join them, Alleluia? Become one of them, Amen? I really don't see myself here, Grief! In any case, the abbey would never agree. There's no legal connection between us and these new communities. It would be necessary to leave the order.

And that's something I'm never going to do of my own free will. The contract I signed was with God. Maybe I misled myself; maybe I was misled: no matter. My vows are the only fixed reference point I have left. I'll be faithful – even if it means instant death.

"But God, Brother Irenaeus" – the quavering voice is precise and clear – "God doesn't want you to die. You must live – find a means of living."

He often talks to me conversationally at these times of his own order, the Dominicans. He tells me of his own venture through life and that of his brothers. They're not monks; they're "mendicant brothers"; freedom's their most precious possession. Intellectuals, preachers, workers, artists, they've always been in the front line, up where the action's taking place. There's no standard Dominican: their order is made up of personalities that find their own situation, their own equilibrium, according to what they are – prima donnas, rebels, who stand together because they are all of the same breed: pioneers, iconoclasts, explorers.

I listen to the faint voice in the semi-darkness. I listen, but say nothing.

Is it still winter, or already spring in our sleepy village? I'm no longer sure. The path ahead seems ever more confined; I can only see walls to right, to left, in front.

255

Now I've done what it's any monk's duty to do. I've written a long letter to Father Gerard, my Superior, the one who held my hands within his, the one in whom I placed all my trust.

I'm playing the game.

I'm seated in my room. On the table, a sheet of paper with the abbey's letterhead. It's Father Gerard's reply. I read and reread it till I know it by heart, incredulous.

Brother,

I have your letter, and I thank you for it. Like you, I live without past or future, contenting myself with the present. Live one day at a time. No one, monks least of all, can escape the loneliness and futility of a life lived without love. I would so much like you not to have to get through this Easter without Christ!

Each day I go to the cemetery, to the resting place of those who are truly alive, and I commit you to them...

If someone ever compiles an anthology of empty language, of wooden church-speak, I will submit that letter. Only one sentence has any significance: "Each day I go to the cemetery, to the resting place of those who are truly alive..."

No. I'm used to the way the Church expresses itself: but in this case, no. Those who are truly alive are not in the cemetery. Those who are truly alive are living, trying to live. Unconsciously Father Gerard has unmasked both himself and the sect's philosophy at the same time. It's not a school of life, but a school of death. "You will arrive..." Is this the meaning of the phrase in the Rule on which I had staked my existence so long ago?

I have showed this letter to the old Dominican. He says nothing, just smiles: he's familiar with the wooden language, he's not surprised. Then he gently raises his toad's eyes towards me:

"But then, if you want to remain within the Church, if you want to be faithful to your vows... I understand: that's right, it's the linchpin of your life... Well then, why don't you ask to change orders? You know that a member of a religious order can always transfer his vows from one order to another, with Rome's agreement. Why don't you become a Dominican? I could easily see you as one of us. We have a tradition too, and it's one in which you would be comfortable. Think about it..."

7

"Sit down, Brother; I was expecting you."

I have before me, in spotless white habit, the Provincial of the French Dominicans. We're in the Rue du Faubourg Saint-Honoré: here in the heart of Paris the Dominicans own a huge building, including a church open to the public.

The Provincial's offices are on the sixth floor, with a view over the rooftops. Up-to-date furniture, unobtrusive affluence, original paintings by lesser masters – it's clear that the mendicant brothers don't lack for means.

The Provincial agreed at once to see me. The old Dominican, who never goes out, never leaves that dark study of his, did well: he came all this way to talk to his Provincial about me and plead my case.

"Have you prepared a statement?"

Yes. As he requested over the telephone, I've summarized in several pages the story of my life, the abbey, the barriers that are going up, the deadlock I've reached, and my wish to be faithful, but also to live.

"Thank you. Please make yourself at ease while I read."

Thereupon he lights a cigarette in my presence, then leafs quickly through the pages. *Strange how a life can be fitted onto so little paper...*

The Provincial is young, slim and pleasant. He knows he has charm and deploys it in moderation. As he turns the pages, his cigarette burning down in his wiry hand, he emanates a personality that's arresting and authoritative.

"Nothing exceptional in all this..."

His voice, tinged with a southern accent, is husky and friendly.

"Really nothing. I'm ready to accept you into our order, if your superiors agree. We'll have to submit a request to Rome. It'll go through. And you'll have to do another twelve months' noviciate with us: that's the rule. Do you think you can accept that?"

With this man everything seems possible, straightforward, obvious. Yes, I'll do a second noviciate: I've seen men do more. I agree.

"Your father abbot must give his consent in writing: I will ask him for it. From now on I will deal with your case personally. The noviciate is spent in Strasbourg; it'll start at the beginning of September. Go and meet the Father Master there, he'll keep you in touch."

In the July sunshine the Rue du Faubourg seems to be bursting with joy. I want to grab the passers-by by the waist and get them dancing. To live, to live again!

My mother's place is not very far away: quick, I've good news for her! Her son, the son she's been seeing in such a gloomy, sorry state, her little king, is going to regain his appetite for life.

To live!

I've made the journey to Strasbourg. The Dominican Father Master is called Rogatian, of all things. He's jolly and extrovert, with a Georges Brassens moustache, and he plays the saxophone. We spend a long time talking.

"Listen, if the Provincial accepts you, I'll accept you too. We'll ask your father abbot – Father Gerard, isn't it? – for a letter. At the end of the noviciate year, the community here will vote on the novices. If they accept you, you'll be a Dominican. We're expecting six or seven youngsters as novices too. Now, come along, we're going to have a beer."

It's not quite the abbey's style, that's clear. But the weather's hot, and the beer makes a good welcome to Alsace.

Strasbourg. A smart building in the centre: a dozen Dominicans form the community that harbours the novices. Seven young lads have just made the same decision that turned my life upside down twenty years ago.

Everything is organized around the refectory – the sole place of meeting – and the church. Liturgy is minimal (Dominicans are not monks), entirely in French, and tuneful; lay-folk who want mingle with us. This is another world, and I'm immediately feeling comfortable in it. Why, oh why have I waited so long?

After a few days comes the taking of the habit. Father Rogatian stops me in a corridor:

"We've had a letter from your father abbot. It's fine; the Provincial will do the necessary in Rome."

He looks preoccupied, unwilling to speak for longer: the taking of the habit has to be organized, I presume. Everything is going well, that's the important thing.

In a packed church, the Provincial has just presented us with our white habits. He walks along the row of eight novices, who stand facing the altar, and embraces them. He addresses each with the traditional form of words: "Henceforth you will be called Brother…"

He stands before me and in his grave, husky voice says:

"Brother Irenaeus, henceforth you will be called by your baptismal name, Brother Michel."

I've turned a full circle. But why the strained look, quickly deflected?

The aim of those twelve months is to test the novices' ability to live together – and to allow the community, who will vote on them, to get to know them better.

Every morning the Father Master gives an hour's lecture on the religious life. I'm excused most of it:

"We won't inflict this on you, though, you old abbey veteran!"

The ever jovial Father Rogatian wants his novices to be happy. In fact he wants everyone to be happy. He cannot abide strained feelings and deals with them in a summary manner:

"With us this is sorted out with an honest explanation, and a little glass of Vosges white wine, hey presto!"

But why then does he appear to be avoiding me, to be shunning every encounter where I might try to check out with him how things are. *It must be the Dominican way, hey presto! and I suppose he needs to be careful with an old monastery veteran like me. His room is opposite mine – if he has something to say to me, he'll say it, hey presto!*

Each novice is given a small assignment in the community's external mission, alongside a senior community member who will assess him. My assignment is with a group of young people – something I'm used to.

The winter is harsh here, and temperatures arctic. But the refectory is warm. We eat at small tables; meals are lively, with conversations continuing indefinitely over the last little glass of Sylvaner. The wine loosens tongues – as good a way as any of getting to know each other. The food is wholesome, and plenty of it. Anything is an excuse for celebration, for uncorking one more bottle.

Where this affluence comes from I don't know. In any event, the "mendicant brothers" feed their men well. Good heating, car, pocket money – to be so free with the pennies there must be enough of them.

The community seems to have accepted me – or at least no one tells me anything otherwise: there's joking, there's table-chatter, friendly if superficial. Father Rogatian never crosses the threshold of my room.

After six months, a full retreat in the Vosges. The spring, late this year, seems about to explode. In the course of the week Father Rogatian will really have to have a talk with me; I'll know at last where I stand.

"Well, everything's fine, Michel, eh? Do you feel OK with us?"

Rogatian strokes his moustache as we stride together through the garden of the sisters who are putting us up. The retreat is coming to an end.

"No problem for me, Father. But what's your view? Do you think that I'll make it as a Dominican?"

By twisting his moustache so much, he'll end up pulling it out of shape. It allows him a lengthy silence. Could he be embarrassed about answering me? Yet my life now depends on this question.

"Yes, yes, the brothers are happy to have you with us, you can see for yourself... And then, the Provincial is personally monitoring your progress. You'll see that when you meet him early this summer."

The impression of unease lingers on. Why doesn't he look me full in the face? Why isn't he more explicit? He's never one to mince his words.

Strasbourg is shimmering in the first heatwave of summer. The community will vote in a month. After that the brothers will leave to spend the August holiday in one of the order's houses in France.

The Provincial has been with us since yesterday. I meet him briefly.

"Stay on course. After hearing the Father Master's report on each of you, the community will vote. You know Church law: the vote is final; I have no power to overrule it. But I've every hope; carry on!"

I have received a letter from Father Gerard – friendly, non-committal. He too is leaving it to the Dominicans' vote; he too has every hope.

Come on, this unease that I feel is just the product of my anxiety. In view of what they've said to you, Michel, go forwards without questioning yourself!

Tomorrow's the vote. Every novice has received his posting for August: I'm going to spend it at the Dominicans' house in Nice. I'm to help the community there a bit and take some holiday – something I've lost the habit of.

My train is leaving this evening; there were no more seats later, and Father Rogatian had huge trouble in getting one ticket:

"So leave now; you don't need to be present here for the vote. You can call me from Nice, and I'll give you the result by telephone. Don't be worried; have a good holiday!"

He kisses me, strokes his moustache and moves away without giving me a look. Funny way of saying goodbye... but I just have time to go and have a bite to eat before departing. The house bursar is busy in the kitchen: he's one of those who will be voting tomorrow.

"May I have something to eat, Father?"

"Of course. Carry on; you're at home here!"

"You're at home here"... *Come on, the vote will go fine. In a couple of days I'll be a Dominican, and my life will take a new course.*

8

The Dominican friary is in the old city of Nice. There are only five or six brothers, most of them elderly, who undertake various activities in the town. I shall be serving in the community and taking a holiday, but above all waiting for news from Strasbourg. The voting is going on this very moment. I must telephone this evening. Being a bit nervous, I go for a stroll on the seafront.

It's twenty years since I've set foot on a French beach. Most of the girls have bare breasts: it gives Brother Michel, Dominican novice, tingles in the back of his neck. But, to tell the truth, my preoccupations are wholly elsewhere, eight hundred kilometres away, where my life is in the balance. Of course they're going to accept me. That's obvious: they'd not have let me continue for a whole twelve months and come all the way to Nice, if they'd had any qualms or apprehensions. True, they haven't said much to me during the year, but no matter – that's presumably their way of doing things. I'm coming to them fully trained, ready for service, wanting to give the best of myself: they know that.

Still two hours to go...

Dinner is soon over; half the brothers are away. *Father, may I use the telephone? Of course, come into my study.* The Superior is friendly.

"Hallo? It's Brother Michel here; I'm telephoning from Nice. Can I speak to Father Rogatian?"

"Ah, Brother Michel... Yes, yes, of course. Wait while I go and look for him."

"Michel?"

"Well, Father Rogatian, has the vote taken place?"

"Yes, yes." His voice is nervous, hesitant. "Listen, I'm in an awful hurry. I haven't time to talk to you. But you'll get a letter from the Provincial."

"A letter? Good, but what was the result of the vote?"

"Everything's going fine. Don't worry. You'll be getting a letter. Look, I have to leave. Have a good holiday!"

He's hung up. I don't understand. Why a letter from the Provincial? And why the refusal to answer so simple a question?

Anyhow, he's wished me a good holiday. If there'd been a problem, he'd have told me, obviously.

So I shall wait for the letter – and not worry.

Amid the bustle of Nice the friary is an islet of tranquillity and peace. My room looks out onto a side street. At the end of the dark, cool corridor is a window from which you can glimpse the boulevard and the sea.

The Superior has asked me to give some lectures on the Bible to a group of friends of the friary and to provide cover for the mornings. For the rest of the time I'm a free agent. Each afternoon I explore the aromatic hinterland and became a regular at the Chagall Museum – reconnecting with a beauty that's pure and unambiguous.

For twelve months now I've been pursuing a single trajectory, striving for a single goal – to anchor my life once more in the Church; to keep my side of the contract made in God's presence so long ago; to be faithful. And I've done it without wondering why, without pondering the value of a faithfulness that's cost everything, without asking myself questions. Faithfulness is just not up for discussion.

Later I was to realize that I had kept my eyes tight shut: faithfulness has no meaning apart from the life that it makes possible and which is its justification.

But God – where was God in all this? Only God could give sense to such dogged persistence. But prayer continued to evade me in Strasbourg – there were just long, empty times of waiting, in which I stayed faithful as to the rest.

Fortunately my sexual urges, still anaesthetized, had left me in peace – meagre consolation!

Now I'm awaiting the green light for the resumption of life, and maybe this will give me once more a taste for God.

Yes, everything will get going again, and things will have meaning, direction, importance. I'll once more have a base somewhere, and a purpose. Even my people, the family I've abandoned, need to know that I'm at peace with myself. They're uneasy with this rootlessness of mine.

I'm waiting for the letter.

A week has passed already. On the Sunday the Superior has asked me to preach at mass. He's pleased:

"You'll make a good Dominican. Maybe you'll be sent here to Nice? You'd be welcome here."

Yes, maybe. But first I'm waiting for a letter.

It's almost a fortnight since the vote. Nothing, no letter, no telephone call. I can't bear the silence any longer. I'll telephone Paris, call the Provincial direct. That's not the done thing, but I can't remain like this, hanging in midair. *Of course, Brother, go into my office.*

The room is in shadow; it's very hot. I stay standing and dial the number for the Faubourg Saint-Honoré.

"Hallo, this is Brother Michel, a novice of the French province. Can I speak to the Provincial?"

"Ah, but… the Provincial's away; he'll be back in a week. This is his secretary."

I know that father, a courteous and discreet man. We've spoken together several times in a friendly way. I'm happy to seek his help.

"Good morning, Father. The point is, I've had no news of the end-of-noviciate vote that took place a fortnight ago. I was told to expect a letter from the Provincial, but nothing's come. Do you have any information?"

"The fact is... yes, Brother, the Provincial has written to you; perhaps the letter's gone astray; it's the holidays. But... you haven't heard?"

"No. What is it then?"

"The vote went in favour of everyone, except you. It's not for me to tell you, but I can't leave you in ignorance, that would be cruel. The community voted unanimously against your admission to the order."

I sit down. Suddenly the study seems icy. I feel cold.

"What... but then... I'm no longer anything?"

"No, you're no longer a novice. For us you're no longer anything. The only solution is to return to your abbey. They can't turn you away... Hallo? Hallo? Can you hear me?"

I'm speechless, stunned. Unanimously? How can it be possible?

"Yes, Father... Tell me, I can't stay any longer here in Nice. What am I to do?"

He has sensed my anguish, which is total. A moment of silence. The line crackles.

"Listen, Brother, I'll take responsibility: come back to Paris, you'll stay at the Faubourg. That'll enable you to make your plans. And the Provincial will be here at the end of the week. But you realize that there's nothing he can do about it: the community's vote is final; it's unanimous and clear. There's nothing anyone can do."

"Thank you. I'll be there tomorrow. Thank you, Father."

There's nothing anyone can do... I come out into the corridor; it is deserted. Down there is a patch of light: the window. I go to lean on the sill. The boulevard, which is visibly flooded with sunlight, seems to me dark and empty.

Nothing more, there's nothing more. I don't understand. How can it be? So was that the reason for Rogatian not wanting to say anything? If so, what duplicity, what appalling, abominable double-speak!

"You're at home here... Have a good holiday..."

What game have they been playing? And for how long? But then… they've been in cahoots, they're in tacit agreement, all of them!

In a flash the plot becomes apparent to me; I can't believe it, but it's unmistakable. Yes, it's all been arranged, prepared in advance, well organized. And I've just been a toy in their hands.

"Well, Brother…?"

It's the Superior touching my arm, with a smile. I've been there more than an hour, by the window open to sea and sky.

But I feel that I'm now a different man. The only thing, the only occurrence that could break the bond by which I bound myself, in God's name, for life and for death – maybe that occurrence has now come about.

I have to go to Paris and check my supposition. If it was true… how can it not be true? I feel nausea.

"Well, Brother? The bell for lunch has gone! Are you coming?"

"No thank you, Father, I'm not hungry. I have to return to Paris urgently. With your permission I'll take the night train this evening."

"Ah… what a pity! I was still counting on you. May God protect you."

Yes, but God has nothing to do with this business. It's men that are the problem, and their villainies.

To Paris. There I'll find out.

Another train. Sitting in the corner, my head resting against the window, I can't sleep. Tomorrow, the day after tomorrow, I'll find out. I watch the lights flashing by in the darkness. The lights flashing by, my life flashing by… There's nothing any more, just a slice of existence gone to waste.

I have to find out, get to the truth.

9

It's the end of August, Paris is strolling idly along her sidewalks. The friary in the Faubourg Saint-Honoré is half empty, with plenty of passing visitors. The Provincial's secretary has booked me a quiet room facing the courtyard.

"You can stay here as long as necessary. The Provincial will be here in six days. You're his guest, the guest of the order."

"Guest of the order..." when I should by now have been an active, recognized member. I've put my lightly loaded suitcase down by the wardrobe. All's calm and silent in the house: my presence passes unnoticed. Indeed, I'm transparent here – which gives me several days' respite. And then? Then...

There's a white telephone on the table. I sit by it and bury my face in my hands. Almost all the separate elements now seem clear to me, but I need to link them together and check a few points. I begin a long vigil, alone with my thoughts.

The abbey could not find fault with me. It was simply that, after the period of openness, when the men of the Dark Ages had adjusted to the modern world, a process in the reverse direction had got under way. The pendulum was swinging in the usual manner: the Church was used to such toing and froing: it was this that allowed it to remain the same, unchanged over time.

So it was that the world had seen famous theologians condemned, exiled and reduced to non-persons just before the Council; then rediscovered and acclaimed as expert advisers to the same Council, to which they provided a framework and theoretical underpinning; and then, a little later still, thrust back again into silence and mistrust, their work assimilated and themselves sidelined by the Church.

So the Church sailed on, while these men had nothing left to look forward to but sainthood or despair.

My tale was much slighter. "They've taken the best of you," Father Nicolas had said. Yes. The head that stood out above the rest had to be cut to the level of the ranks.

But it is not easy to cut off the head of a living being. So Father Gerard, man of the Church, had made sure that, lulled by my illusions, I eliminated myself. I could not hold it against him: he was defending his organization, which he had the duty to do, and the power to do – oh, the dreadful effects of power in corrupting a man so!

When in the end I had suggested changing religious orders, he had agreed, no doubt with relief. And he had sent the formal letter, called a "testimonial" in Church jargon, authorizing and facilitating my transfer to the Dominicans.

But then something had come to pass that I had yet to understand. Why had the Dominicans, having first unhesitatingly accepted me, then very quickly evinced the reservations that I had sensed throughout the year, all the way to their final rejection of me?

Here something still escaped me.

The night passed – a fitful sleep, punctured by spasms of waking. I did not attend the morning service, "their" service. But at breakfast the Provincial's secretary brought me a letter and put it down on the table without comment. "To Brother Michel, Paris". The writing was Father Rogatian's.

I went back up to my room, letter in hand. Maybe this was the answer to my questions, the missing link? I opened the letter on the bare table.

You must think me a fine bastard, and you're not wrong…

So far so good! Father Rogatian was spilling the beans at last, in a spirit of mawkish self-criticism. Poor man, that could not have been fun for him.

Several days after my taking of the habit, he had indeed received from the abbey a formal "testimonial" letter in neutral terms.

But the following day Father Gerard had sent another, personal letter. I have never been able to see that letter, but its contents were such that Father Rogatian had immediately understood: it was a damning report that shut the door of the Church on me for ever.

He had shown it to the Provincial. And the two of them had not been able to come up with any solution but this: to let me carry on as if nothing had happened – and leave the matter to the community. Father Rogatian could tell what the outcome would be, but had not had the courage to warn me. Then for a long twelve months he had played that double game, dreadful for him because it had gone against his conscience – to let a man walk towards the guillotine that would certainly finish him off at journey's end.

That was why he had caused me to leave the evening before the vote. That was why he had shunned all communication, because he did not know, no longer knew, what to say. He too had ended up a victim of the clandestine power play.

At the time of the vote he had simply read Father Gerard's letter out. And the community (some, the bursar for example, already knew) had voted against me as one man.

Doubtless sickened to have had to play a part in this game, he had refused to speak to me till the last moment and had retreated behind his Provincial: "You will be getting a letter…"

All was clear, or nearly so. But was it Father Gerard, then, in whom I had placed all my trust, who made sure my head rolled?

I have the white telephone in front of me. It's almost midday: I can still ring him; it's certainly urgent. I want to speak to him, to hear the truth from his own lips. Why, why such double-dealing?

I dial the abbey's number.

"Good morning, it's Brother Irenaeus here. Can I speak to the Father Abbot?"

"Ah… one moment, Brother. I'll go and see if he's in his study."

Silence. Then Father Gerard's voice, muted:

"Brother Irenaeus? Where are you?"

"In Paris, Father. The Dominicans have just voted against my admission to the order: I'm back at square one."

"Ah… that's awful news, awful… How so?"

"At the time of the vote they were read a letter that you wrote to Father Rogatian about me. That was enough to wreck things."

"A letter? I don't understand. I only sent the formal testimonial letter."

"What? You didn't send a second, personal letter?"

"No, never in my life. It certainly wasn't me. Was it from Rome perhaps, or from our Provincial, or from the Abbot Primate?"

His voice is distant, neutral, impersonal. The matter no longer concerns him; the file is closed. I've got the message: there's no point in continuing.

I've hung up.

The Church, always the same, knew what she was doing. I had just seen a fine example of this, at my own lowly level.

Someone had to be eliminated, for whatever reason. The decision was a clear one, perhaps endorsed by someone high up.

But the Church is guardian of morality, and a shabby, rather awkward decision is not to be laid at the door of a single individual who would then bear the clear and unquestionable responsibility.

No, the elimination would originate from everywhere, and from nowhere. Each of the protagonists would be able to pass on responsibility to someone else, and so go on living with a clean and easy conscience.

The leading Dominicans – had they not done all they could? The community, for its part, had listened to a letter and announced the rejection in consequence. But a community is impersonal, and in any case it was the letter that had done it.

As for the letter, its author denied its existence: perhaps it had come from Rome? Go there and ask them.

No, I would not go. I had finally understood. They really had no fault to find in me, but they needed me to leave. After all, what is one life worth against decisions of policy, taken who knows where?

Out!

Night fell over Paris. Daylight would come tomorrow.

Again, a wakeful night. How was I to sleep?

Loneliness, my closest friend...

Goodbye then, Mark, Luisa, and so many others. Goodbye Anselm, goodbye my illusions, my life that has run its course on the riverbank, and that crazy dream that has kept me sleepwalking for so many years...

In the morning I telephoned the secretary:

"Father, I'm grateful for your hospitality. I'm leaving the friary now, this morning."

"What? Won't you wait for the Provincial to come?"

"No. What's the point? We shan't have much to say to each other. You'll give him my regards."

"OK. I understand. Keep in touch, won't you?"

"Yes, of course. Goodbye, Father."

I've picked up my suitcase and gone downstairs without taking the lift. The friary porter hasn't raised his head as I pass. The entrance passage is dark: has he even seen me?

Through the open door I come out onto a sun-drenched pavement. One step forwards... but where to go? "You will arrive!..." I put my suitcase down. It's light, as light as that other suitcase twenty-one years ago...

I own four shirts, two pairs of trousers; a few coins in my pocket; just enough to take the metro – to restart life.

The passers-by on the pavement have the carefree and aimless look that Parisians have in August. I'm still there, standing in the middle of them. They part slightly, brush against me as they pass. *Careful, can't you see? Here, all round me, you're walking over the wreckage of a ruined life.*

On the opposite pavement a group of young girls is moving along laughing. They're presumably coming out of the nearby secretarial school. Their lively voices, their laughter, bring me out of my daydream. They turn the corner of the street and go off in the direction of the metro – skirts swinging, footsteps dancing.

The metro, that's right. At the other end is my mother, my family: they've never stopped being mine. Where else am I to go but to them? My own people...

On the other side, two girls at the back of the main group are holding hands, one a blonde, the other a brunette. They're smiling at the sun. Mechanically, I pick up my suitcase and cross the street.

Epilogue

First letter to Mark

Dear Mark,

Your letter comes to me in this forsaken corner of Africa as the reminder of a past long gone. It's now two years since that August day when I found myself in the street, stripped of everything...

What is there to say to you? I'm alive. I work hard, in difficult conditions. Money won here is dearly earned.

But yes, to you, friend that you are, I shall say something: I've recovered a sense of balance in that area we talked of so often – one that seems to me to embody the most damaging perversions I encountered in the abbey.

The warmth of Africa comes not only from its sun, but first and foremost from its men – and from its women.

I've been made welcome by the women of Africa. "That's simple," you'll say, "the white man's rich, and he pays." No, Mark: these women that are so open to a liaison with a white man are not prostitutes. In Africa love is always given in return for services. Women, who have no life of their own, no possessions, always receive a gift from their partner, if only a symbolic one.

But they can give in return, if one's willing, infinitely more.

With kindness, with understanding, with tact even, they have retaught me my body. No doubt this was because they sensed that I was not just the French colonial trying to have a quick screw, like so many do here; perhaps also because I've been careful to choose my partners.

How they love the language of physical love, Mark, and how well they can speak it! Of course, they only have what they have. But that grammar, which I had lost the use of, they deploy like a mother tongue.

I'm conscious that in your moral code all this is sin. I put this question to you as theologian: isn't it death that's the big sin, the only sin? And your God, isn't he the God of life?

Till later, Mark. *Ciao*.

Second letter to Mark

My dear Mark,

Your friendship continues to amaze me: you're the only one to write to me, the only one, it seems, for whom I still exist in that world where, nonetheless, I lived out half my life.

It's four years now since I was thrown out of the Church, in the circumstances that you're aware of. I have a job and a wife, and around them I've once more begun to live. At last, it seems to me... I'm learning to forget. The hardest part was not the leaving, the incontrovertible failure, the taking stock of disillusionments. (You remember? We were going to be the knights of a new world, where expressions of peace, harmony, brotherhood, purity, inspiration... might become a reality. "You are the hope of the order; you are its life!" Yes, we should have given, we could have given, new sap to that old tree, still standing as it was, and the wild birds would come to build their nests in it.)

No, the hardest part was what followed. I found myself one August morning on the pavement – with nothing, no past, no future, no money. A desert.

In the coming weeks I needed to sleep, eat, find work. I was arriving from another planet; I no longer knew how to get along.

I expected from the abbey, from those who'd called me "Brother", from those to whom I'd given up my life, whose destiny I'd shared... I expected a gesture, an enquiry: "Are you OK? Where are you going to stay? Is there anything we can do to help?"

Nothing. None of those simple, everyday words by which a friend worries for his friend by day or night, or a brother worries for his brother for the morrow.

Nothing. Not a proffered hand, nothing. I had left the sect: I no longer existed. They show greater consideration for their dead, caring for the graves, adorning them with flowers.

No, I was not their brother, nor their friend. I never had been. Behind those deceitful expressions was nothing. They were just clichés, words for display – a snare and a delusion. Brother...

You ask me where I have got to in my relationship with God, whether I pray. You incorrigible evangelist! You're the only one, though, from whom I can accept such a question: the friendship you have shown me gives you the right to ask it of me.

I don't know, Mark, I don't know any longer. God was once the sole motive of my life, my sole love perhaps. Shall I be able to love now – to experience that emotion that governs all the others? With that love disappointed and betrayed, can another love, be it what may, take its place?

I don't know. Yes, I mustn't mix things up, confuse God and men of God. Once I knew so many things about God; I taught others about him (and they learnt from me); but I know nothing of him any more – except that he exists. But *who* he is, and *how* to get through to him – that is something the teacher, the scholar, no longer knows.

God exists. And I suppose that at my last breath, at that second death that's late in coming (the first took place far back on the riverbank) – I'm sure, when that time comes, my last thought will be for him – that force that carries you beyond death, and that sums up every life. God, only love. Absent love.

Well then... I'm not Zola. My life doesn't count for much. But for your eyes – you're a friend, I can say anything to you – for your eyes here is my accusation.

My accusation is that the Church has used men as tools in furtherance of her power. I bear no grudge against those men as individuals. They're captives of a system, of the deadliest ideology that humanity has engendered. Churches or whatever – Catholic, Islamic, Hindu – they're all the same... machines that crush.

My accusation is that the Church has commandeered all that's most beautiful, most fragile in us, and most pathetic: our idealism, our yearnings for sublimity, for honesty, for purity – all that differentiates the human from the animal.

My accusation is that the Church has above all deprived us of the one good that's essential, indispensable to our lives and our societies: God – only to build over him the ramparts of her despotism.

Yes, finally, the Church has robbed us of God, to her own private profit. So who is now to show us the way to him? Where shall we find him, in his pristine freshness?

Well then, Mark, you've won: I never wanted to talk about all this again; but you've managed to touch that old wound, to flush the wolf out of the forest.

I don't hold it against you. Watch yourself, friend: it's a narrow edge between God and nothingness...

That's it, enough. Till later. *Ciao*.

Afterword

I knew in 1985, a year after the monastery had abandoned me, that I would write this book. Between Douala, Libreville and Brazzaville I began making a few jottings. Nothing of them has survived, except perhaps that first sentence, "I have chosen death." This sentence, written posthumously as it were, struck exactly the right note – so many hopes had been dashed, so many ideals betrayed.

* * *

Around 1991 I realized that the relationship we were forging, M— and I, was breaking apart in spite of us. My reaction to knowledge of this fresh setback? It is during this painful period that Parts One and Two were written, and later frequently revised, to heal the lesions that were still exposed.

* * *

"Each day I go to the cemetery, to the resting place of those who are truly alive." Just by her presence at my side each day, M— gave the lie to this sombre expression of a warped ideal. Thanks to her a womanly tenderness has entered my life. I owe it to a woman that I have survived the unseeing, unknowing violence of an organization formed of men.

* * *

At the time of going to press we still did not have a title. I had suggested thirty titles to the publisher, but one after the other they had all been rejected. "Michel," he said to me when the printer was losing patience, "we'll call it *Prisoner of God*; that's a good title."

I protested: God has never taken a prisoner. It's my own prisoner I've been, mine alone – the prisoner of my illusions and of those of an era. But the publisher was right: it was a good title – untrue, but effective.

* * *

I became Brother Irenaeus on 9th October 1962, three days before the opening of the Second Vatican Council. At that time the missions in our newly independent colonies were still thriving. At that time sects were practically unknown in Latin America, Africa, the Philippines and Korea. At that time John Kennedy was President of the United States, the first to be a Catholic. From Acapulco to Seoul the Church, untouched by the centuries, liked to consider herself the sole repository both of God and of human aspirations. Her view of the world, of public morality, of relations between men and women, was widely shared. From antiquity she had inspired our civil law, our customs, our inhibitions, our joys and our sorrows.

When I turned up at the abbey door, the Church still constituted the framework of a huge edifice, the strong, supreme edifice of Western civilization. Twenty years later, when I found myself in the street, both edifice and framework were tottering, though it was impossible to tell which of them had brought this unforeseen enfeeblement upon the other.

* * *

The events related in this book unfolded between the years 1960 and 1980 in a closed universe. They took place at particular dates in particular places; yet *Prisoner of God* far outreaches the cramped perspectives of a Catholic monastery. What was no more than the story of an individual career now looks almost like a historical document, shedding light as it does on a period of transition: the ending of a tacit consensus between a religion and the civilization whose imaginative faculties it had nurtured for centuries – an intricate piece of apparatus that blew apart before my eyes.

* * *

The roots of our civilization, whether one likes it or not, are Christian. But the great tree that those roots invigorated with their sap for so long seems now to be held standing only by its bark.

* * *

The monasteries have always been the spearhead of this civilization. The Church saw them as the realization, through the Rule of St Benedict, of her ideal of perfection. I found this Rule profoundly Stoic: "Death begins at the very point where pleasure begins". This obsession with death does not come from the Gospel. By word and act alike the rabbi of Galilee evinces an utter hatred of death: he has spread around him nothing but healing and life.

* * *

I know now that chastity of body and spirit can only be sustained through the exercise of meditation, so well described by the Buddha. That is why the monasteries are emptying. People are going elsewhere to find ways of gaining wisdom and of purifying the mind. It is to the sages of the East that one has to go to learn the theory and practice of silent meditation – the only form of prayer practised by Jesus the Jew. By continuing still to ignore this meditation the Western Church is seeing the best of our aspirant mystics turning away from her.

* * *

People have criticized me for using the word "sect" of the organized Church. Yet it is certainly a system of sectarian imprisonment that is at issue. I entered freely, and I was free to leave at any time; but I did not do so. The member of a sect imprisons himself in the sect of his own accord, and cannot reverse his decision without admitting the mistakenness of his choice and his own part in the sufferings he has undergone and precipitated. No one takes this decisive step unless an outside force drives him to it.

What took place on the riverbank could have happened in the same way in any evangelical or Islamic sect, or in certain political parties.

* * *

"There is *one truth and one only*, and that is ours; you must share that truth; or else...": that is a sect for you. At many times, in many places, this "or else..." has entailed the most brutal of corporal punishments, with death a happy release. But at all times and in all places "or else..." has meant unending punishment in the afterlife.

From the standpoint of history the Church is a sect that has succeeded.

It took me ten years after recovering my freedom of movement to regain my inner freedom. Then I understood that it was not worth fighting against the past: I had to map a route over those toppled stones. God was no one's private property.

* * *

How many years it took to realize that the Churches – all the Churches – are power machines! – that their unvoiced ambition is to win power, then cling to it at all costs. "Service to God comes first" is the slogan they flaunt – an ideal that believers aspire to and sometimes achieve within the organization. The unselfishness of their quest causes them to miss the falsity of the phrase. I see in it now a pretence that goes deep down into the recesses of the subconscious.

* * *

By "pretence" I am not referring to those who wear mitres, skull-caps or turbans. The pretence I mean is the treatment of a youngster's vital energy which finds itself parked on a shelf, exposed to oblivion's corrosion and to the slow accumulation of dust.

Long ago the clergy knew how to transform that irrepressible energy into cathedrals of the spirit or of stone. We have shaken off this cloak of pretence – maybe it was time – and we find ourselves naked and shivering.

* * *

The Church had taught me Christ; but I had to leave her in order to discover the prophet of Nazareth. This discovery, extraordinarily fruitful as it is, has given meaning to Brother Irenaeus's defeat; it has blown away once and for all the vapours of death. Since then, through the medium of novels and essays, I have been constantly deepening and sharing the reverberations it generates.

In the moral and spiritual desert of humanity, which is what our civilization has become, the rediscovery of the human Jesus is for me a real gleam of hope. This man, solitary as he was yet linked to everything, wanted to humanize the planet by showing it a pathway. Over the centuries a few great personalities – and so many nameless champions – have managed to take this path. For our societies it all remains to be done.

* * *

My aim, dimly perceived, in entering the monastery was to acquire a family that would replace the one I had lacked. But I had to leave the monastery to find, in the most commonplace and often unexpected encounters, those who would give unselfish care, reassuring words, warm friendship or a soothing touch – characteristics of Jesus that some men and some women unconsciously embody, though society at large wishes to ignore him.

* * *

Once stripped of Christian mythology the itinerant rabbi from Galilee is seen to be entirely subversive. He rejected the Church of his time, its rituals and its priests. He yielded to the authority of Caesar, the better to free himself from it within. He defied every restriction, overstepped every boundary of established custom.

A stance like that cannot be maintained within any social structure, be it civil or religious. Jesus did not found a church; and Christianity, as it developed, was a betrayal of him. The day when I began to take an interest in Jesus the Jew I unwittingly set off down a corridor that could only lead to the exit.

* * *

The Gutenberg revolution* fostered the expansion of the various Christian Churches of Western origin. The unifying influence of the printed book brought communities together around its interpreters. Right up to the nineteenth century it was only the intelligentsia that could read extensively. Knowledge came from on high; its dissemination reflected the pyramidal structure of the hierarchies, which it reinforced.

Television, and now the internet revolution, are disrupting this time-honoured model. Communication is now horizontal, without the mediation of the intelligentsia, without *any* intermediary, restraint or censorship. Will this displace the Churches? Virtual communities are already beginning to emerge. People are learning, trading, communicating on a keyboard. But it is only personal encounter that can change lives and produce *metanoia* ("repentance") – a profound internal renewal, an adventurous fresh start, recovery from a harvest of disappointments. If Jesus had been content with Google, would he have left the mark he has done on the world? The vivid, heart-warming experience of an encounter with this man will never be transmitted solely by computer.

* * *

Churches will not disappear. Christian, Moslem, Jewish, Hindu – the history of humanity shows that they have always paralleled the trajectory of civilizations. When a civilization declines, dies or undergoes transformation, nothing of its original Church is left but the outer trappings.

* * *

The word "tradition" comes from the Latin *tradere*, which means both "to hand on" and "to betray". Can one hand on without betraying?

If I have been able to familiarize myself with the Gospels, if I have encountered the personality of the Galilean prophet, it is indeed through the intermediation of the Catholic Church, and thanks to her. She has provided the framework, both social and religious, that has handed on to me whatever is remembered. She has supplied the tools that have enabled me, much later, to rediscover the face of the one she claims to represent. "You will arrive...": to arrive where she professed to be leading me, I had to distance myself from her. Perhaps the same goes for all sects and churches?

* * *

Mine is a generation that has had to adjust to the fastest changes the planet has ever known, but it has still had the benefit of landmarks, reference points, routes through the past, perspectives of what is possible – the benefits, in short, of tradition. When this generation of mine has disappeared, then, who will *hand on*?

In a world that has no values but those it can put a number to, where the most private yearnings for the divine are thrown onto the market like everything else, who will hand on – and to whom?

Michel Benoît, 21st March 2008

Notes

p. 35, *Father, watch your right; father, watch your left*: The famous words of Prince Philip the Bold to his Father King John II at the battle of Poitiers (1356) shortly before they were taken prisoner by the English.

p. 56, *Lord, save us, we perish*: Matthew 8:25.

p. 88, *Deo gratias*: Latin: "Thanks be to God" (Latin).

p. 89, *pax tecum... et cum spiritu tuo*: "Peace be with you... and with your spirit" (Latin).

p. 179, *And there was evening... morning*: Genesis 1:5 *ff.*

p. 184, *God, you are my God; I have sought you since daybreak*: Psalm 63.1 (Vulgate)

p. 246, *Requiem æternam dona eis*: "Grant them eternal rest" (Latin), the opening words of the Mass for the Dead.